1-22-03

# MAKING THINGS BETTER

Anita
Brookner

# MAKING
# THINGS
# BETTER

*A Novel*

RANDOM HOUSE
NEW YORK

All rights reserved under International and Pan-American Copyright
Conventions. Published in the United States by
Random House, Inc., New York.

RANDOM HOUSE and colophon are registered trademarks
of Random House, Inc.

Originally published in the United Kingdom by Penguin Books, Ltd.
in 2002 under the title *The Next Big Thing*.

Library of Congress Cataloging-in-Publication Data

Brookner, Anita.
Making things better: a novel / Anita Brookner.
p.     cm.
ISBN 0-375-50888-0
1. Middle-aged men—Fiction.   2. Midlife crisis—Fiction.  I. Title.
PR6052.R5816 M35 2003        823'.914—dc21         2002069860

Random House website address: www.atrandom.com
Printed in the United States of America on acid-free paper

24689753

First U.S. Edition

*Book design by Carole Lowenstein*

# MAKING THINGS BETTER

# 1

Herz had a dream which, when he awoke into a night that was still black, left him excited and impressed. He dreamed that he had received a call from his cousin, Fanny Bauer, the love of his life. He was to take her to the cinema, she ordained. Eager to conform to her wishes, as he always had been, he shrugged on his coat, and within seconds was elsewhere, as was the norm in dreams of wish-fulfilment. Although it was a weekday afternoon the cinema was so crowded that they had to stand at the back of the auditorium. Fanny was as he had always known her and still remembered her: petulant, with the petulance of a spoilt pretty woman, demanding and discontented. Shortly after the beginning of the film she had clutched his arm and declared that she felt unwell. Again, without transition, they found themselves in the vast café that was part of the cinema complex. Fanny had recovered somewhat but looked uncharacteristically dishevelled, with a large camel-hair coat slung over her shoulders. He was conscious of retaining his eager smile, but felt discomfited. This feeling had something to do with the coat, which he recognized as his own, the coat he should have been wearing. He had no memory of having offered it to her. The coat, and Fanny's malaise, remained closely associated in his mind. It was only when he understood that it was he who had been taken ill that the dream attained its peak of significance. Ailing, smiling, he had offered her his remaining health and strength, and she, not in the least grateful, had carelessly dispossessed him, not noticing that she had done so. This was so akin to their real life association that, if anything, his newly awakened self was conscious of its reality. Brought back to himself he was aware of the smile—of complicity, of acquiescence—directed to the corners of the dark bedroom. Only the relentless ticking of his clock informed him that he had woken up, that this would soon be a new day, all too closely resembling the others, the normal days of his present existence, in which nothing happened nor could be expected to happen.

He had not seen her for thirty years. In the dream they were both young and she was still unmarried, before Nyon, before Mellerio, before his own family had come to England. It was his longing that had made him feel close to her, since he thought about her so often and so much that there seemed to be no distance between them. This longing extended to her parents, whom he preferred to his own. He knew that his own parents were socially inferior, although he suspected that morally they had the upper hand. His mother had never forgiven her sister for marrying out, though by no means observant in her own right. His father, a modest man, deferred to his brother-in-law without ever feeling entirely comfortable in his presence. Yet it was this brother-in-law, Hubertus, who had guaranteed them safe passage out of Berlin. Their house, one of those chic villas that Hubertus was so good at constructing, had all the charm of a more carefree establishment, an hotel, for example, or some kind of resort. By the same token, his aunt, Anna, appeared always on the verge of giving a party. They played bridge, drank cocktails, yet even at his young age he could see that they were merely fashionable, slightly meretricious. He did not know then that they were worried about the fate of their ardent dark-eyed daughter, whose looks were so suspect in the Germany of that time. His own parents were worried, morbidly worried, not about their own fate, but for that of their elder son, Freddy, their musical genius, rather than that of the eagerly smiling Julius. This had brought the two families momentarily closer; there were more telephone conversations than had previously been the case. Hubertus would stay behind; that was never in any doubt. But it would be prudent for his wife and daughter to be moved elsewhere, out of harm's way. Herz's own father, an employee in a firm that made musical instruments, had every faith in his colleagues, in his director, to whom he had pledged his loyalty. How could such loyalty not be recognized, and if necessary protected? His mother, who was afraid of everything, dreamed of escape from the many difficulties with which life had presented her. She, rather than her husband, put her diminishing faith in Hubertus; he rather than her too humble partner would know what to do.

As the boy, Julius, presented himself at his aunt's tea-table, his smile making up for his lack of an invitation (he would overlook this though they might not), he was given the sort of greeting into which he read so much: familiar, if slightly impatient. He had just missed Fanny, he would be told; she was playing tennis with friends, with some of her 'set', but he would stay for a quick cup of tea, his aunt queried, with a lift of her pencilled eyebrow? Useless to wait for Fanny, who would be spending the evening with her friends. The family well? This question was a pure formality, the kind in which she normally dealt. He would sit humbly in their glass and chrome drawing-room, with its pale wood and white curtains, comparing its discomfort favourably with his parents' flat, all subfusc and dim, the furnishings still those of his grandparents who had ruled their loyal daughter and meek son-in-law not entirely mercifully, and from whom Anna, the disloyal daughter, had parted with few backward glances. Her marriage to a Protestant was considered an act so terrible that she was never to be forgiven, although Hubertus was a good man whose discreet allowance had ensured a comfortable old age for the tyrannical elders who continued to vilify him. It was probably a matter of survival to agree with them on this. Nevertheless the moral discomfort that this brought about made Hubertus and Anna seem an enlightened pair, as perhaps they were, and their house a haven of modernity, for which he craved. Even if Fanny were not at home—and she so rarely was—he could sense her presence, picture her picking up her tennis racquet, follow her in sympathy as she issued into the bright afternoon. The image was so gratifying that he would count his unscheduled visit a success, taking home impressions to be added to his meagre store, and already looking forward to another similar afternoon, when surely, one day, she would be at home and delighted to see him.

Fanny Bauer! In the dream she had been young, pretty, a heart-breaker, her fickle behaviour part of her charm. In the dream his own age was indeterminate, but he recognized the smile, which in fact had never left him. When he finally reconciled himself to a day like any other he knew, without a shadow of a doubt, that he was seventy-three years old, 'retired', as they said of old people with too little to do, and that Fanny would be a year older. In fact when he had last seen her, in Nyon, at the Beau Rivage, she was already altered. He had sought her out after his divorce, with the intention of asking her to marry him. He had found a stout dignified woman who did not even possess her mother's chic. 'Julius!' she had said. 'What on earth are you doing here?' And he had made his request, far too early in the proceedings, without the proper setting or preparation, to have it waved away by a still pretty hand. He did not tell her that he had followed her progress by dint of some unnecessary detective work, for what was there to discover? He already knew that Fanny and her mother had, by virtue of Hubertus's prudence, been dispatched to Switzerland, to the most peaceful and neutral of lakeside towns, until things improved. He knew that equally prudent Aunt Anna had found her daughter a husband, an architect called Mellerio who had taken them both on, installing them in his ugly villa, from which they escaped as often as they could, to eat cakes at the English tea-room or to sit on the terrace of the Beau Rivage, to which they quite naturally retired after Mellerio's death from a fall when he was inspecting one of his own buildings. The sale of his house and of his business had left them well off: the hotel suited them, or rather hotel life suited them, was appropriate to a deracinated existence which could surely be only temporary. They were safe, more than safe, for the time being, but in fact never went home, for home no longer existed, flattened by Allied bombs, and Hubertus no longer alive to make plans for them all.

Calmly Fanny had rejected his proposal, not unkindly, simply demonstrating that she was better off as she was. She did not speak as if she had a lover, nor did he suspect her of living an irregular life. She was placid, comfortable; she played bridge with women friends, looked after her mother in the suite they shared, still frequented the English tea-room or sat on the terrace before retiring to make alterations to her appearance and thus ushering in the evening. She was practically Swiss now, just as he was practically English, but their childhood had left its mark. That was why he was so grateful that part of them remained untouched. More realistically he could see that she would never exchange Nyon for London. He accepted defeat, joined Fanny and her mother for dinner at their habitual table, and left for home the next day. Neither of them had thought his visit anything out of the ordinary. He had returned home to an empty flat, promising to keep in touch. This he had done sparingly, unable to identify the stout calm woman who was Fanny in late middle age with her younger dark-haired dark-eyed self. Therefore he was more than happy to have encountered her in his dream, intact, unchanged. Even in the dream he had not possessed her, yet, untouched, innocent, he preferred it so, or was conscious of having decreed that this should be. At heart he was still a young man, a boy, even, to whom adulthood had come as a surprise and had never ceased to be a burden.

In retrospect even his visit to Nyon—his only visit—seemed to possess a kind of charm. This had more to do with his own initiative than with the reception offered. For he had still been relatively young, able to make decisions, or maybe trusting more to chance than he was ever willing to do in normal circumstances. Fanny's rejection of his proposal did not alter his impression of adventure, of acting on an impulse that impressed him as heroic. For both of them her refusal was final. He knew that he would never see her again. He wrote to her, keeping her in touch with news of the family, such as it was, but received few replies. Eventually a letter came informing him that her mother was unwell and that she was to marry again, the two pieces of information logically linked. Her new husband was a German businessman; she had met him at the hotel where he was on holiday, and in due course she would move back to Germany with him, to Bonn. She seemed to have no qualms about this return. Assured of protection, she disregarded the wider implications. But that had always been part of her charm: her utter selfishness. And this same selfishness gave her a character to be reckoned with. She was no longer the young beauty whose tears usually ensured that her wishes were met. He did not blame her. He wrote congratulating her, and then the letters stopped. He had no new address for her, relinquished her symbolically as well as emotionally. He no longer knew anything about her, whether she was ill or well, whether, in fact, she was still alive. For some reason he sent a card to her, care of the Beau Rivage, one year after their last communication. It was met with silence, as he knew it would be.

Thinking back to the dream, the details of which were still clear in his mind's eye, he reflected that everything was retrievable, or so it seemed. He frequently dreamed of his parents, but not with the weary impatience he now felt for them, and was entitled to feel now that he had somehow survived them. In dreams he was once more the tender affectionate boy he had once been, able to tolerate his mother's complaints, his father's humility, his brother Freddy's assumption of superiority, always with that eager placating smile, trying to make things better. How much of his life he had wasted in this attempt! Making things better seemed to have been assigned to him as his life's work, particularly making things better for Freddy, to whom he had been something of a guardian, although he was the younger brother. How he had admired Freddy and his prowess at the violin! How he loathed them in retrospect! As far as he could remember Freddy had always been regarded as a genius, largely by his parents, but it was true that he had enormous facility and was easily persuaded to perform. His youth and his poetic looks had prevailed easily on agents and concert promoters, and soon Freddy's engagements became a priority in their little household. He played well, but confined himself to easier popular pieces—Sarasate, Saint-Saëns—acquired a certain wider prestige, was a name, a prodigy, whose gifts might or might not last. It was not his gifts that let him down, but rather his temperament. He was unequal to the concert platform for which his parents destined him, developed nervous trouble, a tremor in his right hand, and with the collapse of his future willed himself into a kind of invalidism which in time became ineluctable. This was not helped by their translation from Berlin to London, where his father found employment in a record shop; visits to the hospital or the nursing-home had absorbed all his free time, time that might have been put towards his studies. But these, once interrupted by the change in language and curriculum, never really flourished, and were in any case not a priority. Freddy was the priority. He now marvelled that he had never questioned this.

All gone now, all over, and himself the survivor. As he eased himself out of bed he reflected that survival was a mixed blessing. It involved surrendering that once young self to time, and time taught harsh lessons. Only the moments one managed to save from time were acceptable, and those were not always in one's gift. Yet the dream had restored him momentarily to his younger self. How quick he had been, how candid! He no longer remembered how he had looked, but knew the eager confident smile which had faded somewhat with age and experience. There was no one now on whom to lavish that smile, yet on occasions it still preceded him, seemed to announce his future cooperation in whatever was decided. He knew he was alone, that he must rouse himself, make a cup of tea, prepare himself for another boring day. This pacifying routine brought no rewards, was often accomplished with a sigh, and, worse, had to be eternally undertaken. Solvent, and as healthy as he could be at his age, he nevertheless knew that his journeyings were nearly over, that he would remain in this small home he had made for himself until he was eclipsed, he hoped far from indifferent eyes. Sparse now, but not noticeably diminished, he could still convince anyone who cared to look that he was a viable concern. To a careless observer he seemed to be making out a good case for survival. But his heart still ached over the intervening middle years, which were ones of curatorship, of his parents, of Freddy. Their deaths had not emboldened him to strike out on his own. Even his resolute holidays were accompanied by a feeling of sadness, for he knew that he would always have to return to accumulated sadness, the sadness of his stricken parents, the sadness of those visits to Freddy in hospital, in the nursing-home, and finally to that windswept Quaker establishment, half hotel half rehabilitation centre, where he had languished (where both of them had languished) until Freddy's death. The memory of those weekend visits would, he thought, be with him beyond the grave. All the deaths were natural, yet all had an aura of horror. It was their lives rather than their deaths that were regrettable, and all the frustrated love that had failed to sweeten their end.

Even at his age he still felt the hurts of childhood, the ever-present anxiety represented by the family which was in his charge. For he had been the only viable member of that small unit, mismatched, divided, uncertain. His father's life had been one of unsought duties, of which pacifying his disappointed wife had been uppermost. He had left for his humble employment as a shop assistant with the relief of a man let out of prison, leaving Julius to take charge of his diminished household, until another vacancy in the shop offered Julius the same reprieve from domestic sorrow. And the shop had been his eventually, when the owner, Ostrovski, a fellow German despite his name, retired to southern Spain. Ostrovski had been his first and last benefactor, had befriended him, had taken him to the Czech club to meet others in the same boat. Exiles, Herz had had time to reflect, were the original networkers. At the time he had not recognized the generosity of feeling this represented; he was reading his way through *Palgrave's Golden Treasury* and exiles had no place in his new English life.

Now, retired himself, he almost wished he still had the shop to go to, so that he could take his place in the early-morning streets with fellow workers. Instead he would go out to buy his newspaper, would read it carefully over breakfast, and then go out again to buy something for his lunch. He was no cook; there was nothing to prevent him eating out, but he felt conspicuous on his own and pre-ferred to return home until he could think of a further excursion to occupy the afternoon. A gallery would do, a bookshop in the centre of town. It was a laborious life, lived with caution. He no longer had the heart for those solitary holidays, his suitcases relegated to the storeroom in the basement. He welcomed the night hours, even though he slept badly. His parents had gone to bed soon after their evening meal. By eight-thirty their meagre flat was silent. Now that silence was being replicated. He too went to bed early, recognizing the despair that had prompted those par-ents to do so. At moments like these his habitual smile fal-tered, as it had done all those years ago. Dreams were his only reward, his only birthright.

Bathed and shaved he felt more confident, applied the pomade and the cologne that did little for his appearance but conformed with some gentlemanly ritual that must also have been a family characteristic, belonging to more spacious times before their translation to reduced circum-stances. In this way he could confront the day, would re-peat the grooming process with the brushing of his coat and shoes, with the final smoothing of his hair. The street beckoned, with its illusion of life, of company. At moments like this he envied no one, indeed he knew of few people to envy. Solitude had bred a stoicism which he hoped would see him through. He patted his breast pocket to assure himself that his pills were in a safe place. He did not consider these pills to be serious, but at his age, he supposed, everyone took pills. And the young man who was now his doctor had looked at him so trustingly, rather as if his own health depended on Herz's obedience. And it was not raining for once. He thought he might telephone his former wife at some point and suggest lunch or dinner. Although they had parted without regret he still looked forward to seeing her, and thought she felt the same. The divorce had been amicable. He thought of it as the one good thing he had managed to bring off. So did his exwife. The memory brought a certain grim amusement. Strangely there was no bitterness. When he thought of her, which was not often, the smile found its place once more. Lunch, he thought, then a film, if she had the time. Thus armed with purpose he went out to buy *The Times*.

# 2

As he stepped out into Chiltern Street, under a cloudy sky, Herz could see that this was to be a day for memories. Dreams he would have to postpone for future nights. He reflected, as he always did, on the strength of that early imprinting which left so many faces intact. He could see, as if he had just left her at the bus stop, his mother's friend Bijou Frank, who always came to tea on Saturday afternoons, when he was with Freddy in Brighton and his father at the shop. They were living in Hilltop Road at that time, in a flat that was too big for them. They had stayed there when they first came to London because Hubertus, who had many contacts, had arranged it through a friend of his. This friend happened to be a connection of Ostrovski, the owner of the music shop which had taken them both on. So that in their early days they were entirely dependent on Germans, and on what had been decided for them in Berlin.

This eased the transition to a considerable extent but had kept them from making new friends. In any event they had not felt welcome, had been aware that critical eyes surveyed them in the street. Neighbours made no approaches. It was charitable to suppose that they had as yet little idea of circumstances in Germany. The flat was rent-controlled, which did something to disguise the fact that it was ultra respectable, bourgeois even; at some point they would have to leave. When this happened—and everything was uncertain, undecided—they would, advised Ostrovski, be better off in the flat above the shop in Edgware Road. This flat was small, too small, but it had the advantage of belonging to Ostrovski, who had taken on something of a godfatherly role. His mother suspected that Ostrovski wanted the Hilltop Road property for another of his protégés, a woman, no doubt, but they were in no position to dissent. And in Edgware Road his father would avoid the long walk which was his only recreation, his only diversion. Again there was no way in which to point out that a move would not be entirely desirable. They were dependent on the kindness of strangers, even if this kindness took the form of decisions over which they had no control.

It was in Hilltop Road that Bijou Frank visited his mother, on those terrible Saturday afternoons when he kept Freddy company. He could see her now, as plainly as anything: a small tremulous figure in her decent black coat and the stolid felt hat that overshadowed her anxious little face. She too was a contact from the old days, although she had been in England for some time, had married an elderly Englishman whose stultifying love had isolated her from the sort of company for which she craved. A widow, with more than adequate means, she had found herself virtually disabled from normal contacts, was more than delighted to meet Trude Herz in the local bakery, swiftly agreed to renew what had never been more than a vague friendship, was relieved in fact to have found a female confidant after years of attendance on a man she had not chosen. He had chosen her, she explained to her new-found friend, and never willingly allowed her out of his sight. She was free of him now, but not free of his influence, as nervous and as circumspect as if he were still watching her every movement. Although she was competent enough in other respects, she was frightened of most things and took comfort in Julius's presence when he walked her slowly to the bus stop and waited with her until the bus arrived. This was a courtesy he would never dream of shirking. In any event his mother insisted on it. So that even on radiant summer evenings, when young men of his age were preparing to enjoy themselves, he was imprisoned by Bijou Frank's little hand on his arm, and her slow steps, and her murmurings, which had all to do with her concern for his mother's health (which was indeed poor), and her own despair at their present circumstances. Freed at last by the arrival of the bus, he would wait and wave for as long as she remained in view. It was her last sweet smile that went part way to reconciling him to the further duties that awaited him at home.

Bijou Frank was a good friend to his mother, and he hoped that his mother was as good a friend to Bijou, who seemed, and was, devoted. He was spared much of their conversation, which he supposed consisted of Bijou's marital experiences and his mother's hypochondria. Each listened eagerly to the other, while waiting her turn to speak. Yet these occasions revived something of his mother's assertiveness, before the advent of Freddy's mysterious opposition to his destiny, or rather to the destiny she had decreed for him, had dealt her such a cruel blow. She would dress more carefully than usual, would prepare a dish of small delicacies, would retrieve, for a brief interval, the manners of a Berlin hostess, would in fact rise above her circumstances in a way she was never able to manage in the intervals between Bijou's visits. She was greedy for Bijou's company, but would never allow this to show. Nevertheless it was a friendship of some weight, though had they still been in Berlin they might not have seen each other more than a couple of times a year. The tea-table, like Bijou's hat, which was never removed, reassured them both that standards were being maintained, that worldliness had not entirely deserted them. This reassurance was perhaps their last link with their former lives. They knew this too, and treasured the knowledge.

'And how is our dear friend this evening?' his father would enquire after his return from the shop, gallantly professing friendship on his own behalf while silently longing for a restorative glass of schnapps. This he was not allowed, for a further ceremony had to be enacted, a thimbleful of cherry brandy in which he joined the ladies. This was the signal that the visit was about to be concluded, that he, Julius, was soon to usher out again with Bijou on his arm.

'Well, thank you, Willy, and yourself? Your work?'
'Fine. Perfectly fine.'
'What news from over there?'
'What do you expect? Best not to think about it.'
'I try not to. But it's not easy.'
'It will not be easy for a long time.'

Here his mother would break in, saying that they must all try to live in the present. This she managed to do in a somewhat uncanny fashion, disguising her resentments and anxieties by concentrating on her physical condition, which she allowed to overshadow the physical condition of her husband, her younger son, and Freddy, in whose rehabilitation she appeared to place exaggerated faith. That her faith was misplaced Julius had had reason to reflect once more that afternoon, while sitting with Freddy in his barely furnished room in what he privately thought of as the hostel in Brighton which Freddy showed no disposition to leave. Both Julius and his father knew that when Bijou Frank took her leave Mrs Herz would revert to her former self, would remove her necklace and her earrings, and as like as not change into a dressing-gown. The inquest on Freddy's health would take place later that evening, when they were all exhausted, and would be exhaustive. What did they know of those bleak Saturday afternoons? What did he allow them to know? Making things better was his task, his obligation, and eventually, after another glass of cherry brandy, his mother would allow herself to be encouraged to go to bed. Their supper would consist of the smoked salmon canapés and the little macaroons that had been laid out for the guest. The guest, as if suspecting, had eaten sparingly. In some ways she was a delicate-minded woman. They were all careful of the friendship, for it was almost the only one they had.

But even those exhausted Saturday evenings were a relief after the day that had preceded them. Those Saturdays! Even at the age he had become, even on the verge of extinction, as he supposed himself to be, Herz hated weekends. Sundays were just possible; on Sundays he took a walk, stopping off at churches for a few minutes, to see if he liked the programme, as it were, and, inevitably, wandering out again as if he knew that he was out of place, or rather that his place was elsewhere, in some harsher environment. God was not present for him on these occasions, but then he knew that God was not to be approached in so casual a fashion. It was the absence of Jesus that saddened him, for surely he should have felt some sort of call? His ancestral religion, which he did not practise, seemed to him an affair of prohibitions, of righteous exclusiveness for which he could see no justification. He would have welcomed some sort of approach, some sort of solicitation, but it was not to be. Although resolutely secular in outlook, as were his parents, he had been expelled from Germany as if guilty of some ancestral flaw. And he supposed this to be the case, for he was not filled with love, as he knew that Christians were, rather the opposite. For example, he felt a dawning hostility towards his brother. And what had he to do with the puerile sentimentalities that surrounded the Infant Jesus? He knew that he had to make things better, but without supernatural aid this seemed too difficult for him. He supposed that he would do his duty, since that was what was required of him. Nevertheless if he had known of some kindly deity he would have requested some sort of temporary exemption from the task, just enough time to get his own life on its course, and allow him to exert a choice.

In later life he marvelled that his parents had had so little idea that pleasure and freedom were due to the young. He excused them finally, for their own youth was somehow unimaginable, as if they had been careworn adults as soon as they were born. He felt pity for them, an exasperated love, a kind of acceptance, but he also knew that he had not come into a proper inheritance, the inheritance of the truly young. Nor had Freddy, despite the indulgence they had lavished on him. In later life he came to understand that Freddy was braver than himself, for Freddy acknowledged his resentment of those parents who had set him on so vertiginous a course, one that he was not able to sustain. Freddy's nervous breakdown, if that was what it was, had more to do with rebellion than with genuine suffering. That he had become ill was not in any doubt, yet in his mother's desire to attribute the illness to Freddy's artistic temperament, to nothing more fundamental or more radical, to discontent, in a word, was part of her blindness, and of her continued favour. This made Freddy's incarceration bearable, acted as an interval in which she could make new plans for him. It was also part of her blindness that she could not see that these plans were no longer necessary.

Saturdays, therefore, were surrounded by melancholy. He would make his way, by bus, by train, and by another bus, to the outpost where his brother now had his being. It was a house which had formerly been a private hotel, now converted into a long-stay facility for those in need of refuge. There was some nursing care, but patients, or residents, were expected to look after themselves, under the benevolent guidance of Mrs Walters, who owned the place and lived on the premises. This excellent woman always greeted Julius with every appearance of a good will he knew to be genuine. It was another instance of the mystery of the Holy Spirit, for Mrs Walters was religious. Freddy, on the other hand, showed little good will, was probably unaware that Julius had given up his free time to visit him, received the newspaper and the bag of fruit without apparent appreciation, and waved his brother to a chair as if preparing to give an interview to a journalist. His habit of

referring to 'my mother' and 'my father' also had something autobiographical about it. He seemed to be kept
going by the fantasy that he was still a performer, a prodigy,
yet at some point in their conversation the fantasy broke
down and he would dissolve into tears. That was when
Julius himself felt tears rising, not merely for Freddy but
for the wreckage of his family.

'Don't cry,' he would say. 'You look so much better.
Here, have some of this chocolate.' And the shaking hand
would reach out eagerly for the offer of sweetness that he
thought was still his due.

His looks were altered, his hair thinning, his body slack
and unused. Yet he was not discontented, except when he
referred to the past. Retrospectively he felt the monstrous
injustice of those artificial expectations, seemed to prefer
this small bare room to the home he had once known,
seemed to be at ease until the time came for him to ani-
madvert against those pressures which had brought him to
this place. This was the ritual that informed these visits,
and the complaints were always the same.

'I was too young,' he would say. 'I didn't know how to
refuse. I was sick before and after every performance. Even
so my mother forced me to practise, sat in the front row—
in the middle of the front row—whenever I performed.
My father went along with it, although he could have
saved me. But he had no character. And my mother always
overruled him. A terrible woman.'

He did not ask how any of them were getting along.
Imperceptibly the tone had become grandiose, dismissive,
for the benefit of the imaginary interviewer. Except that
Freddy did not seem to know that the interviewer was in
fact his brother. The soliloquy was routine, but Julius never

heard it without embarrassment. In vain he would look out of the window, at the white sky. It was as cold in the room as it had been out of doors. Even on the rare days of sunshine the winds were penetrating.

'Don't you get bored?' he would ask, in an effort to break the monotony of the afternoon. Boredom and discomfort were the essence of the place. 'Don't you want to do some sort of work?'

At this Freddy looked evasive. 'I help out here,' he said. 'In the kitchen sometimes.'

'You could do that at home.'

'I couldn't leave Mrs Walters.' He looked agitated. 'I could never leave Mrs Walters.'

'You will have to at some point. We can't afford . . .'

'They'll give me a job here. That way I can keep my room.'

This was what in fact had happened. They gave him a small wage to help out as a general assistant, mainly as a cleaner. The rags and polishes made his hands rough and swollen but did something to arrest the tremor. The shame of this was unbearable to Julius, yet he knew that there was no alternative. If they were to move to the flat over the shop there would be no room for Freddy. Exert good will as he might, Julius could not accommodate the thought that he might once again be displaced by his brother. Therefore he kept quiet about the arrangements, merely told his father that less money would be needed for Freddy's upkeep. His father had looked at him sharply, then subsided. 'The heartbreak,' he said. 'My beautiful boy.'

'You'll have to go now,' Freddy would say. 'It's nearly time for tea. I said I'd wash up afterwards.'

'I'll see you next week,' they both said, as if this were

somehow necessary. They embraced at the door of Freddy's room. In that embrace there was something of the fervour of two originally loving siblings. Then the visit would be over.

Julius accepted that his parents were unequal to the task he shouldered every week. Those parents (and Freddy too knew this) were too fearful of confronting the shipwreck of their hopes, and lived an obstinate illusion of normality in absolute denial of the facts of the case. It was a tactic which had ensured their survival, and one on which they fiercely relied. The burden was shifted to their younger son, who became guardian to all three of them, unaware of his own entitlements. Yet on the way back to the station he was habitually engulfed in a sadness that coloured the entire landscape. It was then that the full tragedy of Freddy's life appeared at its most significant. And it was not yet over: his decline from cherished prodigy to general handyman would take place without interruption, without intervention. For he had been young enough to believe in all-powerful agencies which would somehow reverse a process so ineluctably under way. He accepted without question that Freddy no longer wished to listen to music, but thought that art should not let one down in so deliberate a fashion. Art was surely the key to a better world, yet Freddy had renounced it as if his engagement with it had been a mere flirtation, and moreover a flirtation which had failed to develop into a mature relationship. His mother still listened to music on the radio, beating time with her hand, and they were, after all, surrounded by music in the shop, but for his father and himself it held no message. What held a message was Freddy and his rebellion, which had ended in an almost willing acceptance of defeat. Or was there freedom in that defeat? Was Freddy in some ghastly way appeased? It was as if he had cast off his previous life and with it all those earlier attachments which had filled it. It was Mrs Walters who was his new parent, and Julius saw no value in trying to bring him home, in all senses of the word. 'My mother' and 'my father' had become almost mythical personages, quite without application to the present day, and Julius himself too humble an interlocutor to arouse much interest. It was probably preferable that he should not be disturbed by echoes of the wider world, but Julius wondered what would happen if and when his parents died. Would that occasion some sort of reawakening, some cataclysm of buried feeling? That was to be avoided, if possible, for he could still break down again. And what would happen if Freddy were to die before his parents was not to be contemplated. The ruin of two other fragile lives, of three, if he were to count his own, would be complete. He had no doubt that other deaths would follow swiftly, and his own need to make things better, the task to which he still gave his loyalty, would be exposed for what it was: a wish, a vain wish that his efforts would be crowned, if not with glory, then at least with a sense of honour.

Fifty years later, a lifetime later, Herz reflected that Freddy's gift, though phenomenal, had been unsettling. It seemed a kind of autism rather than a genuine passion. Audiences had watched, fascinated, as different emotions chased themselves over Freddy's face, as if the unconscious were visibly at work. He had seemed totally unconnected to what he was feeling or experiencing, as if those experiences were taking place in another dimension, remote from everyday circumstances. Attendance at his recitals was always eager, but as if in response to a phenomenon, a fairground spectacle. The return to everyday life must have been painful in the extreme. No wonder he had had to stop playing, to stop vomiting, to stop being translated elsewhere. No wonder he had broken down. And once his illness had been accepted he had seemed lightened of a burden, as if nothing more could be expected of him. Even his mother was somehow aware of this, although she kept up the fiction of his recuperation for reasons of her own. Despite the horror of those visits Julius could see that there was nothing to be done, and would leave Brighton with no sense of a duty discharged but rather of the enactment of a ceremony over which no one had any control. His own emotions, though extreme, had had to do with himself, as if he were one of those victims in the French Revolution who were tied to a dead body and thrown into the river to drown. He had been sacrificed, in helpless attendance on someone who had in many ways already passed out of this life.

Herz wondered if all old people came to such knowledge when there was nothing to be done to remedy the damage. He wondered if the people he passed in the street ruminated on lost causes, as he did. There was little value in such reflections; they were a function of the passing of time, and so beyond applicability. What control could he exercise even now on those sad Saturdays, except to recognize that he was their legatee? Try as he might to divert himself he could never escape the suspicion that he should be elsewhere, that he should not be shopping in Marks &

Spencer but walking resignedly along an empty road, his collar turned up against the wind from the sea. It was only when Saturday was over, and he was sitting in front of his own undoubted television, in his own verifiable flat, that he could relax. Yet even then he was half prepared to go out again, to see Mrs Frank to the bus stop, postponing his life once again in the vain hope that someone would restore it to him.

Freddy had died in a hospice, with only himself in attendance. As he had hoped, the parents had died before him. Julius had wondered whether to tell Freddy that these deaths had taken place, and had finally done so. Freddy was by that stage very weak, drifting in and out of consciousness, but he had appeared to understand. As if united in family piety they had held hands. It was when their hands grew cold, in unison, that Julius knew that Freddy's life was over. Once again he had not seemed discontented. His features had taken on the strange remote fascination that he had manifested when he was playing. It was as if death itself had made its presence felt in the remote days of his success. Only this time it was clear that he felt no fear.

# 3

Late in the afternoon Herz telephoned the garden centre where his former wife now worked and asked for Mrs Burns. Josie had reverted to her maiden name after the divorce but had kept the married style. He found this perfectly acceptable; he could appreciate that marriage, even a defunct marriage, conferred a certain dignity on a woman, and women nowadays were, or seemed to be, rather anxious to define their status. Besides, she was to all intents and purposes a married woman, comfortable with her condition, perhaps even more so than she had ever been as a wife. And she was of an age when dignity counted: the single state, despite all propaganda to the contrary, still had something sad about it. Widows were in a different category. He suspected that Josie would have been quite contented as a widow, but was still sufficiently attached to him to have alighted on what she saw as an ideal definition. He knew that their divorce had separated them; he also knew that they would remain friends. Indeed they had always been friends, even more so than husband and wife. Their marriage had lasted a bare two and a half years and they had parted without rancour. He still looked forward to seeing her from time to time, in the relaxed manner which had become habitual to them both. They met occasionally,

without undue anticipation on either side, but took some
kind of reassurance from the unchanging nature of such
meetings. Nothing had been lost; they remained more
than acquaintances, allies in fact, with the sort of familiarity gained from intense though brief physical proximity.

'Josie? Julius here. I wondered if you could manage
lunch next week?'

'Love to. Monday's my best day. We're not busy on
Mondays.'

'Next Monday, then. Sheekey's at twelve forty-five.'

'See you then. Goodbye, Julius.'

He liked her businesslike tone on the telephone. She
was a woman without prevarication, one who spoke her
mind in an instinctive, almost inoffensive manner. This was
what had led, indirectly, to their eventual separation. He
suppressed a lingering feeling of shame as he remembered
the attempt he had made to deflect her outspokenness. For
himself he had not minded; for others he had minded too
much.

With a sigh he went to the mirror and surveyed himself, as if preparing to meet her straight away. She had
thought him handsome, 'distinguished', as she put it, and
might even think so now. The great attraction for him was,
and always had been, her physical ordinariness, although
she was a pleasant-looking woman and might have made
more of herself. This she clearly thought either unnecessary or impossible. In any event she presented an efficient
if slightly unkempt appearance which he was always mentally tidying up, anxious for her to have her hair expertly
cut, to put some colour on her lips, even to wear the scents
he took pleasure in buying for her. But she laughed those

away, and continued to content herself with a vigorous wash before facing the day. He found her natural smell exciting, although part of him was comprehensively disappointed that she did not resemble the pampered women he had been used to in his youth, with their painted nails and faces. His aunt Anna, for example, was always perfectly dressed and coiffed, and if the continued effort made her seem a little bad-tempered he appreciated that too. Instinctively he preferred women who made much of themselves, were capricious, flirtatious even, though he knew that such behaviour had gone out of style. Josie, with her bushy hair and unadorned face, which he had loved, had not altogether displaced the image which he would, somehow, have found easier to understand.

But they were old now, their looks no longer a bargaining counter. In the mirror he saw a sombre thin-faced man who could no longer be confused with his younger self, his eager smile eclipsed, more by solitude than by experience. In truth he felt himself to be as unprepared for life as he had been in his youth, though he tried to be as competent as he had always been, or so he supposed. He knew that he stooped, that he tired swiftly, that he could no longer walk as far as he had been accustomed to do, that he felt the cold to an abnormal extent. This chilly spring, these long light evenings, made him as fretful as a child, disturbed his sleep to an extent that made him anxious to get up and begin the day, even though that day was as empty as the night had been. He thought back to the nights he had spent with his wife, but without a flicker of desire—strange, since they had been such enthusiastic partners. He had been anxious for continuity, for permanence, after years of fleeting relationships, garnered opportunistically to satisfy his appetites. He was as idealistic about marriage as any young girl, could hardly believe his good fortune in finally acceding to the married state.

And he had wanted someone to be kind to him, to look after him, and to allay the sadness he seemed still to feel, a sadness which had nothing to do with hardships and disappointments but was rather an inheritance he did not fully understand. To attribute this sadness to early privation seemed to him not quite to explain it. Certainly there were legitimate sadnesses which were perfectly obvious, but the sadness had outlasted the various phenomena that had provoked it, so that now it was not only ineradicable but somehow renewed each day by the condition of old age. Those cold nights in an unwarmed bed were not only physically uncomfortable but emotionally, even morally, unbearable. This was not how things should end. And he felt bound to conclude that his divorce, while reconciling him once again to his solitary dreaming state, the state in which he still cherished Fanny Bauer, had brought about a diminution in his perception of what life still had to offer.

It was not even that his wife had satisfied every imaginary requirement, had embodied all his fantasies about companionship, stored up from youth. It was even simpler than that. She was robust, practical, normal, and in the early days she had seemed to have normality in her gift, so that he himself felt healthier, heartier, more optimistic, more enthusiastic as he went about his various tasks. Above all he did not have to compensate her for anything, console her for unhappiness, make things better . . . Although it was she who had demanded the divorce he knew that the fault was his, the original fault, like original sin, which might not have been detected at first glance. They were mismatched, but not in any obvious sense, despite their utterly different backgrounds; they were mismatched by virtue of their needs, though these needs had for a time been miraculously met. That he had failed her was abundantly clear, even though he was not technically guilty of any misdemeanour. Others perhaps were guilty, but he could not entirely blame those others. He reflected that to act out of need is always fatal. He tried to give himself some credit for not letting his own need compromise his sense of fairness. In that way he was still able to look forward to his next meeting with his wife. Their affection for each other had not soured, had if anything increased now that need no longer entered the equation. He sighed as he thought of the long week to be got through before he saw her again.

They had met in circumstances that had been so unexpected, so mysterious, and yet so humdrum that it seemed appropriate to mention fate. He had not at first paid much attention to the woman standing in front of him in the queue at the bank until she had asked if she might borrow his pen to write a cheque. Conscious of the shop's takings, which he had in a canvas bag kept for this purpose, he had smiled briefly but had made no attempt to engage in conversation. It was only when they left the bank at the same time that he sought to offer some acknowledgement of her presence. After a couple of anodyne remarks ('Lovely day', 'Yes, isn't it? At last.') they were alerted by a crash in the street beyond the bank's double doors, and instinctively ran out together to see a young man on the ground and a taxi driver standing over him. A large fuming motorcycle on its side, just in front of the taxi, explained the crash, though the taxi driver's part in it was, and was to remain, unexplained. One or two people had gathered, and there was talk of the need for an ambulance. 'Let me through,' said the woman who turned out to be Josie. 'I'm a nurse.' She bent over the boy, who seemed to be eighteen or nineteen and was clearly concussed, and asked, 'Can you hear me? What's your name?'

'Richard,' was the very faint reply.

'Don't worry, Richard. We'll take care of you.'

Already someone had issued from the bank, saying proudly that an ambulance was on its way.

'Don't touch him.' Her instructions were given in a kindly but authoritative manner. 'I think he's broken his shoulder.'

It seemed entirely natural that the two of them should join the boy in the ambulance, and even wait in the hospital until he had been found a bed. With the arrival of a doctor (exhausted, and looking about as young as the patient) he put his hand under her elbow and steered her away. The incident seemed to have taken place in a dream; already he felt he knew her as well as he knew anyone.

'Would you like a cup of coffee?' he asked. She declined, saying that she had to go to work. It was with a feeling of regret that he saw her go.

After lunch he sent his father upstairs to the as yet untenanted flat above the shop for a rest. This he did every day, aware that what had become routine for them both confined him until the late afternoon, when his father would make an increasingly mournful appearance, unwilling to renew acquaintance with a commerce he despised. They would greet the odd customer with enthusiasm, grateful for the opportunity to make a little conversation. In the absence of customers they put up with each other but said little. Their proximity both at work and at home was oppressive but also comprehensible: there was no need to talk. Julius watched without comment as his father became more negligent, his hair disarranged by his recent siesta, his handkerchief trailing from his trouser pocket. There was little to be done; they were both too fundamentally disheartened to look for any kind of improvement. It was almost a relief to know that his father was incommunicable for a couple of hours, barricaded in sleep on the bed which had been left in the flat and which Ostrovski had used for the occasional assignation during the day. They had no idea what he otherwise did with himself. The shop, of which he was the uninterested owner, he was more than glad to leave to the assiduity of the father and son, went off to play cards or to visit one of his girlfriends, turned up from time to time to see how they were getting on, more in a spirit of curiosity than anything more considered, suggested a cup of coffee, and, after satisfying himself that the business was being looked after, disappeared again into the busy street. They suspected that their days in Hilltop Road were numbered, that Ostrovski would dispossess them without a qualm, satisfied that he had found them alternative accommodation. That this accommodation was inferior—dark, dusty, up a creaking staircase—did not seem to be negotiable. They all knew this, but his father was too polite to complain, or to express disappointment. It was not disappointment that they felt; it was, once again, despair. Willy Herz knew that his wife, who had yet to see the flat, would shriek with horror, declare it impossible, and, worse, would make no effort to make it habitable. That would be his task. How many times in his life had he had to mobilize his wife into some sort of energetic action, aware of her unhappiness, which was now also his own? The flat would do very well for him, but only on condition that he was on his own. His secret wish was to be a bachelor again, for it was only as a bachelor that he could have confronted this new life. The task of making his beloved wife happy was beyond him, as it was beyond everyone now. He dreaded the day when his unhappiness would break cover, was grateful to Julius—not his best-loved son—for his tact, realized sorrowfully that Julius had been sacrificed, and, short of a miracle, would continue to be sacrificed, by virtue of a family bound together by grief and with no prospect of rehabilitation.

During the afternoon hours, with little to distract him, Julius's thoughts returned to the morning's incident, concentrating on the boy's frightened face rather than on the so capable nurse. Richard, he had said his name was. Perhaps he had surrendered him too quickly, anxious as he had been to remain with the nurse? He resolved to go back to the hospital as soon as he had finished work, would ask the boy if he needed anything, would promise to look in again. This visit made him surprisingly happy. Divested of his leather accoutrements Richard looked younger than he had first appeared, was perhaps no more than seventeen. He had managed, he told Julius, to get a message to his mother and father and had told them not to worry. Julius thought this surprisingly mature of him and said so. The boy looked gratified. In his hospital gown and with the heavy dressing imprisoning his arm and shoulder there was little he could do for himself. 'They're very kind here, but they're so busy,' was his only comment. Julius went away to buy him a few necessities from the hospital shop, and told the boy that if he wanted anything he had only to say so. There was a moment's hesitation, then came a request for a motorcycle magazine. He promised to bring it in on the following evening, prepared to leave, got up, and saw the nurse—his nurse—advancing from the end of the ward. He was suddenly overjoyed. They stood on either side of the bed and smiled down at Richard as if he belonged to them both. Then, when visiting time was over, they said goodbye, promising to come again. He wondered how to further this rather odd acquaintance. But there was no need to wonder, as it turned out, because as soon as they were in the street she turned to him and said, 'I'll have that coffee now, if you've got time.'

'Delighted,' he said. And he was.

In the course of that first tentative meeting he learned something, but not much, about her. She did private nursing, was under contract to a nursing agency, shared a flat in Wandsworth with two other girls. It seemed a little early to discuss their heredity but she told him that she had been brought up by her grandparents after her widowed mother had gone back to work, and had had a perfectly happy childhood in Maidstone, where her mother, now retired, still lived. 'You're not English, are you?' she disconcertingly observed, so that he was obliged to tell her something of his background. Then she thanked him for the coffee and stood up to leave.

'Will I see you again?' he had asked. She had smiled. 'Almost certainly, I should think.' After a second visit to their patient he had invited her out for a meal, after which they made use of the flat above the shop, to their mutual satisfaction.

He was impressed by her honesty, both in bed and out of it. Used as he was to polite evasiveness on the part of his father, to regrets on the part of his mother, he thought he might find this difficult, but instead found it liberating. Josie was vigorously natural, in a way that impressed him as foreign. He had not come across this style before and thought it characteristically English, an opinion which he held in the teeth of much evidence to the contrary and which he never revised. Within days he knew that he wanted to marry her, wanted her comfortable confident presence in his life as a bulwark against future sorrow. The only problem that he could foresee was introducing her to the habits and customs that held sway in Hilltop Road, to the early nights, to the company of no one more excit- ing than Bijou Frank and Ostrovski, who looked in occa- sionally on Friday evenings, 'keeping up the old traditions', as he claimed, though they were none of them obser- vant. Even his mother had abandoned her former intran- sigence, and had written to her sister care of the Beau Rivage in Nyon, the Nyon she had never visited, nor was likely to visit. But he need not have worried, for they had both adored Josie, seeing her, not unreasonably, as a sym- bol of life and health, 'a breath of fresh air', as his mother said. And it was somewhat to his surprise that Josie, with her exuberant forthright manner and her untidy hair, had made such a good impression. As, he was the first to con-

cede, were his parents. His mother had bestirred herself
and cooked a proper meal, which Josie ate with every sign
of enjoyment. Their first meeting could not have been
more auspicious.

'Lovely place you've got here,' said Josie. 'Bit different
from . . .' The flat above the shop, she was about to say.

He silenced her with a warning glance, but saw his father hide a small smile and turn away to hide a larger one.

'Oh, Julius has shown you the other flat, has he?' said his
mother, unaware. 'Yes, well, we shall have to come to terms
with it. Of course it's hardly what we're used to.'

'Must you move, then? Can't you stay here?'

'The owner, Mr Ostrovski, whom I'm sure you will
meet, wants it for himself, though as an inveterate traveller
he will hardly be here.'

This was an old grievance, but how could they oppose
Ostrovski's wishes? His life was mysterious to them, his
motives obscure. Yet he was their patron as well as their
employer; there was no way in which they could argue
their case. Without him they would be without either
home or employment. They had not the means to move,
although the shop more than paid its way. Julius privately
thought that if he were in charge he would introduce some
improvements and look further afield for sources of in-
spiration. In order to do this he would have to persuade
his father to retire, though that might be difficult to see
through. If retired, his father could take those long walks
he had always loved, and once Josie was installed might
come home to a warmer welcome, certainly a more interesting one, than he habitually received from his wife. That
wife now had two spots of colour burning in her cheeks,

and drank a cup of coffee, though it always made her tearful. It was the rising tension caused by her excited state, which Josie interpreted with professional detachment, that prompted her tactful announcement that it had been a lovely evening. She thanked her hostess profusely.

'Where did you say you worked?' asked his mother.

'I do private work, look after people in their own homes.'

'Ah!' breathed his mother, with a beatific smile. 'How lovely that must be for them!' After that it was more or less settled.

That night, after he had put Josie into a taxi, he went to bed and dreamed that his brother Freddy, wearing a striped jersey and a porter's cap, was bad-temperedly sorting through a large pile of books that he wished to remove from this shop or library, whatever it was. They were for his own amusement, he implied, and instructed the assistant or librarian to parcel them up. 'Have you got a lorry?' he enquired, in the same bad-tempered way, though Julius, who was lurking in the background, thought that a van might be more appropriate. The main thing, when Freddy was in this mood, was to keep out of the way, yet the dream had no application to real life, in which Freddy rarely read anything more substantial than a newspaper, and sometimes not even that. He awoke with a feeling of weariness, told himself that he was shortly to be a married man, and resolved to be less attentive to his family's wishes. Retired, his father could do more for them all; in fact his father's putative retirement took on a certain inevitability in his mind. Changes needed to be made, and he was in a mood to make them.

He wanted a change, that was the truth of the matter. They all wanted a change. Even Josie wanted a change. She was tired of nursing, tired of being in all day, wanted to be out in the fresh air. He made no objections, was hardly in a position to do so. In fact he liked the idea of her being at home, keeping his mother's discontent at bay. It was decided very suddenly. When they announced that they had slipped out and got married his parents were not surprised. His father produced a bottle of champagne from a cupboard in their bedroom and they drank one another's health, amazed that change had been brought about so easily.

For a time changes went on being made. His father retired, with some relief, and Julius had the shop to himself. His mother kept house again: roast chicken appeared on the table, cold fried fish *à la juive,* fruit compotes. Josie seemed to enjoy her new position as daughter of the house, and was good-hearted enough to play her part when his mother, relapsing into one of her former malaises, required her attention. They got used to hearing her cry, 'Josie! Josie!' from her bedroom, even as they were preparing to go to bed themselves. Everyone's health seemed to improve, despite his mother's protestations. And the young people, as his father referred to them, delighted in their intimacy, the new indulgence that had been granted to them. Despite his mother's efforts Josie still looked slightly unkempt, but Julius found this oddly attractive, and in any event without her clothes he thought her magnificent. She played her part; he would always be grateful to her for that. And she seemed pleased with her new life, pleased to have left the flat she shared with others in the same boat,

pleased with the favours granted her, the love. Even the
odd invasion of their privacy seemed acceptable; they
had their own quarters at the other end of the flat, were
not too much disturbed by the proximity of the Herz parents. Their marriage seemed the ideal solution for everyone.

It was the move to Edgware Road that settled their fate.
Here again Josie was invaluable. She commandeered the
woman who cleaned the shop and got her to put the flat
to rights. Without any authorization she removed several
pieces of furniture from Hilltop Road and installed them
in their new cramped quarters. She did her best to rally
them, to keep up their spirits, though without much success. Their bedrooms were no longer separated by a substantial corridor. His mother's former good humour faded,
his father absented himself as much as he could, though he
did not tell them what he did with his free time. Bijou
Frank explained that she would no longer be able to visit
so frequently, as the journey was now inconvenient. This
distressed Mrs Herz, perhaps more than it distressed Bijou
Frank, as his mother, always hypersensitive, observed. Their
health, which had been so gratifying, began to suffer; again
Josie complained of the lack of fresh air. Then his mother
caught a cold and bronchitis developed, and it seemed as if
Josie had become a nurse all over again. Their nights were
more disturbed, by noises from the street, from the other
bedroom. Julius was embarrassed by his parents' night
sounds, by their occasional arguments, and worse, by his
mother's appeals for help, for a remedy, for consolation. Josie
would get up with a sigh, her good humour in abeyance.
They would settle down again, but not for long. 'Josie!

Josie!' would come the cry, the endless solicitation. It was love his mother wanted, and did not notice that that love was fast fading.

And then it was gone. When Josie announced that she was leaving Julius could hardly blame her. He was tired of fielding his mother's renewed complaints, saw that various incompatibilities were beginning to surface. He too wanted some peace, saw no alternative to reinstating the family as it had been before its brief renaissance. He would take care of them, since he had, as always, to make things better. And his father seemed ill, failing. And his mother had not quite recovered, would need his full attention. He almost wished Josie out of the house, in order to spare them all. 'I love you,' he said to her, as he watched her packing her cases. 'Yes, well,' she replied. 'In other circumstances, perhaps.' He kissed her goodbye: it was the most solemn moment of his life, more solemn than his marriage. She too was moved. It was that moment of genuine emotion that confirmed for him that he had been a married man and was one no longer.

## 4

'Salmon fishcakes! My favourite!'

He smiled. He had ascertained that they would be on the menu when he had made the booking. After this he had felt a diminution of interest, as if, the preparations for the occasion once made, nothing more needed to be done. He would have been happy, indeed happier, to let the lunch go ahead without him. But that was the way of it these days: all the pleasure was in the anticipation, very little in the enactment. He thought that all old people must feel this, this slight sinking of the heart when the time came for social interchange, when the need to be 'positive' (Josie's favourite word) imposed its iron rule on a nature more given to reminiscence than to normal human curiosity.

An additional reason for his slight depression was the conviction, conveniently overlooked when he was on his own, that Josie would do her strenuous best to rally him, to cheer him up, as though his delicate sadness were some kind of an affront. She had, she had once told him, always been 'marvellous with old people', from which category she excluded herself, although she was now sixty-six and technically a pensioner like himself. But she still worked, he reminded himself, in that garden centre where she seemed to have found her métier, as if nursing had been merely a false start. And that was what divided them, for her days were busy and his were empty, filled with routine tasks, with activities so modest that they would hardly register on the scale of her undertakings. This put him at a moral disadvantage, one more reason for keeping out of harm's way, although the niceties were still to be observed.

'Busy?' he asked humbly.

'Very. Bedding plants mostly. And I've got a delivery this afternoon. I'll have to leave you fairly sharpish. I'm in the car park, luckily. Otherwise . . .'

This was the only sign that she too was growing old, her failure to utter a proper sentence, as if time were too short for all the formalities of normal speech. Yet she looked much as she had always done. Her crinkly hair was now grey but her complexion was almost ruddy, witness to those days spent in the open air. Her light eyes, always her best feature, were still fine, but coming upon her unawares, as he might have done, he would have taken her for some kind of mutant, verging towards the masculine. Her shoulders had rounded and grown thicker, her hands larger and less cared for. As she buttered a piece of bread he noticed that the last two fingers of her left hand were slightly bent. But it would not do to mention this, for health could only be dealt with in the most general terms.

'Keeping well?' he asked.

'Oh, fine. You know me.'

He noticed that she did not ask him about himself, but that he recognized as part of her strategy of being positive. She would not shoulder his burdens, not even if he were in dire distress. Suddenly he acknowledged his reluctance to play his part for what it was: a sort of disenchantment. What had seemed like a good idea in his reclusion was fast turning into a disappointment. He put this down to the impact of reality on a dreaming nature but could not entirely rid himself of the conviction that something had gone out of this relationship, and that the memories he had of it now appeared erroneous. She had been ahead of him in perceiving their incompatibility: she had a primitive practical intelligence which reached conclusions before he did and was adept at avoiding regrets. Her self-centredness, which he had always admired as a sign of health, protected her from many of life's more awkward revelations, protected her too from feeling undue sympathy on another's behalf. Perhaps she was too vivid a reminder of the past, one of the few people from times gone by who was still alive and in visibly good health. Again he felt a surge of gratitude for her sheer viability. There was no danger of mournful reflections in Josie's presence, for the simple reason that she armoured herself against them. She would fail to pick up his signals in the interest of her own survival. He could not but think this an admirable, an enviable trait. To engage in a proper discussion of the sort he craved would have her bristling, on the defensive. He would have to content himself with admiring her, as he invariably did, admiring even those features he did not normally find admirable.

This was the way most of their meetings were conducted now: lunch in a good restaurant and an attempt, on his side, to recapture former intimacy which was usually unsuccessful. It was a parody of courtship which had not been necessary in the early days of their acquaintance. He

supposed that what he still wanted from her was some sort
of recognition that he had played a part in her life. She
seemed to have no need to reassure herself that his presence was the presence of an old and valued friend. Positive
thinking had reinforced her separateness. He saw with a
shock that her good will could not now be taken for granted.
Bowing his head in confusion, he understood that she was
slightly bored, that she might manufacture an argument just
to keep boredom at bay, that she accepted his invitations
because she felt that something was due to him but would
have been much more comfortable with the odd telephone
call, or none at all. And she was busy, he reminded himself, perhaps too busy for these old-fashioned ceremonies.
Mainly, as always, he blamed himself for misconstruing her
willingness to accept his invitations. By doing so she could
cross him off her list of obligations. A prompt acceptance
would put paid to further arrangements . . . And she had
always had an excellent appetite. And he was always careful
in his choice of a decent, even a prestigious restaurant, so
that she would not too much regret what she might even
have considered a waste of time. He still cherished the illusion that he might call on her in case of need, of illness.
Now he saw that this was indeed an illusion, one that he
had cherished for far too long. And she would not make it
any easier for him to ask for her help. Her famous positive
thinking, like an insurance policy, covered only herself. He
wondered if she had had other partners. 'Partner' was the
term she used when speaking of the manager of the garden centre. At first he had thought this a purely business
term. Now he saw that 'Tom', about whose health he must
also enquire, was rather more than that, that this thickset

woman sitting opposite him had captured the heart of another. This struck him as part of life's plan, a plan from
which he appeared to have been excluded. Yet the joke
was on himself, and, as if seeing it for the first time, his
smile grew broader.

'And how's Tom?' he asked, as the waiter poured the
wine.

'Tom's fine,' she said steadily. After that they felt easier
with each other, as if a vital piece of information had been
filed away. Fortunately their food arrived at this point.
Some of his pleasure returned as he saw her delighted appreciation. In that at least he had not failed her.

Nevertheless he would have been happier on his own.
He stole a brief comprehensive look around him and settled on two women lunching together at an adjacent table.
They were, he supposed, sisters, or sisters-in-law, certainly
not working women. He supposed them to have met for a
day in town, if women still did that sort of thing. They
were properly, that is to say, formally dressed in a way that
he recognized, and heavily made-up in a way he supposed
appropriate to the wealthier suburbs. Their red-nailed hands
bore wedding and engagement rings. Sisters, he thought,
rather than sisters-in-law. Not always on good terms, as
witnessed by that slight furrowing of the brows, that whisper of discontent, yet fine women, indispensable to each
other. Anachronisms, spending busy idle wealthy days,
such as his aunt Anna had spent at the Beau Rivage, with
her daughter as a guarantee of her respectability. Not so
easy for a woman to represent respectability these days, he
reflected, patting his lips with his napkin. Now, like Josie,
they worked hard and accepted what protection was avail-

able. And became harsher and more confident in the process. He had a sudden memory of the dinner at the Beau Rivage, after his impetuous and wrong-headed proposal. He had never told Josie about this, nor would he, though he had frequently longed to tell someone. How elegant the women had looked, both in black! How he now wished that he had stayed longer, given himself a second chance! He should have obeyed that almost unimaginable impulse and stayed, simply not come home. But not to come home had struck him then as now as against nature. Not to come home was to disappear from view, as he had never had the courage to do. And home had been so longed for, so aspired to, that he knew that he would never have had the courage to abandon it, not even for a lifetime of future felicity. That too was an illusion. It was sheer common sense to stay with what one knew.

It was strange how the Nyon episode was somehow secret. It was not a guilty secret; on the contrary, it fulfilled the function of a youthful indiscretion of which one is somehow proud, although he was already a middle-aged man when it had come about. The sheer unlikelihood of Josie's understanding it had reinforced his desire to keep it to himself. The ladies in their black dresses . . . This memory was not communicable. And there was no need to confide in Josie, who certainly did not look to him for confidences. The less he told her the less she seemed to want to know. His deaths, those of his parents, of Freddy, he kept to himself. When he had measured the extent of his solitude he had sought her out, had briefly courted her understanding. He was more ashamed of this than of the Nyon episode. She had responded, but 'positively', urging

him to take up various activities in which he had no interest, and if anything congratulating him on his new status as
a completely isolated and unattached person. 'Now you
can please yourself,' she had said, as if this were the only
conclusion to be reached. It was then that he had inaugu-
rated the custom of inviting her to lunch three or four times
a year. He thought it a duty to be observed, a civilized duty
which kept open lines of communication, though little
was communicated. His father's death from cancer, his
mother's decline, had no need to be dressed up in mournful colours: they both knew, in their different ways, that
those deaths were a release. A release which she acknowledged but he did not. He still felt those hands grow slack
in his, still metaphorically stood at their bedsides. By definition anyone who was not with him at those moments
was a stranger. And his grief and subsequent loneliness
were no cause for congratulations.

Over coffee they both mellowed, aware that this somehow disappointing occasion was nearly at an end. He felt
apologetic, as if it were his fault that their normally com
panionable exchange had not taken place, had let them
down, in fact. He recognized that Josie had no reason to
blame herself for this; indeed she rarely blamed herself for
anything, and quite rightly. Guilt was not merely a weakness, it was misleading, casting one's entire life into doubt.
He could hardly, at this point in their relationship, explain
himself to her, marvelled that she had once accepted him
for what he was, or rather what she thought he was, some
sort of exotic, different from her normal experience of
men. His status as an exile, which she recognized rather
more than he did these days, had intrigued her, had given

him some sort of romantic aura, the only element of romance conferred on a character on which he himself had
no illusions. And how could he now make up for lost time?
He was grateful that she had not been present to witness
those deaths, of which in truth she had known nothing.
He had telephoned her with the news that his parents had
died, only to be briskly cheered up, as if that were the
proper response to sad news. He could not explain to her,
nor would he attempt to do so, how he had held his dying
mother's hand, knowing that the end was near, and remained silent as she had whispered, 'Freddy? Freddy?' And
when it was all over, when the final death had taken place,
when he had known that Freddy at last had been removed
from his life, he had indeed felt relief, but it was a relief
that had something terminal about it, as if he too had died.
That was how he had continued to feel, not as a survivor,
though that inevitably was a part of it, but as death's assistant, marked out from an early age to be present at rites of
passage which contained no illusions of rebirth. That was
why he was half contented with his present solitude, recognizing it as something merited, something that was his
due, and moreover something that would not fail him. On
his own he could manage better than he had ever managed
in company of any sort.

He saw her glance at her watch, as she had done once or
twice throughout the meal, and bestirred himself to bring
matters to a close. He signalled the waiter for the bill, scrutinized it, and added a large tip. They must end on a pleasant note, though both were aware that it might be some
time before the occasion repeated itself. He asked her what
her holiday plans were, aware that this was a low point in

the conversation, in any conversation. They were going to Greece, he learned, though only for ten days; it was so difficult to leave the garden centre to others, and she did not altogether trust the assistant manager. He tried to imagine Tom, whom he had met, exposing his already crimson face to the Greek sun, saw Josie's undisciplined hair unravelling even more completely in the heat, was momentarily glad that he was in the centre of London and likely to remain so.

'I wonder you don't travel any more, Julius, now that you've no longer got the shop to worry about.'

He was grateful for this show of interest, although he recognized it as a familiar counter, one which she could offer without compromising her own independence or indeed departing from her half-reproachful encouragements. Do not tell me of your loneliness, was the subtext of her reproach. No one need be lonely! There are tours you could go on; you could even take a cruise! She did not need to say this out loud since she had said it all before, but he could see, from the combative light in her eye, that she would go on saying it for as long as she thought it necessary.

'I've done all that,' he said mildly. 'I quite enjoyed it, though not in the way you would. I have never sat on a beach in my life.'

'No, well, you wouldn't, would you? What did you do, then?'

'I went to cities. At first I went to all the glamorous ones: Venice, Rome. But I did in fact feel rather lonely there. Then I realized that I didn't have to go to these places, that I was happier in small towns of no particular interest. So I picked the ones in which I could please my-self, without witnesses. France, mostly. I was more or less contented when I could just amble round a church, and then sit down and drink coffee and read the local paper, half-hear other people's conversations.'

'Sounds hilarious.'

'Oh, you'd hate it. But carrying on like this seemed to satisfy me. And the places I chose had a certain charm, though not of the sort that would appeal to you.'

'Did you ever think of moving somewhere abroad?'

He smiled at her. 'I feel as if I am abroad already. Lon-don is still strange to me, though I have lived here since I was fourteen years old. Somehow it still doesn't feel en-tirely like home. And now that I don't travel any more . . .'

'That's a mistake, Julius. You'll just turn in on yourself.' She paused. 'I take it you live alone?'

He smiled again. 'Of course I live alone. I'm an old man. Who would have me now?'

She cast around her, picked up her bag, having done her best to rally him once more.

'You were a good-looking man,' she said. 'Women could still find you attractive.'

'I don't hanker for female company.'

'I was enough for you, I suppose?' Her tone was mock-ing, but there was a wistfulness behind it.

'You were enough for me. I was very happy with you. I'm only sorry that you weren't happy with me.'

'It was the whole set-up, though, wasn't it? Your par-ents, and that funny old girl who came in on a Saturday and never took her hat off. It got to me after a time. And even that was better than Edgware Road.' She shuddered. 'I don't know how you stood it.'

'I had to stand it. Now I'm happy that you've made a life for yourself, found someone who can take you on holiday, take you out . . . I manage. I'm not discontented. Don't worry about me, Josie.'

He reached for her hand, glad that this brief exchange had cleared the air between them. But now he was tired, and thought she must be too, although in her case tiredness would be compounded with relief that he had not reproached her. Though eager to proclaim the rightness of her decision to end their marriage, if challenged to do so, she was nevertheless not eager to dwell on it. In this, he thought, she showed signs of a belated maturity, although in a way he regretted this for her sake. In his experience maturity rarely brought cheering insights. Better the eagerness of youth, before the world had done its worst. His smile faded. He pressed her hand and then released it. They had after all not completely disappointed each other. And it was time to leave, before further reminiscences disturbed their fragile equilibrium. He glanced meaningfully at the next table, where the two women who had earlier caught his attention were now arguing vehemently. Josie followed his gaze, then nodded at him.

'They will have a rotten afternoon of it,' he said, guiding her out into the street. 'And they had planned it all so carefully. It was to have been a treat for one of them, though not, clearly, for the other. I dare say they will cut it short and go home to Weybridge. Oh, your car. Where did you say you left it?'

'In the car park. Don't come with me. I know you hate it.'

'Well, if you're sure. I'm always afraid of getting locked in.'

'Goodbye, Julius. Thank you for lunch. Keep in touch.'

'Yes, I'll keep in touch. Good to see you, Josie. Oh, and have a good holiday.'

He watched her stride away, noting with some sadness her thicker shoulders, the fact that she was slightly bent. With an effort he straightened himself, pushed back his own reluctant shoulders. They were old; it was all over. She would have told him not to be so defeatist, that, compared with so many, he was fortunate. He knew that, but it made no difference. His own equilibrium rested on such slender foundations that he also knew that undue reflection would disturb them. And now he was truly tired and wanted nothing better than to be at home, where no one but himself could register his decline.

He decided to walk back to Chiltern Street, knowing that this was foolhardy, yet anxious to test himself. He stood for a moment, irresolute. The day was fine, windy, but with a mild sun. He set off down St Martin's Lane, turned instinctively into Cecil Court to look through the second-hand books, and spent a restful few minutes away from the crowds. He was no longer used to company, that was the problem, could not function well in an atmosphere of talk and activity. Even the pleasures of the restaurant had tired him, even the company of Josie, although he was glad that she had re-established herself as a dear girl, barely recognizable now as the fresh-faced nurse whose presence he had so craved, almost as soon as he had had time to study her across a café table on the very first evening of their acquaintance. But that was how it should have continued, he thought: meetings in cafés on random evenings, as if they were actors in some black-and-white film, preferably French. In that way they could have injected an element of romance into their fortuitous association. He realized that he had been too keen to drive the relationship to its logical conclusion to speculate as to what a woman might want. Besides, his knowledge of women was so slight that this was in the realm of abstract thought. As far as he knew women were divided into two categories: those like Fanny Bauer who tormented one and those like Josie who offered refuge from such torment. Now he saw that this was less than fair to either of them. They were both, in their different ways, similar at heart. Both were opportunists in the best possible sense, able and willing to turn matters to their advantage, even if by the most traditional route, by marriage. It was entirely possible that he had failed them both, by not endowing Josie with that missing element of romance, by not being less romantic, less impetuous, more of a solid prospect, in his approach to Fanny. He had picked the wrong moment to act the lover, should have turned himself for the occasion into a sober citizen. As for Josie, she had seen her advantage in solid prospects: the respectable setting of a family she would soon outgrow, the bourgeois comfort of a flat that would soon prove to have been merely a temporary refuge. And no romance, he reflected, could have survived Edgware Road and the cramped quarters barely adequate for one ménage, let alone two. The strain had told very quickly, so that it was almost a relief to him when she made her decision. And by that time Fanny was simply a mirage. He could still see her as a girl, that was the strange thing, as if the intervening years had no substance.

He wandered back down St Martin's Lane, thinking he

might go to the National Gallery, might look at the Claudes and the Turners for half an hour. He did this from time to time, applied himself to a pleasure that had outlasted all the rest, yet aware that art was indifferent to whatever requirements he might bring to the matter. He still had in his mind Freddy's contempt for his former calling, and worse, his boastful negligence, his repudiation, as if art had proved fallacious in some way, as if it were preferable to be the equivalent of a playground bully, a ruffian, rather than the suffering aesthete he had been in his former life. Herz hoped that there was no real need to choose between these two extremes, but thought that there might be. It was informative that after seeing Josie he felt the need for something incorporeal, as if the one ushered in the need for the other. Yet after a calming half hour he would be aware of the sound of his own footsteps and would long for company of the simplest kind. The sight of children, sitting cross-legged on the floor and listening to a lecturer explain a picture to them, made him want to join them, if only for a minute or two. Yet in today's sad climate an adult man approaching a group of children was no longer an innocent sight, even though a man as old as himself might be thought to be above suspicion. Unfortunately nobody was above suspicion these days. It was a matter of prudence to behave with the utmost circumspection, as if one's guilt and folly, the accumulation of a lifetime, might in an instant be exposed to the public gaze. And how could one recover from that?

Finally, more hesitant now, he decided to give the National Gallery a miss. He would keep his favourite pictures for another day, a better or a worse day, it hardly mattered

now. Now he would go home, but not on foot. He had
noticed that he was becoming a little unsteady. That was
why he had largely given up travelling. He was afraid of a
collapse in a foreign city, saw himself lying on a pavement,
surrounded by unknown faces. Such a thing had never
happened, but he had begun to fear the day when it might.
He was safer now at home, for home had become his ultimate refuge. In the taxi he decided to telephone Josie that
evening to thank her for their lunch, and once again to
wish her a pleasant holiday. That was the right note to end
on, he thought, and then, in a panic, asked himself why
he should be thinking of endings. Nothing was over. In a
couple of months' time they would meet again, and be
glad to. It was the best that could be done for the situation
in which they found themselves. In a way it was the best he
could do for both of them.

# 5

By the time Herz reached Chiltern Street the sun had clouded over and the wind freshened, foreshadowing a dull evening. He put his key in the door and stood for a moment in the little hallway, experiencing as usual both relief and a sense of anticlimax. He was still not used to the silence that greeted him, although he had craved that silence at various points throughout a day which had proved exhausting. He moved slowly into the kitchen and filled the kettle, then, abandoning the notion of making tea, moved equally slowly into the sitting-room and settled himself gratefully into a chair. Adventures such as his lunch with Josie now proved disappointing, yet their conversation had agreeably filled the afternoon. Now there would be no more conversation. He looked around him as if seeing the flat for the first time, unusually aware of its constraints. It was too small, but being small was, he supposed, ideally suited to one who lived alone. On this cold May evening it took on the proportions of a cell, decreed by some invisible agency as appropriate to a lifestyle which could no longer accommodate company. He supposed that it was the best thing that had ever happened to him, and wondered why, at moments like these, at the end of the day, it was no longer gratifying. Its work was done: all that was left for him to do was to come to terms with its restricted amenities, and to reflect, as always at such times, that it was foolish to expect mere living conditions to supply a degree of contentment which only humans could furnish.

And yet he loved the flat. Its coming into being he regarded as nothing short of miraculous. He remembered as if they had taken place yesterday the events that had brought it about. Once again it was Ostrovski who was the provider, as if he were the unlikely convenor of their destinies. One day he had paid a visit to the shop, looking as he always did simultaneously prosperous and ramshackle, his over-large coat slung over his shoulders, his hands playing with one of his numerous sets of keys. Even in winter he was deeply tanned. Herz had greeted him with his usual mixture of deference and resignation. Ostrovski was, in that unsuspecting moment, still his employer, and, if such duties could be ascribed to him, his patron.

'Make coffee, Julius. I need to talk to you.'

He had done as he was told, preparing to hear the usual diatribe against the harshness of the economic climate, his impatience with the property market, with which he had mysterious dealings. It had been rumoured that Ostrovski owned several shops in various parts of London which he bought and sold as the fancy took him, always on the lookout for the end of a lease or a failing business, news of which would reach him in his perambulations or while drinking coffee with cronies in the cafés he frequented or in those odd clubs in which card games took on the function of a day's work. Herz knew nothing concrete about him, supposed him still to be living in Hilltop Road, looking more mournful now that he was old, no longer the cocky entrepreneur keen to spot a gap in the market. He commanded considerable funds, that much was clear, and yet his income was insubstantial, as likely as not to vanish overnight. He seemed never to be in a hurry, yet his eyes were sharp, observant. At any moment it seemed as if he might disappear, move out of town, as if his misdemeanours had caught up with him. Yet Herz had never heard a whisper of complaint against him, no suggestion of illegality. He behaved like a minor financier, but with a hint of penurious origins. His dealings were as ever obscure. As far as anyone knew he operated alone, making the best of uncertain beginnings, which he had managed to supplement by native shrewdness. He was an unavoidable fixture in their lives, and although neither Herz's mother nor his father had liked him they had been forced to trust him. This was never a comfortable position; they suspected him of various irregularities which might or might not land him in prison, but as far as they knew his reputation, which they suspected of being damaged, had not so far caught up with him.

It was that bleak time after the deaths, after the divorce, after Nyon, when life in the shop had had to fill Herz's days and for which in a way he was grateful. It was the sameness of those days that had compensated for the rawness of recent years. Every morning he descended the stairs from the flat to open up; every Friday he took the week's money to the bank. Yet this was no longer the modest outfit that his father had nurtured for so long; it had become busy, almost prosperous. Herz had supposed that he would take care of it for as long as Ostrovski was satisfied with him. He had no thoughts of owning it, but had come to terms with it as a fact of life, of his life. He gave Ostrovski his coffee and prepared to listen to the usual nostalgic reminiscences of those evenings in Hilltop Road at which he was an almost assiduous visitor, almost assiduous because he was so adept at hiding his true purpose that they never knew whether he felt anything for them at all or was, as Herz suspected, lonely.

'I'll come straight to the point,' he had said. 'No point in keeping you in suspense. The fact of the matter is that I've sold the business. The whole property, in fact. Had a very good offer and accepted it.'

'But why? It was doing so well. At least I thought so.'

'Make no mistake, you've done wonders with it. No, it's nothing to do with you.' He shrugged off his coat. 'Look at me, Julius. How old would you say I was?'

'I've no idea.'

'Eighty-one.' He waited for some rebuttal. When none came he dropped his uneasy manner and looked uncharacteristically sombre. 'I'm getting out,' he said bleakly. 'I've had enough. All these years I've been wheeling and dealing I've never been happy. I always wondered why. And now I know. I'm not well, Julius.' He laid a tentative hand below his rib cage. 'Tried to overlook it, as one does, but there's no doubt about it now. I'm looking at the end. The next big thing.'

'The next big thing?' Julius had echoed.

Ostrovski ignored him. 'I've got a place in Spain, as you know. Marbella. Might as well spend my days in the sun as in this perishing climate. I'm getting out, liquidating my assets. So you'll be on your own, dear boy, free, for the first time in your life. You've been a good son, I've never doubted that, too good, perhaps. Sorry your marriage broke down, but that was all part of it, wasn't it? Now you've got a chance to be your own man. I've seen to that.'

'You mean you'll give me a reference,' he had said, his tone carefully neutral.

'I mean I'm giving you what I paid for this outfit in the first place. Of course prices have gone up since then. I've taken this into account.' He mentioned a sum that sounded unreal. 'You can look for a flat of your own. Take what you want from here, not that you'll want any of it. Truth to tell I always had a bit of a bad conscience about you. They favoured that brother of yours, didn't they? Well, now you can make up for lost time.'

'I can't take this. All this money.'

'You can and you will. It'll buy you something small but comfortable. And there'll be a bit left over. Wisely invested it should take care of you for the rest of your life. Ask my nephew about that. Name of Simmonds, Bernard Simmonds. He's a solicitor, perfectly straight sort of guy, though bloody uninteresting. He'll advise you. I should get in touch with him as soon as possible. He'll have the flat in Hilltop Road, by the way.'

'I can't take this money,' he had repeated.

'It's all perfectly legal, if that's what you're worried about. And why not have it now, instead of waiting till I'm dead?' He grimaced. 'Why wait?' he said. 'Simmonds had the same reaction, couldn't believe I was doing the decent thing. But I always wanted to do the decent thing. The times were against it; that was the beginning and the end of it. I had to claw my way up, and I don't say I didn't enjoy some of it. Only it ends badly, Julius, remember that. You end up looking on, reduced to less than half of what you were. I dare say I shall do as well as I can, out in Marbella. In the sun there's less need to think. And I want to get rid of the past, just live in the present, or what remains of it.'

'Are you sure? You might be lonely.'

'Of course I'll be lonely. But there's a loneliness that comes with age anyway. There's nothing I can do about that. And there's a sort of club there, all ex-pats, all on their last legs, all making quite a good job of it. It'll be like going back to school. Absurd!' He gave a harsh laugh. 'Anyway I've put you in the picture. You've got about a month to sort yourself out. The new owner will dispose of the stock; I've given him a few contacts. Wants to open a hairdressing salon, I believe. I didn't want to go into his plans; I've lost interest anyway. I just want my place in the sun, for as long as I've got. As I say, take anything you want from here. The two armchairs are quite good. And that little table. Belonged to my mother.' Tears filled his eyes. 'Don't let me down, Julius. Do as I wish. That way it won't all have been in vain.'

'I don't know how to thank you,' he had said wonderingly.

'No need. I can't take it with me, can I?' He wiped his eyes. 'I suppose this is our last meeting. Get in touch with Simmonds if you need anything. Now get me a cab, there's a good fellow. Got some packing to do.'

On the pavement he seemed frail, unlike his former self. The transformation was already under way. 'Hilltop Road,' they both told the taxi driver. Then it seemed natural to embrace, as they had never done in the old days, natural for Julius to stand waving, until the cab and Ostrovski were out of sight.

The suddenness of Ostrovski's announcement seemed

to have obliterated any response. Julius went to his small desk and scrutinized the invoices and accounts, the contents of which he knew by heart. But it was no good; he could make sense of none of it. His working life, it seemed, was over. Not quite what I expected, he had admitted to himself in the course of the afternoon. Yet he had expected nothing, and had been endowed with freedom, a freedom for which he was entirely unprepared. And he was relatively well off, though he would have to check with this Simmonds person that the gift was perfectly regular. He seized the telephone and dialled the familiar Hilltop Road number. The call went unanswered. The next thing to do was to find out the address of Simmonds's office, and make an appointment to see him. Then he would have to find somewhere to live. The prospect posed even more difficulties; he had never exercised his own wishes in this respect. From Berlin to Hilltop Road to Edgware Road all his homes had been chosen for him. And home was such an emotive concept that he doubted whether he would be able to live up to it, to make a place for himself in a world where people exercised choices. On an impulse he hung the CLOSED sign on the door and went up to the flat. He had grown used to it, in a resigned, almost philosophical sort of way: he had not looked this particular gift horse in the mouth, although it had brought about unwelcome changes. He had been told to take anything he wanted, but he wanted nothing. He noticed a shabbiness he might otherwise have overlooked. The wallpaper had faded; the windows needed cleaning. He would take the two armchairs, and the little table that had belonged to Ostrovski's mother, more in the interests of Ostrovski than himself. In that sense there would be some continuity. The rest he would have to buy. The prospect of a new bed, unslept in by anyone before him, filled him with a timid pleasure. Ostrovski had said something about a month. In that time he would have to find somewhere to live. Even more difficult, he would have to school himself into new habits, work out how to spend the rest of his life. He was after all at an age when most men retired, and no doubt they were all faced with the same daunting prospect. So much time! How on earth was it to be filled?

At eight o'clock that evening he telephoned Hilltop Road again and was answered by Bernard Simmonds. So he actually existed; this was a good sign. And Simmonds was encouraging. There was no doubt about the money: it was properly gifted, and there were legal declarations to prove it. 'Unusually generous, I agree, and almost unheard of these days. But he was better off than any of us suspected. I'm talking serious money here. I know, I know; it takes a bit of getting used to. If I were you I'd look for a property before the prices go up again. Don't hesitate to get in touch with me if you need advice. We're in the same boat, you know. I'd been paying rent here; now I own the lease. Incredible.'

'Where is the money?' he remembered asking helplessly, a memory at which he blushed for several days when forced to think of it.

'In your bank. It's all there, don't worry. Now you'll want to put it to good use. Between ourselves I think it would be better if you found something as soon as possible. Things will not be too comfortable at Edgware Road. New owner, and so on.'

'But the business. The accounts. The stock.'

'The new chap has appointed a firm of accountants to

take care of all that. Liquidators, I suppose. But it's all fair and square. In fact you're free to leave.'

But he did not feel free. He felt bereft. As the evening darkened and the shadows gathered in the small sitting-room that had been home he felt somehow deprived of a birthright, the right to work. He felt newly alone in the world, wished for a family, an imaginary family, more like an audience, composed of people who would applaud and endorse all his actions. He had never known such people, half-knew that this was a fantasy left over from adolescence, or further back, from childhood. He went to bed, slept fitfully, would have welcomed a dream, however unpleasant. He got up before five, anxious now to be out of the place, out in the air. He would have breakfast at the all-night café on the corner, then try to work out some plan of action. In the early-morning light the familiar street looked strange, uninhabited, although there were muted signs of activity, as shopkeepers opened their doors to take in supplies. The coffee had a valedictory taste; he was in no mood to eat. As the sun rose slowly on what might prove to be a beautiful day, he paid, exchanged a few abstracted words with the café's owner, and turned back to what was no longer his home. Raising his eyes from the pavement which he had apparently been studying, he saw with a pang that a van had drawn up outside the shop, that the door was already open, and that inside men were engaged in some sort of activity, one of them apparently going through his desk.

'Good morning,' said a hearty man who seemed to be in charge. 'Thought we'd make an early start. Don't mind us. I'm afraid you've ceased trading. We should be gone by this evening. But we'd like to take possession in, say, ten days'

time. That should give you time to make your arrangements, if you haven't already done so, that is. Now, if
you'll excuse us . . .' He turned briskly away. The interview
was at an end.

Herz had gone out again, drunk more coffee, and
waited for the nearest estate agent's doors to open. The girl
who seemed to be some sort of secretary still had her coat
on, and was obviously preparing to make herself a cup of
tea. He took no notice. 'I need a flat,' he said tersely, more
tersely than he thought he had it in him to say. 'Two
rooms, kitchen and bathroom. Independent central heat-
ing. Balcony. As soon as possible. Today in fact.'

She looked at him in surprise. 'You're in a hurry,' she
observed. 'Tea? I can't get going without it. Take a seat.'

He took a seat. Outside the windows the day was now
fully fledged, young men with briefcases striding along
with an air of purpose. He was no longer that sort of man,
not that he ever had been. He had taken only what had
been ordained for him, and would go on doing so. This act
of buying a flat seemed to him a monstrous aberration, but
presumably people did this every day of the week. Buying
and selling, getting and spending were the order of the day.

'I'm Melanie,' said the girl. 'My card. I can show you
two properties this very morning, if you're free. I've got
Clarence Court and Chiltern Street. Both very central,
both in good repair.'

'I don't like the sound of Clarence Court,' he said, re-
covering some composure. 'It sounds too dainty. I'd like to
see Chiltern Street, if you don't mind.'

'Sure. It's a lovely flat. The last owner put a lot of work
into it.'

'Why did he leave?'

'She. Got work in the States, left in something of a rush. It's only been empty for a couple of weeks. We're handling the sale: she left everything in our hands. So if you like it it's all quite straightforward. Shall we go?'

As soon as he saw the flat all his doubts were resolved. It was on the second floor of a narrow building which had been well maintained. The ground floor was occupied by a dress shop, the first by what he supposed was a work-room, from which he could hear a chatter of voices. The flat itself was small, admittedly, but light and calm. Some-one, the previous owner, no doubt, had laid a hardwood floor and installed a miniature kitchen. The windows looked out onto Chiltern Street at the front and onto a small patio at the back; as he peered out he could see two girls install themselves with coffee cups. This gave an illusion of com-pany which might be welcome. There was little room for additional furniture: he would need only a bed, and per-haps two more chairs. The bed was a priority; the rest could wait.

'I want it,' he said simply.

'Great. If you'll come back with me to the office my boss should be in by now. I told you about the lease, didn't I?'

'The lease?'

'Rather short, I'm afraid. Eight years.'

He calculated. With a bit of luck he would be dead be-fore the lease ran out. 'I'll take it,' he said, with an air of fi-nality that convinced them both.

He hired a van, packed his clothes, and prepared to leave, though the actual leaving might take some time. Edgware Road now belonged to the past. He could hear men moving about downstairs in the shop, but they no longer disturbed him. He was in a hurry to be gone. If necessary he would sleep in one of the chairs until the bed arrived. All this had happened rather more quickly than he had anticipated, as if under some kind of enchantment. The afternoon of the following day was spent on purchases which gave him a thrill of ownership. 'Household Requisites', he read at the entrance to one of the departments of a large Oxford Street store. He was a Householder! He was entitled to Requisites! He felt the same thrill in the supermarket, where he had shopped for years with massive indifference. 'Traditional Afternoon Tea' and 'Breakfast Coffee' convinced him that he was at last part of the community, with breakfast and tea adequately recorded. Without compunction he went back to Edgware Road, and removed sheets, towels and cups, piling them into plastic bags. After a last look round he placed his keys on his denuded desk and stood impatiently on the kerb, waiting for a taxi. In the new flat he threw open the windows and surveyed Chiltern Street, which seemed agreeably well-behaved after the clamour of Edgware Road. Again he heard sounds of life from the patio, which he supposed was one of the amenities reserved for the seamstresses. Their conversation, which was in a language he did not recognize, was the only sign that he was not entirely alone.

By the end of the week Ostrovski's mother's table and two chairs looked well against the sunlit wall of the sitting-room. Flushed with success, he went to John Lewis and bought two more chairs, a television, a bedside cabinet, and three lamps. At home, as he now thought of it, he made up the bed which he had bullied the shop into removing from the window, and hung his clothes in the small cupboard. As far as he could see he needed nothing more. He was almost disappointed that the process had been so speedily accomplished. He telephoned Bernard Simmonds to give him his new address, got no answer, and sat down to write to him. This meant that he would have to acquire some sort of desk. It was a reprieve. Happily he set out again for another day of purchases. Again he was lucky. Apparently everything was available to those with time and money. This was a new dimension for him, one formerly unsuspected, or, if suspected, not for his participation. Now this had changed: entitlement again. The time for deference was over. He spared a thought for Ostrovski, promised himself that he would keep in touch. Then he cancelled the past, marvelling at how easily this was done, wondering why the past had kept him in its grasp for so long. In his euphoria he felt new-born, looked forward unrealistically to new friends. Already the landscape was familiar. It would be up to him to make the next move. What that might be he had no idea, but felt confident that it would present itself.

But melancholia, once given house room, is difficult to dislodge. After a couple of months, after having dined with Bernard Simmonds and greeted Mrs Beddington, the owner of the dress shop, after shyly smiling at the seamstresses, only to hear them giggle as he walked on, he found himself once more enveloped in dream and memory, as if they alone could furnish him with information. Though he did not exactly miss his former routine, he regretted that he had so little to do. His days were composed of artificial outings: a newspaper and the supermarket in the morning, and in the afternoon a bookshop or a gallery. He told himself that many were in the same boat, but pitied them, thought wistfully of families, of ideal families, with gardens to occupy them and grandchildren to cherish. Even the Claudes and Turners which he had so loved began to let him down, evoking only a half-remembered response. This seemed uncannily reminiscent of Freddy's evolution, and, beyond that, of the apathy of his parents, whom he now loved and deplored in equal measure. He lived like a recluse, for that was how he thought he must, as if his destiny had reclaimed him. As time wore on the future seemed less accommodating, continuity not to be taken for granted. He revised his expectations, resigned himself to living in an uneasy present. The past took on a new refulgence, became momentarily precious. He was grateful for any additional information that his mind could supply, half-aware that he was now involved in a process that was almost certainly restricted, and caring less and less, as day followed day, that this might be so.

## 6

Custom decreed that Herz should take a holiday. At least
he supposed it was so, since snatches of conversation in the
supermarket and the café where he had taken to drinking
his morning coffee revealed an unknown world of villas,
apartments, *gîtes,* boats, and families overseas, and proved
that the city was emptying, a fact which he had observed
for himself in his modest perambulations. Even Mrs Beddington, the owner of the dress shop, had come up to in-
form him that she was joining her sister and brother-in-law
in the south of France and to warn him about the burglar
alarm, of which he now seemed to be in charge. The chatter from the workroom had diminished in volume and he
supposed that some of the girls had gone home, to homes
he had difficulty in imagining. He himself felt isolated in
the middle of all these plans, elaborated over a cold winter
and an even colder spring. Without holidays, it seemed, he
had no currency to offer, no travellers' tales, no amusing
mishaps, no suntanned face to be presented to his usual
constituency of casual acquaintances, and was reduced to
questioning others about their plans. These plans seemed
to him exhausting, yet they served to galvanize the year's
activities into purposefulness. Having no plans of his own
to offer in exchange, he accepted that his role was to be a

useful audience. His smile dutifully in place, he played his part, but began to weary of it.

His past holidays would hardly pass muster in this dialogue. Those quiet days in small towns, even in suburbs at the end of a bus route, did not make for interesting anecdotes. In Amboise he had listened to a family party discussing a relative's will; in Auteuil he had quietly sympathized with an elderly man on his way to a doctor's appointment, but he was outside of all this, not a participant, and what was a holiday without fervent participation? And he was newly aware of frailties when faced with a major undertaking: again the vision of himself on the ground looking up to a circle of attentive faces presented itself and grew ever more compelling. He clung to his routine, although it bored him, and the days seemed long. Nor did he appreciate what others might see as an altogether enviable leisure. He had too much time at his disposal, and frequently found himself standing at the window, scanning Chiltern Street for a sign of life. He had no appetite for anything, tried to sleep in the afternoon without great success. Such brief dozes merely served to bring back the past, so that when he emerged, with a stale taste in his mouth, his grasp on the present seemed diminished and his resolve significantly weaker. Yet in the long silent afternoons it was hard not to succumb, and although this conclusion of the day's preoccupations was ill-advised it seemed to be a habit that was growing on him, without his encouragement. And if it was easy to slip into sleep in the sunny days of summer, how would he fare in the winter when darkness came early and the outside world retreated?

To counter this all too symbolic descent into the shadows of his mind he took to walking in the evenings in order to tire himself out and to make his rest more appropriate, more excusable. After his supper (it could hardly be called dinner) he emerged into Chiltern Street and began a rambling peregrination of his immediate neighbourhood, hoping to catch life on the wing, and to make himself into a semblance of gentlemanly old age which others might find acceptable. But there were no spectators, only young people drinking and laughing outside pubs or eating pizzas with a crowd of friends. No one expressed any interest as he walked up Gloucester Place and down Baker Street, or even went as far as Oxford Circus in the vain hope of urban company. The park beckoned but it would take him too far from home and darkness would catch him out. Besides, he was unsure when the park gates closed, and imagined, with dread, being locked in, forced to spend the night on a bench, his hair awry, like any other vagrant.

These evening walks fulfilled a purpose, which was to exhaust him, but were accomplished without pleasure. For this reason, as much as for any other, he began to envisage wider excursions, yet these seemed pointless without the prospect of company. Patience had worn him out, yet he knew that his solitary way of life was the only one that suited his temperament. He could, with a little courage, take himself abroad again and sit in the odd unfashionable church or discover the upper floor, usually deserted, of a largely unattended museum, and if he did so, as he had done so many times, he would undoubtedly derive some mild satisfaction from the experience. But then he would have to return to the small hotel, where a hard-faced proprietress would hand him his key without the sort of greeting that he craved, would not question him about his day or enquire about his prospects for the evening, and he would be obliged to go out again, to seek a solitary meal, and to apply himself once more to observing others. And always in the knots of people strolling past him in the streets he would hear snatches of conversation that would intrigue him, make him anxious to know more, even to interrogate those passers-by who had momentarily distracted him; he might then register an unfamiliar reaction—frustration? anger?—not at his inability to participate but distress at the impermeability of others, of all those who did not wish to hear his plans, know his preferences, his tastes, so absorbed were they with their own.

If he were honest with himself he would admit that he had truly enjoyed only one holiday in his life, and that was when he was eight years old. He had the photograph to prove it. He was with his family in a fiacre in Baden-Baden, being driven down the Lichtenthalerallee towards the Casino, where they would drink coffee to the sound of a small orchestra. He could still remember the sun shining through the branches of tall trees, and the amazing size—amazing to him at that age—of the rhododendrons that bordered the road. He could remember the stately creak of the fiacre as they made their way, in the company of similar families, towards the Casino and the enactment of the leisurely morning ritual. The photograph, which he had scrutinized exhaustively, showed a laughing child's face and a hand clasping that of his mother. He could see, as he could hardly remember, that they were comfortably off, secure and harmonious; there was a nursemaid in discreet attendance, probably in charge of his brother, and he remembered her name: Marie. He knew, though this lacked the immediacy of the photograph, that other activities awaited them: walks in the Schwarzwald, with polite greetings to other strolling couples, the heavy appointments of the expensive hotel which so delighted him, the sentimental tunes played by the Casino orchestra, his father's cigar, the lavish meals which would now be frowned upon by today's dietitians, the multiplicity of doctors devoted to one's health and well-being, and who prescribed spa water instead of pills.

That world no longer existed, or if it did would have undergone a change; it had indeed come to an end as his own childhood ended. A braver man might go back to measure these changes, but he was no sociologist; the world he wanted was the world reflected in the photograph, and the laughing face that, for as long as he could remember, only ever now relaxed into a mild smile. Even the smile had become modified with age. The smiling boy had become a polite adult; the smile now had something dutiful about it, as if it were expected of him; he would continue to offer it but without conviction. It was a smile that no longer expressed eagerness but was a suitable feature in his dealings with others. Preparing to listen, to sympathize, he would acknowledge the return of his habitual smile, while all the time registering his lack of joy. That, it seemed, was now in default, was even inconceivable. He accepted this, as he accepted the distance between past and present, wondered whether this feeling was unusual, regretted that there was no way of conducting an enquiry. After examining the photograph he had the fleeting feeling that he was in the wrong country. This was not a welcome reflection. His situation was commonplace. But that occasionally made it extraordinarily difficult to recognize as natural.

He dreaded becoming like the man he saw in the supermarket every day (and who saw him) and who, though respectable, was somehow to be avoided. He seemed always to be seated on a chair near the checkout, his stick planted between his knees, his expression disapproving. He was given to expressing his views on the government to anyone who would listen, and, in a raised voice, to those who would not. Attempts had been made to move him on, but as there was no reason why he should not be in the place these were largely unsuccessful. He was given a wide berth, although what he had to say, or rather to proclaim, was attractive, inasmuch as it was vigorous. He was a fount of moral criticism, with accusations of hypocrisy, of mendacity, delivered with some authority, as if he were in the streets of ancient Athens and had a coterie of impressionable young men. Women took no notice of him, although the girls at the checkout, who, Herz noted, frequently changed places with each other, either wearily assented to his denunciations or laughed without constraint, depending on their degree of kindness or complicity with each other.

For this man there was no complicity; there was none in Herz either, although the man's madness was such as to excite pity and terror, as tragedy was supposed to do. Herz turned his head aside when passing the man, aware that he had been singled out as a confidant. But in fact everyone had been singled out as a confidant, but without success. The extent of this man's solitude was perhaps not particularly obvious except to those who turned away from him, unable to bear the reflection of their own. And yet the man was smartly, even foppishly dressed, which implied that someone was in charge of him. And no doubt one would pass him in the street without a second glance. It was only in the supermarket, with the prospect of a captive audience, that he launched on his accusations. No one seemed safe from his disapproval: all came in for scathing commentary. The most frightening feature of his diatribes was the sensation that they were somehow merited. Even those with a clear conscience felt uneasy, not perhaps on their own behalf but on that of all those government ministers who were being castigated. Why was there no one to rebut his accusations? Where, in fact, were those government ministers, who might be called upon to shed a kindlier light on the issues of the day? A sense of wrongs not righted pervaded the immediate vicinity of this man whose stick seemed ready to strike out, though this had never happened. One reached the street with a relief which had little to do with a chore successfully accomplished. One reached the street willing to embrace the mass, to subside into a comforting mutuality, to dismiss the disconcerting spectacle of the unassimilated, of the unsleeping moral conscience, which, if not checked, might lead to acts one was not anxious to witness.

It was encounters like these, minuscule in themselves but repeated on an almost daily basis, that made Herz feel in need of some protection. Again he invoked that imaginary chorus of encouraging relatives, or, more satisfyingly, because verifiably real, that doctor in Baden-Baden to whom his parents had taken him because he was underweight and who had questioned his eight-year-old self with grave professionalism, with what had seemed like magisterial competence, weighing, percussing, listening, and finally pronouncing a completely reassuring verdict. To be given a bill of health by such a sage was more curative than any regime, although he had had to endure the spa waters, which had no discernible effect but at least did no harm. In Baden-Baden, and even in Berlin, the sun shone, and he might be sitting in his aunt Anna's drawing-room in a haze of excitement, waiting for his cousin Fanny to appear, although when she did she was usually bored and dismissive. In the absence of those strong sensations he was without compensation, and also without purpose. It seemed childish, at the age he was now, to seek rewards for fidelity to those early impressions, yet his life as a grown man had been fashioned by the need to cherish the sensations which had formed at least some part of his character, and to regret, to the point of pain, that they could never come again. Now his sensations were muted, and it was wiser that they should be, in case he turned into the man in the supermarket and railed against his fate, or perhaps fate in general, and recognized the despair he was so anxious to conquer.

He would have liked to discuss these matters with just such a sage as the German doctor, or with an ideal interlocutor, unfortunately unavailable. People went in for such things on television these days, or in the Sunday papers. Television would be the ideal medium. He would be questioned by a sympathetic interviewer, in what circumstances he could not imagine. What he could imagine would be himself discoursing on the persistence of early memory, of images that had stayed with him throughout his life. He would be seen, on the success of such a performance, to be worth consulting in the interests of general enlightenment, would go on—always with encouragement—to describe the Casino at Baden-Baden, its rich debased rococo decoration, so perfectly suited to the spirit of the place, or, more ambitious this, to give an account of his travels, of his artistic delights, Schloss Bruhl, near Cologne, or the house that Wittgenstein designed for his sister in Vienna. Asked back yet again he would be memorable on the Claudes and Turners in the National Gallery, on which his opinion would prove invaluable. These were matters on which he had reflected in the course of his evening walks, but on which he was obliged to remain mute. The existence of such an audience remained his most persistent temptation. His real audience became as strange to him as the people in the supermarket who ignored the man with the stick. Such indifference, with which he was obliged to conform, remained the order of the day.

Instead of which he discussed holiday plans with Bernard Simmonds, whom he met for dinner once a month. Or rather he discussed Bernard Simmonds's holiday plans, which were expansive: he had rented a house near Cortona, to which he had invited different friends, at weekly intervals, to ensure the maximum of variety. This sounded punishing to Herz, who could only tolerate one person at a time, and that at well-spaced intervals. He marvelled at Simmonds's capacity, which seemed an integral part of his youthfulness. He was in his mid-fifties, and looked it, but had the tastes of a much younger man, as these holiday arrangements bore witness. He had a girlfriend who stayed at Hilltop Road in the time she could spare from her various business assignments, which took her to Hong Kong a great deal. Simmonds was proud of her, but in fact just as pleased when she was not there as when she was in residence. He was gregarious, spoke of parties, weekends, plans for the holiday after next. Astonishingly, he had no objection to Herz's company, rather evinced a liking for it, but always consulted his watch to make sure that he was not late for another entertainment, which might have been scheduled for what Herz thought of as an advanced hour. He was not an interesting companion, but he gave the impression of being affectionate. In his smiling demeanour Herz could see something of Ostrovski's odd loyalty to his lame-dog protégés. The association was made comfortable by the fact that neither required anything of the other. Simmonds was his solicitor, and charged hugely. That way there could be no hint of patronage.

Herz could have wished their relationship were more sustaining, more speculative, rather more like those television interviews in which his opinion was sought on a variety of subjects. He was mollified by the impression that he fulfilled some sort of function for Simmonds, some quasi-parental function, simply by virtue of being older. He was a surrogate elder towards whom Simmonds felt an old-fashioned, almost naïve respect. Herz had little experience of dealing with younger people but understood instinctively that one kept out of their lives as much as possible but was curious and indulgent towards them. Hence the exhaustive questioning on his part—the holiday plans were an example—and Simmonds's equally exhaustive replies. It was a matter of discretion not to talk about oneself. To do so would be to shock Simmonds with the prospect of what awaited him.

It did not, of course, have to turn out that way: he would not make the mistake of supposing that Simmonds resembled himself, or that decline was the common lot, the destiny in which all were united. In that prospect at least there might be a degree of compensation. Instead of which all were cast adrift on their own, could barely signal to one another their knowledge of what was overtaking them. The only resource in such circumstances would be the young, their children, if they were fortunate enough to have them, or, if they were not, those like Simmonds who were kind enough to tolerate their company. Here too circumspection was called for: one painted a picture that would not disturb, gave an edited view of oneself that would prove acceptable. In that way one could pass muster. The confession that fought its way out, the inevitable complaints and regrets, must be stifled so as not to inspire distaste, or more frequently boredom or impatience. The trick was to remain separate and restrained.

'So when do you leave for Italy?' he queried, picking up his fork.

'End of next week. If you want anything get in touch with Deakin. He knows all about your affairs.'

'The will . . .' said Herz. 'Ostrovski's will. How can I ever forget that? I feel unworthy, ashamed, even.'

'The money he left you? No need. I benefited too, re-member. We were the only legatees. Well, he had no family living.'

'He referred to you as his nephew.'

'Nothing like. A second cousin only, and one I hardly

knew. He used to blow in from time to time to see my parents.'

'He did the same to mine.'

'He was lonely, of course, although he had all those businesses he was juggling. In a way he liked to be unattached, or rather unobserved. Nobody ever knew his real circumstances.'

'What was his background?'

'Nothing he was very proud of. Ostrovski wasn't his name, of course.'

'What was it?'

'Abramsky. I did some research. He was a self-made man in every sense of the word. Yet he liked to keep up some sort of fiction that he had friends: my parents, your parents. That was all he had. And nobody had much time for him. His manner was fairly off-putting. He looked up to your parents, by the way, thought they were aristocratic.'

'They weren't,' said Herz.

'They were to him. You've no one left, I take it?'

'No one, no. My marriage, as I think you know, ended in divorce.'

'I won't make that mistake. I've seen too much of it. Helen and I agree on that point. No marriage, no children, no divorce.'

'I wonder if you're quite right about that.'

Simmonds shrugged, looking suddenly weary. 'I won't say there hasn't been the odd discussion. But she likes her freedom. Women do these days; they don't seem to suffer. I sometimes wonder if men don't suffer more. But we're together, we have fun.'

'Fun?'

'Distractions are easy to find. We travel a lot. And because we're not together the whole time we're always
pleased to see each other.' He looked wistful, as if foresee-
ing a time when he might miss her. But, thought Herz,
there would be those distractions. Perhaps eternal restlessness was the answer, just as eternal vigilance was the price
of liberty. Rest would not only descend on one too soon;
it would be unwelcome when it did.

'Your generation is quite different from mine,' he
smiled. 'You seem to have everything mapped out.'

'It's all a matter of communication these days. You need
never really be apart: e-mail, mobile phones, and so on.'

'But I wonder if that really keeps you together. Some
things can't be put into words.'

'Most things can.'

'I was thinking how the smallest changes are often the
most subtle. How one unconsciously reverts to what I suppose were one's origins. Nowadays I find myself eating the
sort of food I had at home. And it's not a conscious decision. I do it instinctively.'

'You want to look after yourself, you know. You're
looking a bit thin.'

'Oh, I'm fine.'

'You should take a holiday.'

He smiled. 'I look forward to hearing about yours. Shall
I get the bill?'

'Let me.'

'With all this money it's the least I can do.'

They parted on the usual good terms, Herz waiting on
the pavement until Simmonds's car drove off. Then he
walked to the bus stop, remembering, in spite of himself,

Bijou Frank and his first experience of servitude. He smiled. How had she lived, poor Bijou? And when had she died? There had been no notice in the Deaths column of *The Times,* although there was no reason why there should have been. It had been an obscure life, dignified by a sort of loyalty. That was what he missed, the sort of loyalty observed by people who had little in common but their origins, but who understood each other in a more rooted way than the rootless young could ever understand. He understood it now, almost wished those lost connections back again. He was not trained for freedom, that was the problem, had not been brought up for it. He had done nothing more than glimpse it. The irony was that he now possessed freedom in abundance, but did not quite know how to accommodate it. And it was, it seemed, too late for him to learn.

At the bus stop he was suddenly overcome by a feeling of unreality, so enveloping as to constitute a genuine malaise. He placed a tremulous hand on his heart, and seconds later wiped a film of sweat from his forehead. He stood for a moment, trying to regain his composure, glad that there were no witnesses. He had no memory of the journey home, in a providential taxi. In bed he felt better, ascribed his faintness to the second glass of wine he had imprudently drunk, but slept badly. The morning came as an unusual relief, one that he had barely expected.

# 7

'It was like a cloud descending,' he explained to the doctor. 'Like being enveloped in a cloud, or indeed a cloudy substance. Opaque, you know. I couldn't otherwise explain it, although I had to explain it to myself. The only thing I could think of was Freud's experience on the Acropolis.'

'I'm sorry?'

'Freud reported a feeling of unreality which overtook him when he was visiting the Acropolis. He was alarmed, as well as feeling unwell, although he didn't go into that. Then, being Freud, he worked out an explanation; he was uneasy because he had gone beyond the father. In other words he had achieved a way of life—moneyed, cultivated—which would have been denied to his father. He had overcome his father's constraints. Freud knew that his father would have had no access to the sort of excursion he was taking; therefore he had in a sense betrayed him, outclassed him. The theory is very beautiful, don't you agree? I too have gone beyond my father, who was a hard-working and unhappy man. Do you think I might have experienced something similar?'

'When did you last have your blood pressure checked?'

'Oh, some time ago. Your predecessor, Dr Jordan . . . What happened to him, by the way? A young man . . .'

'He went to Devizes to take over his father-in-law's practice. Couldn't wait to get out of London. The pressures on GPs in London are formidable.'

'Yes, one hears a lot about that.'

'I'll just check. Roll up your sleeve, would you?'

On the wall behind the doctor's desk hung an inept watercolour of boats at sunset.

'Your own work?' he enquired politely.

'My wife's.'

'Ah.'

'Our house is full of them. It's rather high, I'm afraid. Too high. I'll give you something for that.'

He consulted his computer. 'I see that Dr Jordan prescribed glyceryl trinitrate. Have you used it at all?'

'Those pills one puts under the tongue? No. I don't use anything. I prefer not to. I think I only saw him once. Dr Jordan, I mean.'

'They will help you if you have a similar experience again. Silly to ignore the pills. They are there to help you.'

'Oh, I carry them around with me.' He patted his pocket. 'But I prefer to know what's happening to me. What, in fact, is happening to me? I'm not really ill.'

'You are not a young man. Have there been other episodes?'

'Not really. A little faintness sometimes. I've only consulted a doctor once, I think.'

Again he thought of the German doctor in Baden-Baden, who had literally laid on hands. Herz placed a protective hand over his heart. The doctor did not see the gesture, being occupied with his computer. In that instant Herz determined not to consult him again. He was no doubt quite adequate, but in Herz's opinion did not have the artistic, even the poetic sympathy that would enable him to understand another's malaise. And his malaise lingered, not in any physical sense, but again in the shape of a cloud on his mental horizon. All his life he had been, not robust, but resistant to illness, obliged to spare others the knowledge of his own weaknesses. And there had been weaknesses, but overcoming them so as not to disturb his parents, even his wife, had been his overriding preoccupation. In this way he had built up a certain immunity to physical distress, though conscious all the time that such defences could be breached. So far he had not succumbed to major illnesses, for which he could take no credit, or to minor ones, for which he could. In his experience a good night's sleep would enable him to fight another day, and generally he had been proved correct, but lately he had slept badly and sometimes woke in a panic, his heart knocking. It was at times like these, in the very early morning, that he was grateful that he lived alone, could perform the morning rituals slowly, during which time his heart would settle down. As the day wore on he experienced no further tremors, put such tremors down to a nightmare from which he had not woken, but which had been sufficiently disturbing as to make itself known in the form of an inchoate disturbance, largely of the senses. He told himself that altered perception, such as that occasioned by a nightmare, might have physical reverberations. At the same time he was anxious to capture any information that might have been vouchsafed to him in the course of that forgotten dream.

The previous evening's occurrence had alarmed him

sufficiently to arrange to see the doctor, but now that he had done so he decided that the incident was at an end. This consultation had disappointed him—the computer, the watercolour, the curious air of distraction that coloured the doctor's attention—displeased him to the extent of inspiring a certain anger. This was unusual: he was not given to anger. But he felt his politeness threatening to desert him. He would have appreciated more of a dialogue, was conscious of demanding more than he was likely to receive, recognized this as part of his unavailing desire for closeness, intimacy. His Freudian comparison had fallen on deaf ears, yet to him it was a matter of some significance. If he could ascribe the weakness of the previous evening to some profound metaphysical cause he would feel sufficiently heartened to carry on the struggle. If, however, it proved to be some sort of physical mishap he was on shakier ground. For all his faith in remote as opposed to immediate causes he knew that the mind cannot always outwit the body, and that the body that one took for granted could at any moment reveal itself as fragile, and worse, treacherous. He preferred to consider the knocking of his heart to be caused by anger at what he thought a dull-witted performance, regretted once again the grave seniority of the German doctor—so long ago!—even regretted his previous fortitude, which now threatened to desert him. He did not want to die, still less did he want to succumb to illness, yet that was the condition of seeking help. And the help that was available was to his mind inadequate. Above all he was conscious of boring this man, of wasting his time, not merely by presenting routine symptoms, common, he supposed, to all old people, but by

seeking to interest him in speculations of a no doubt dis-
credited nature. Freud was old hat now: young people, especially young doctors, had no time for him. He turned his
anger on himself, felt confused, foolish, prepared to leave,
aware that the interview was over, that the computer was
even now spewing out a prescription, that he was in alien
territory, where only the verifiably physical was important,
and all theory could be ignored.

'I want you to take a blood-pressure pill every day, and
to come back in a couple of weeks' time. People of your
age should take blood pressure seriously.'

'You think that's all it was, then?'

'At this stage I can't say. You seem fit enough.'

But how could he know? As an investigation this left
much to be desired. Above all it had proved to be strangely
tedious. He tried to imagine the doctor at home, with the
watercolour-painting wife, and the requisite images failed
him.

'I expect you will be going on holiday?' he asked, in a
last effort to establish some kind of mutuality, on the doctor's terms, if necessary.

'I've had a couple of weeks. I prefer to go away in the
winter. Get away from all the winter ailments.' He laughed
conspiratorially.

At once Herz understood this man. He was simply not
cut out to be a doctor, loathed medicine, loathed the care
he was obliged to take, even loathed himself for this kind
of emotional failure. This would account for his morose
attitude, his preference for the computer over the living
body, his all too palpable conscientiousness.

'A medical family?' he enquired, testing his theory.

'Yes. Clever of you to guess that. It was assumed that I would carry on where my father left off.'

'Difficult to disappoint him, I suppose?'

'Oh, yes.' In his voice Herz heard a lifetime of thwarted wishes.

'It is indeed difficult to fight one's family's expectations.'

And you would rather be doing something else, anything else, he thought. You would have preferred your freedom, and you were denied it. You made a good enough job of necessity. You minister to the sick in your own way. But in fact it is hardly ministering. Nor is it art. And surely medicine is the highest of the arts? What Claude and Turner cannot tell us is in your hands. It is a priestly task. And a man of true discernment would have turned down his wife's watercolour, though this might have provoked marital disharmony.

'Keep the other pills by you,' said the doctor. 'Place one under your tongue if you experience any more discomfort.'

He stood up with an air of relief, handed over the prescription. 'My nurse will check your blood pressure. Just pop in in a couple of weeks' time.'

Herz put the paper in his pocket. He would take the pills, or rather give them a try. In the interests of science he would have his blood pressure checked by the nurse. After that he rather thought he would do no more, would prefer to rely on his ancient knowledge of himself in order to confront whatever ordeals might have been prepared for him.

'I suppose Freud is completely out of date now,' he queried, as he reached the door.

'Completely. Goodbye, Mr Herz. Take care.'

Out in the sunny street he felt less exasperated, although a lingering consciousness of disappointment remained. He remembered having noted a small public garden off Paddington Street, the only amenity in this district other than the too distant park. He would sit on a bench and think things through, in company with other old men, and old ladies too, perhaps. The weather had proved surprisingly stable: after a lacklustre spring the warm days shaded off only gradually into breathtaking evenings, although the darkness came earlier now that it was August. Now it was difficult to ignore the scattering of fallen leaves or reports of drought in the newspapers, impossible though it was for anyone to wish for rain. It was enough to issue out each morning into sunshine to dispel thoughts of what was to come. Of the coming winter he refused to think. He sank heavily onto a wooden seat, the paper crackling in his pocket. He would take it to the friendly chemist whose advice he had always found reassuring. For the moment it was enough to sit with the other old men, and the old lady reading the *Daily Mail,* with whom he felt solidarity. He would perhaps exchange a few remarks with them sooner or later, about the weather, naturally: he would not make the mistake of discussing Freud, or related matters. That had been a mistake. He felt confused, wondered if others noticed, blamed himself for advancing into alien territory, for revealing an undue curiosity. But how to live without it? After years of dutiful obedience, of deferment to the will of others, he saw this timid examination of ideas as a permitted emancipation. He no longer had to make things better for everyone; that was his conclusion. He could read, speculate, entertain impious thoughts. He could reach conclusions that would have seemed unwise in the days of his obedience, for it had been obedience rather than servitude, and therein lay a certain residual sweetness. He was not sorry that it had come to an end, but the contrast between his life as a worker and this disturbing freedom was hard to assimilate, to manage.

He would, as always, have liked to discuss the matter, in the interests of genuine enquiry, with one or other of his elderly companions in the sun, and regretted, as always, that the thing was impossible. He would be looked on as an outsider, and worse, someone whose eagerness to make friends revealed him as no more than an ageing schoolboy. Yet if he had had the courage to break through that invisible barrier how enriching the revelations might be! But it seemed to be agreed, in this small space, that the utmost privacy should be observed. Indeed the faces he saw were stern, none relaxing into the half-smile of reminiscence. The silence being observed reminded him of chess players, or rather those he had noted, through a similar confusion, in a café in Nyon, as he was about to board his train, after his so polite meeting with Fanny and her mother at the Beau Rivage. He realized that the sadness and humiliation he had felt on that occasion had prepared him for a lifetime of the same, of repeated episodes of defeat. That was the essence of his sentimental education.

Yet what he felt now, sitting in the sun, was more like a new frustration, based on little more than an inability to talk things over, or rather a prohibition against such an exchange. He was accustomed to spending time on his own, was not exactly lonely, but was aware of an absence of ideas, such as might have been the currency between like-minded people. And surely those around him were in the same category as himself? Perhaps it was the absence of a proper meeting place, a café, for example, such as would have been found near a similar public garden in any continental town. He felt suddenly hungry, looked around him, saw only a pub, which was not to his taste. He had never liked pouring cold liquid into his stomach, as younger men seemed to do. With a sigh he got up, decided to eat lunch at an Italian restaurant in George Street, thought it too far to walk, settled for a sandwich and a glass of wine. He would buy an evening paper and return to his seat in the afternoon, spend the day there, in fact. He did not want to go home.

The memory of the previous evening's disturbance had faded until it was almost acceptable. That it had been an occult manifestation, a message from the unconscious, Herz had no doubt. It was the doctor who had sought a routine explanation and in so doing had removed the air of mystery that had proved such a rich source of associations in the past. The doctor could not, in the end, explain it any more satisfactorily than could Herz himself, had somewhat ostentatiously stuck to his brief, had advised taking the pills. But Herz knew that behind his life, the life he lived now, in Chiltern Street, in Paddington Street, in this garden, stretched unexamined territory, most of it compounded not only of his own mistakes, but of the mistakes of others. What if Fanny had consented to marry him? How would they have lived? On his salary? Impossible. He too would like to have lived at the Beau Rivage, thinking such a place a dignified representation of his life as an exile. His malaise had been a reminder of that condition: useless to ascribe it to any other cause. And short of consulting a specialist in these matters there was no way in which this extremely interesting phenomenon—interesting to him— could be elucidated.

That he had been willing to take his malaise seriously, sufficiently seriously to consult a doctor, he put down to an anxious susceptibility which he habitually masked with a smile. The smile was his disguise, and also his defence: it proclaimed him to be a harmless, even a well-meaning person, of whom favours could be asked, by whom favours would be granted. That was what he had come uncomplainingly to be, but there were unanswered questions. He could, he knew, have been different. He remembered saying to Simmonds that in later life one reverted to one's origins, and he had been a romantic young man, even a romantic middle-aged man: how else to account for that flight to Nyon, and that fidelity to a mirage of his youth? And that after an all too prosaic marriage, which he nevertheless viewed with some indulgence. He still felt an affinity with Josie, with her appetites, with her acceptance of him, so soon relinquished. And so easily! This was the difference between them. Even now he sought some spark of recognition from her, while allowing that none might be forthcoming. The attention he reserved for her was all on his side; he accepted this, just as he accepted that she rarely thought of him, was satisfied with the life she had made, saw her marriage as a stage she had passed through, as others passed through adolescence, leaving him an old man sitting in the sun, among others of his kind. He felt no rancour, only marvelled that he had so little to show for what had seemed to him a longed-for permanence. It had not left him much diminished; the reality had passed, the illusion resisted the change. He still longed for an ideal companion, to be enjoyed in an ideal landscape. He saw it as a form of retirement from the world, a private state which would remain a secret, half-wish, half-dream. Though it had faded it had never left him. In the most primitive, the most archaic part of his mind he still cherished it, wondered, even, how to bring it about, while at the same time knowing that he had had his chance. He did not see, at this stage, how he could have acted differently. He accepted that his defeats were honourable, while at the same time wondering how much honour he had wrested from his experiences. He felt sadness, even shame, certainly regret, but also felt as if his part had been written for him, that certain cosmic laws were in operation. Quite simply, he was unalterable. The cloud that had enveloped him on the previous evening was, he thought, a reminder that he had wasted his life.

In the afternoon the garden filled up with a different cast. Two girls, on an opposite seat, had the absorbed excited expressions of women discussing men. Their preoccupation drove him back to his own. Josie had been the reality principle, Fanny the pleasure principle. Freud again. Pity that young doctor had paid him so little respect, but then there had been no ideological background to his work. That was what had been missing from that consultation, a lack of context. Then he told himself that he was being ridiculous: a busy London doctor had no time for discussion, and if it were to have been a discussion what had he, Herz, to contribute? Better to discuss the pressures, the lack of resources, that seemed to be the matter of most complaints, or so one heard. Doctors were always being interviewed on the evening news about their circumstances, warning of crises, of emergencies. It seemed impossible to ignore these matters; one was asked to sympathize with doctors rather than with patients. This appeal for public sympathy annoyed Herz, who was, as ever, searching for another kind of sympathy, one less indignant than intuitive. He sighed. A man at the other end of the bench (one guarded one's space) looked up and asked, 'All right, are you?' 'Oh, perfectly fine,' said Herz, charmed. 'And don't worry. I won't interrupt your reading.'

The man—rather striking, in a dark blue shirt and cream trousers—laid aside his copy of the *Telegraph,* and said, 'I've actually read all I want to read. In any event the sun's too strong. Better to make the most of it, I suppose; they forecast rain.'

'Oh, surely not. It's been a perfect day. I hadn't noticed this little garden before.'

'These public gardens are a blessing to those of us who live in flats.'

'Quite. I shall probably find my way here again.'

'Could do worse. The morning's the best time. But there are always things to do in the morning.'

'I have been here all day,' Herz said wonderingly.

'You had the best of it, then. If you don't mind I'll finish this before I go home.' He took up the paper again, after which Herz sat stiffly, anxious not to impose.

He wished he had brought a book with him; he would do so if he came again. But his thoughts had been too absorbing and too unsatisfactory to be altered by another's perceptions. He reminded himself that Thomas Mann's short stories awaited him at home: old-fashioned stuff but that was what he preferred these days. And he had to get to the chemist with his prescription. With a sigh he prepared to leave, though he was not anxious to be on his own again. The man with the newspaper looked up and nodded. 'Nice to have met you,' said Herz, which was, he thought, the appropriate formula for leave-taking. 'Have a pleasant evening.'

'And you,' said the man, surprised. No further rendezvous was implied.

Slowly, reluctantly, he made his way home. The red-brick façades of Chiltern Street glowed in the last of the sun. Herz was tired now, though he had done nothing all day. He longed to postpone thoughts of pills and other purchases, and to settle down for a quiet half-hour with Thomas Mann. In the flat he made tea, found some biscuits, aware that if he were to be responsible for himself he would have to eat more. The 'occurrence', as he thought of it, now imposed itself once more, but worse than the feeling of illness was the baleful memory of being stranded in the street, of the almost accidental arrival of the taxi, and the uneasy thought that without it he might not have been able to get home. This unfortunately coincided with the Thomas Mann story he had most recently read, in which a poor lunatic makes his unsteady way to the churchyard to visit his graves and in so doing excites the mirth of passers-by, who witness his eventual collapse and call an ambulance. The story ends inconclusively, although the reader knows that the man's fate is sealed.

It was very sad, and more than sad, disturbing, yet it was

only a few pages long. In fact all the stories were sad or disturbing, and it was hard to discern the art behind them.
Only their authority prevailed. It would not be wise to
read further on this particular evening, lest the dread that
came off the page communicated itself too vividly. Herz
realized that he was in a vulnerable state, tried to revive the
anger he had felt in the doctor's surgery, and failed to do so.
He knew that the consultation had been abortive; worse, it
had hurt his pride. No real harm had been done, but he
knew he would not go back. Whatever ensued, he would
have to manage himself. It was this thought that lay behind
all the others.

He finished his tea, and with an air of resolution took
his prescription to the chemist. 'Are these any good?' he
asked, as the packets were handed over.

'Well, I take them myself. A lot of people do.'

This was all the reassurance he needed. If he was at one
with others no harm could come to him. Walking home
again, and limping slightly with tiredness, he longed for
bed. But to go to bed was to succumb. Moreover he was
no longer sustained by his dreams, which had a tendency
to turn menacing. The past once more made its way into
his consciousness, and all the remembered faces—dead or
absent, it made no difference—came back to haunt him.
They had vanished into their own concerns, thought no
more about him, abandoned him to a lonely end. Still he
longed for a return of love, for it seemed to him that he
had remained faithful. From beginning to end he had been
the lover, yet love had let him down. He dreaded coming
face-to-face with that thought in the watches of a sleepless
night.

Resolutely he turned on the television, watched a gardening programme, a cookery programme, a serial about policemen, and one about firemen. The exercise had done its work; he was now back in the present. He switched off with relief, took a long bath, subsided thankfully into bed. Sleep would come, sooner or later, and whatever information it brought would be considered rationally, without self-pity, and not until light had dawned on an ordinary and ordered day.

# 8

Herz had dreams of leaving. Not at night, in the safety of his bed, when there was no possibility of going anywhere, but on his walks, in the morning, and again in the evening, when he was newly aware of the decline of summer into autumn. The year had changed decisively; there was no longer any possibility of sitting in the public garden. This garden, he saw, had done duty for wider horizons, more substantial landscapes, such as he remembered from his travels, however these now appeared to him in retrospect. Frosts in the morning and a growing early twilight brought into focus the perspective of lightless winter days, when he would be forced to endure his own company for hours on end. He told himself that nothing had changed, that he still had the freedom to come and go as he pleased, or alternatively that he need make no changes. The flat oppressed him when he thought of the time he would have to spend in it, yet when he was out of doors, and newly aware of the alterations in the light, and particularly in the evenings, when he heard passers-by hurrying home, he felt a thrill of anguish as he contemplated his own arrangements, the so careful management of his time, the long day, the even longer and by now habitually sleepless night. Yet the evenings were beautiful. Blue vistas of streets seemed to usher in the night to come with a poetic intensity which he was forced to admire, but in an abstract fashion, as if the curtain were to rise on a drama of classical implications from which, once again, he was excluded, not only by his shadowy presence but by a lack of sympathy, going through the motions simply by virtue of obeying impulses the origin of which was almost forgotten.

He looked at the windows of the travel agency and saw advertisements for great journeys to the other side of the world. There, in those so misleading posters, he saw young people drinking on beaches or trekking with rucksacks in difficult terrain. Their youth was an essential part of the attraction, yet he could see, or was informed, that older people made the same journeys, or a modified version of those journeys, spending their money after a lifetime of careful thrift, and enjoying a confidence they thought they had lost. All these holiday adventurers were in pairs, even the grey-haired couples who seemed to offer their own challenge to Herz, as he lingered, trying to penetrate their silent worlds. Such undertakings were not for him, and never had been; he had followed a solitary path, aware of, but not part of, the families he had passed and to whom he was attracted. Not that he had ever actively sought their company. They had seemed to him like objects in a museum, exhibits that he might contemplate, seeking an explanation for the enigma of the past, and the greater enigma of the present. He knew that he had managed his life as best he could, that he had been a hard worker, a faithful son, a husband no worse than any other, yet that his life had failed to yield the ultimate satisfaction, so that he advanced into age with a feeling that he had it all to do again, that he was still an uncertain youth, seeking a way into experiences that would confer fullness. Then he could almost welcome closure, knowing that he had attempted all that there was to attempt, and need feel no regret for the paths he had not followed.

His desire now was not for the banal charm of distant places but for escape from the thoughts he knew too well. He saw himself in the sun, in some version of the public garden in which he had passed his summer afternoons. He even foresaw the possibility of staying away indefinitely, for he knew that he would not be missed. From time to time he might send a postcard to Bernard Simmonds, to Josie, to Mrs Beddington in the shop—'Enjoying the break'—to put them off the scent, while all the time planning his disappearance from the scene. At this thought, hidden behind all the others, he took fright: surely this was not his real intention? Surely it was possible to leave home in a less adventurous sense, not from life as he knew it, but from circumstances which he now recognized as irksome? There was, after all, a simple pleasure to be derived from sitting in the sun, from reading the local paper, from drinking a glass of wine, and to such pleasures he was surely entitled. His idleness no longer bothered him, but he did not enjoy it as much as he had thought he would. And as the days grew colder, and the sun sent only a fugitive gleam through increasing cloud, he told himself that he was not ready for the greater eclipse of winter, that he needed some purely animal warmth to prepare him for the long months ahead.

Some of this he said, in suitably disguised terms, to Ted Bishop, his cleaner, on loan once a week from Mrs Beddington, as they sat drinking their tea. Ted Bishop did little cleaning, but his offer to help out had been irresistible; in any event Herz found him companionable and did not mind the smell of cigarettes that engulfed the flat after his departure. Sometimes he brought his two-year-old grandson with him, but the child soon got bored, which meant an early departure for both of them. Herz knew that he was too tentative an employer to lay down terms of engagement, knew that Ted Bishop saw him as essentially harmless, not able to object to the child stamping delightedly on the hardwood floor, half-suspecting Herz's desire to enfold the child, to calm him, and watching him with a lazy eye that missed nothing. On this particular morning, after a bad night, Herz welcomed Ted Bishop as a human presence, while knowing that in doing so he blurred the distance between them, together with their separate status, in a way that was not entirely appropriate, and not even welcomed by either. In Berlin servants had known their place: the parlourmaid, the daily cleaner, the caretaker. Even in Hilltop Road there had been an amiable woman who came in three times a week and stayed largely out of sight. He did not flatter himself that Ted Bishop would be likely to conform to this pattern, nor did Ted acknowledge the slightest loyalty, although he was extremely well paid for the little he did. He had a variety of ailments which prevented a great deal of activity. This had two results: Herz could check his symptoms against those of Ted, and, more important, could derive some sort of encouragement from Ted's arthritis (which he did not share), from Ted's dyspepsia (from which he was also free), and from Ted's breathlessness, demonstrated to dramatic effect when asked to clean the windows. To Ted, and to Ted alone, he confessed his own occasional breathlessness, knowing that this was a dangerous route to take, but tempted to abandon high principles and sink into a miasma of head-shaking ruefulness which would almost certainly afford them both some degree of comfort.

'You enjoyed your holiday, Ted? Corsica, wasn't it?'

'Never again,' was the reply. 'I went for my daughter's sake, as I told you. I looked after the boy. I didn't mind that so much. It's hard for her, being on her own; she's still young enough to want to enjoy herself. But it was a bit much in the evenings, when she wanted to go out. And the food didn't agree with me. I was glad to get home, know what I was eating, have a read of my paper, go down the pub. To tell you the truth I didn't feel so good when I was out there. I didn't tell my daughter, and the boy en joyed himself, but she'll have to find someone else to take care of him if she wants to go away next year, single mother or no single mother.'

'Only I was thinking of going away myself.'

'It's not that I can't see her point of view. But I've got myself to think about, haven't I? I'm not a well man, and I've got responsibilities, know what I mean? She's got a good job at the hairdresser's, but she doesn't earn all that much. And she likes to go out in the evening, leaving the boy with me. So there wasn't much point going all that way to do the same thing, was there? But she needed the break, I could see that. Did you say you were going away?'

'Well, I thought of it.'

'You sure you're doing the right thing?' He patted his chest. 'You want to be careful. I don't know that it's wise, travelling at your age. There was a man on the plane coming back, had some sort of an attack. They gave him oxygen. About your age, he was. Then there's the food, always causes a bit of an upset. You're well placed here, aren't you? Have a bit of a rest when you feel like it, do your bit of shopping. If I were in your shoes I'd be inclined to stay put. Better the devil you know.'

In that instant Herz decided to go to Paris.

This decision, seemingly random, remained firmly lodged in his consciousness. It became more elaborate as he moved through his uneventful day, a day of cloudy skies with which he felt a sudden overwhelming impatience. On his walk to the supermarket it became more pronounced, more focused. He was tempted by the idea of a further exile, since that was to be his lot. He would go to Paris and seek out the small hotel where, years ago, he had sown a few wild oats. Paris, initially, had been a place that was out of range of his family's constraints, his mother's vigilance. His brief holidays had encountered no serious opposition at home, no encouragement either, but once there he and his companions of the moment had enjoyed a genuine freedom. This he remembered as he picked out his small loaf, his packet of ham, his cheese. There was no need for extensive preparation. He would take his raincoat and an overnight bag, and join the train like any other innocent passenger. Once in Paris he would make for the small hotel where he liked to think he would be greeted with a smile of recognition. Mme Roux: that was the name of the owner. From her he had received the sort of kindness that only strangers can bestow. There was no need for him to explain himself to her: she had seemed to look with favour on his youth and on that of his companions. Of the latter

he remembered very little: they were simply co-signatories
to a short truce in the eternal conflict of everyday circumstances. They too had been kind, offering no reproaches,
no recriminations, demanding nothing that he was not dis-
posed to provide. A sort of sophistication had been observed, as between equal partners who knew the limits of
the contract. Only when he reached home had his euphoria faded, but that had more to do with life at home than
with the fact that the enjoyment was over.

Something of the same feeling pursued him through
this particular day. Diminishing expectations set in once
again. He could hardly blame family circumstances on this
occasion, for there was no longer any family to receive
him, to pointedly ignore his brief absence, to emphasize
his father's fatigue as once again they assembled for an evening meal that was far from any kind of celebration. Back
in Chiltern Street with his small purchases he revised his
plans. He would initially go to Paris for the day, on a sort
of reconnaissance; he would visit his old hotel and enquire
about monthly rates. He would test the atmosphere, see if
he felt welcome. It would be an experiment, by which he
need not feel bound. In the course of the day the vision
faded, as other preoccupations intervened. It would soon
be winter; what would he do with himself all day, far from
the comfort of his flat? Ted Bishop's warnings sounded
once more in his head. Accidents could not be ruled out.
Yet he persisted in envisaging some sort of freedom from
constraints which were no less real than they had been in
the past. It was not memory that constrained him; old
habits of mind were still annoyingly intact. He almost
wished that there was a family to which he might return,

for as he knew from past experience, and also from inner conviction, return would be the hardest part of the entire endeavour. Would it therefore not be wiser to eliminate the idea of return altogether?

On the morning of his departure he woke from an unusually heavy sleep, wishing only not to move. It was in a spirit of absentminded determination that he left the flat and made his way to Waterloo. The same protective indifference saw him onto the train, provided him with a newspaper and coffee, reminded him that he could do as much or as little as he desired. Mild English countryside glided past the window, just such mildness as had greeted his family all those years ago, and had made them if not exactly welcome, if not, ever, at home, at least unchallenged, unexamined. He had grown to value English incuriosity, which perhaps—native colouring—accounted for the indifference he now felt.

Once arrived he took the Métro to St-Germain-des-Prés, for that was where he had taken his girlfriends. They had marvelled then at the effervescence, the sophistication, as they sat in the Flore or the Deux Magots surveying the glittering evening. Their supreme good fortune, in those far-off days, was to have been alike in their expectations; the naïveté of youth had protected them from potential disappointment, not only with the adventure, but with each other. And their instinctive kindliness, a kindliness he had not encountered since, ensured that they would part without recrimination. They were humble employees like himself, would wave to each other on their way to work, would smile acknowledgement and pass on. In that way they attained a level of sophistication denied to many more worldly women, and more, a sort of grace that had to do with unspoilt expectations, and with the brief experience of something like authentic happiness.

He ordered coffee, looked about him with no particular shock of recognition, realized that the true balefulness of age was an inability to bring those memories back to life, to rekindle the intensity of the past as it had surely once been felt. Now he sat, in only mild contentment, in the familiar setting, mindful of the time allotted to him, glancing frequently at his watch, feeling the colder air but unwilling to put on his raincoat. He signalled the waiter for the bill and got to his feet, reassembling himself with some difficulty. Suddenly this excursion seemed pure folly. There was no way, feeling as tired as he already did, that he could spend further days like this one. He should never have left home, should have realized yet again that he must have a thought for his continued existence, that he had been right all along in being cautious, prudent, circumspect, taking his idle walks, sitting in the public garden, sparing his waning energies, his time, his life. This was no age to take chances. He had had a dream of youth; he had had a memory of sunlight, of energy, of faces as young as his own had been. But those faces, if he were to see them again, would be old, spoiled, and worse, indifferent. It was this indifference that now enveloped him. He thought he might even make his way back to the station and catch an earlier train home. For it now appeared to him as home, with all its small comforts. He stood on the pavement, irresolute, buffeted by passers-by. The sky had darkened during the time he had spent in the café. It looked like rain.

But, obeying some obscure instinct, he stepped off the pavement and turned not into the Métro station but across the street, walking rather more urgently now, his raincoat over his arm. He was making for St-Sulpice and for the haunting image that he remembered from his first ever visit to Paris, an image of two men wrestling or dancing in a forest clearing, a hat flung down by one of the wrestlers, a dusty train of men and horses disappearing into the distance: Jacob and the Angel. The scene would lose none of its power or its mystery for being viewed so many times. So it proved. Jacob's head was still down as he attempted to butt his strange adversary in the chest; he looked brutish, unenlightened, but courageous. He needed his courage to confront the angel, who had the grace and stature of a fully grown man, one who would inevitably win this particular fight. He would win it not by superior strength, though that was manifest, but by the ardour of his gaze directed at Jacob's unseeing head. What did that gaze imply? It was not rebuke, still less retribution. It was, rather, the reminder of eternal surveillance. As Herz remembered the story the fight ended in a draw. Jacob had come out of it rather better than might have been expected, had shown a kind of understanding, had demanded a blessing. This fact alone signified acknowledgement, even grace. Nothing more need be demonstrated.

Yet the angel still remained the conqueror, by virtue of his beauty, his strength, the enactment of his task, which was surely, then as now, to carry out the terms of his employment? This he had done, for the benefit of the spectator, if not for Jacob himself. No one who had witnessed the fight (those hapless voyagers departing on their horses had not even been aware of it) could remain unconvinced that at one time, in the remote past, in no time at all, perhaps, there had been mythic certainties, apparitions, prophecies, but that even then such interventions had not been quite clear. Herz, in front of the picture in the semi-darkness of the chapel, stood in awe: had he been wearing a hat he would have removed it, as Jacob had done, to ready himself for the fight. So that there were confrontations that were benign, a fact which Jacob had recognized, by demanding a blessing rather than dying of fright. But whatever fear he might have felt was not in the picture. What was there was not even loving correction—that came much later. What was there was parity, equal status, and a lack of astonishment. This matter-of-fact struggle seemed at one with the certainties of that strange time. And the fight had been concluded without hard feelings on either side. Yet that ardent angelic gaze, that effortless muscularity, denoted powers that Jacob could not even imagine. For all his easy victory he was marked for life.

Mystified, gratified, and somehow heartened, Herz stood for a moment in tribute. He had few beliefs, certainly none that would carry him to a peaceful conclusion. Yet Jacob was his ancestor, in more ways than one. He regretted that he had never engaged in a similar struggle, had neglected the promptings of that so remote antiquity. Yet faith, such as he had never possessed, even as a child, must surely foster a facile optimism, a notion that someone was in charge, that he, Herz, was worth nurturing, if only by admonition. He saw the saving grace of religion, which was to succour, to console, to provide an illusion of reciprocity which all desired. Yet better a stoical pessimism, a hard look at life's realities, and most of all a determination to enjoy that life, certainly to value it. Jacob's advantage was to have been the object of a visitation, one that he did not, perhaps could not, understand, was not meant to understand. He had done the right thing, had asked for a blessing, rather in the spirit of one accepting an unexpected compliment. And the angel, after a successful mission, would rejoin his equally athletic colleagues and await further incomprehensible instructions, rather in the spirit of a highly trained soldier obedient to his superior officer and to the ethos of the company into which he had been conscripted. Only his unearthly gaze revealed him to be of a different species. In his realm, perhaps, all were similarly endowed.

In perhaps equally mystical fashion the visit declared itself to have been concluded, its high point reached and overtaken. Now Herz would simply go home, all thoughts of further exile expunged from his mind. Absurd to think that he might move to Paris; absurd to imagine that the hotel would be as he remembered, that the original owner was still alive. Absurd above all this persistence of memory in circumstances that were radically altered. He no longer thought in terms of a reluctant return, of the glum evenings that had reclaimed him after his so brief adventures. His former companions would be old women now, who thought of their early forays indulgently, if at all. In the here and now, to which he had a duty, such company was not to be had, and unseemly longings must be stifled. In that moment, imbued with the spirit of the chapel, he accepted the prospect of endless solitude, and, in a mood of heightened awareness, embraced it. There would be no revelation, no combat with a divinely appointed stranger.

He would endure, for as long as he was able. That was the only message he was likely to understand.

On his way to the station he stopped for a glass of wine, and applied himself to observing the lives around him. But the well-known formula failed to work. Apart from the hour spent in St-Sulpice this had been a futile exercise. New initiatives were no longer within his reach; he must live on the old ones. Only one more event of note was foreseeable, and he supposed that Bernard Simmonds would chronicle that. He must remember to leave some sort of instruction. Around him the evening was beginning to get under way, people stopping off after their day's work, meeting friends, talking on their mobiles. The globalization, of which he had read so much, was here in evidence: Paris was no longer the paradoxically tender-hearted place that he remembered, but as busy, as noisy, as London or New York. Even the population looked different, more emphatic, less hierarchical, social distinctions more blurred than they had been thirty years previously. The picturesque Paris of his, and, he supposed, everyone else's imaginings was being eroded by a new breed intent on the market, on performance rather than on ideas. He had once been of an age to sympathize with students, though never a student himself. That had been the ethos of that earlier time, the years of his brief freedoms. Now he was merely an outsider, and the bohemians of yesterday were now men in suits, with metal briefcases. As a comment on the passage of time he found them woefully lacking in poetry.

He looked at his watch and started: it was already five o'clock and his train left at six. He hurried into the Métro and stood shoulder to shoulder with the crowds, feeling the familiar flutter in his throat, as if his heart were trying to escape. He reached the Gare du Nord with only ten minutes to spare, was hurried to his seat, and leaned back cautiously, his hand to his chest. The train left on time, and beyond the dark window the lights of Paris bloomed and faded; soon the landscape was flowing past in the opposite direction to the one taken that morning. His capacity for experiment had become extinct in the course of this inconsequential day. He wondered now what had possessed him to set out when he had had no reason to do so, was glad that he had told no one, that he need not explain himself. Later, he knew, he would recover, might mention, but without attaching undue importance to the fact, that he had gone to Paris to renew acquaintance with a picture that had once impressed him. In that way he might invest his poor adventure with a certain urbanity. But he knew that he would make no similar attempt in the future. Much as he still acknowledged larger appetites, he knew that he could no longer satisfy them. The silent striving figures of Jacob and the angel were still vividly present in his mind's eye. He supposed that they would offer themselves for reflection in the days to come.

In Chiltern Street he sank down thankfully into a chair, his raincoat still over his arm. He was too tired to eat, or even to go to bed, too tired to plan ahead, grateful that no further tasks awaited him. Later, lying flat on his back, he reflected that at least he had seen the thing through, tried to retrieve some dignity from the experience, without success. As he turned on his side he reflected that the courageous thing to do would be to repeat the experience, and in that way derive some pride from what would be difficult, as if displacement were merely a test of character, as he supposed it might be. He was not fully awake, but not yet shading into sleep. 'You know the Delacroix in St-Sulpice?' he might remark to Bernard Simmonds when they next met. 'A particular favourite of mine. I popped over to see it a few weeks ago. I find I remember it with the greatest affection.'

## 9

Herz arranged the photographs on his desk, intent on examining what the past had contributed to his strange joyless present. He looked round the room to see if it were ready to welcome in some impossible but unknown, unhoped-for guest, saw that it was, as ever, immaculate, and with a sigh turned to the mute oblongs he habitually kept in a folder, in a suitcase, obscurely, and which he was now resigned to concealing forever. He felt a distaste, but also a curiosity that always accompanied this particular investigation: the photographs, of no conceivable relevance to anyone he currently knew, were to him a painful record of people whose hold on his affections had dwindled to almost nothing.

Yet he was bound to those people, had been formed by them, had now exhausted their legacy, such as it was, and considered himself the recipient of their various discontents, in comparison with which his own seemed somehow lightweight. It was a feeling of unworthiness, as if he had somehow got off scot-free, that contributed towards his ambivalence. Even the photographs served as a reminder of complicated familial unhappiness. He did not intend to look at them again, would put them away forever, to be thrown away after his death with the rest of his belongings, but conceived it as a duty to pass them once more in review before locking them away in the suitcase which would in turn take its place in the basement room he shared with others at the back of Mrs Beddington's shop. He half-hoped that unseen hands would dispose of them when the basement was emptied, just before Christmas, by dustmen coming to collect their annual tip. It would be something of a relief to know that the suitcase had gone, so much so that he would not enquire as to its whereabouts. The act of putting the suitcase in the basement would be a catalyst. He would have relinquished it, and with it the past. That was all that mattered.

Here was his mother, in evening dress, preparing to attend the annual dinner that was held at his father's firm, hierarchical in her finery, and with an expression of triumph on her face, which had been beautiful. That triumphant expression was what he remembered best, yet there had been few occasions on which it could have been seen. She had been a discontented disappointed woman, too long constrained by her religious parents, and obliged to marry for reasons of her own emotional survival, envious of her more worldly sister who had cast off the parental shackles with apparent ease, and seemed to be none the worse for it. Consumed with longing, she had kept up a façade of sophistication; a failed pianist, she had played in improvised concerts in her own drawing-room, so that visitors were obliged to listen respectfully and to compliment her. Herz remembered his own childhood embarrassment as she took off her rings and sat down to play, even to his school-friends, who would be expected to sit in silence when it was against their nature to do so.

Here was a photograph of her seated at the piano, turning to her unseen audience with a smile on her handsome face, in which it was possible to discern a wistfulness behind the mask that was never laid aside, so that it came almost naturally to her to patronize her few friends. She had survived the transition to England rather better than any of them, writing to her sister Anna to tell her how comfortably they were situated in their new home in Hilltop Road, and purposefully ignoring his father's drastically reduced circumstances. By that time she had placed all her hopes in Freddy, whose virtuosity would eventually elevate her to a position that would enable her to triumph once more. All this fantasizing was, he knew now, directed against her sister, the thorn in her side, whom she suspected of enjoying the happiness that had always eluded her. Here she was with Freddy, her hand possessive on his shoulder. How alike they were! Large-eyed, solemn, as if they were obeying some occult instruction, whereas in fact his brother's reputation had foundered as soon as his health gave way, so that in England he remained unknown, a fact overlooked by his mother who perceived a sublime future for them both as soon as he recovered from the illness which she ascribed to his delicate nerves, but in the lightest possible sense. He had not recovered, did not appear to be unhappy with his fallen status. His strange decline had not been recorded by any camera. He had been eclipsed, or had eclipsed himself.

Here was his mother as a child, posing with her sister, their arms entwined, as he never remembered them being in adult life. They had the stricken consumptive look that children had in such posed photographs, their eyes enormous, their abundant hair loosely tied back, condemned to sit at home until released by some man or other, for in those days liberation came in the form of a husband, subsequent on a meaningful introduction by a third party, in this case their mother, or more probably their father, who would know about such matters. It was not possible to deduce from those two solemn infant faces that one sister, the less pretty of the two, would escape such controls, would in fact meet her future husband quite simply crossing the street—the street!—as a schoolgirl, would endure family rages, the condemnation of her parents, and would marry him when she was eighteen, after who knew how many clandestine meetings, to live happily ever after, until the exodus from Germany separated them forever. By that time some slight rapprochement between the sisters had taken place. Herz surmised that it must have done, for that was the time when he was in love with his cousin Fanny. Sharper than any photograph was his memory of those afternoons in his aunt's drawing-room, waiting for Fanny to join him, as she so rarely did, and his awareness of the contrast between the light of his aunt's villa and the dark flat to which he must return, and which he knew would resound with his mother's piano and his brother's violin.

Here was his father as a young man, also solemn, extremely handsome, long before marriage had condemned him to worship at one impossible shrine, obedient to both parents and parents-in-law, never allowed to enjoy his life as a man, his spirit already broken by excessive obedience, willing, by virtue of that same obedience, to be inducted into a marriage which was to be proved unhappy throughout its tortuous evolution. That handsome young face had

mutated early on into something a little too anxious to
please, growing careworn under the strain of contributing
to his wife's fluctuating moods, and already bearing the
burden of knowing that the family's safety was compro-
mised, and that exile was inevitable. His stifled fears had
made him excessively indulgent towards his children, particularly towards Freddy. Sometimes tears would come into
his eyes as he contemplated the boy practicing. It was he
who bore the burden of Freddy's illness, so much so that
he could not bear to visit him, and was glad to depute that
task to Herz himself. In that way both mother and father
had renounced Freddy, out of a terror (or was it a conviction?) that Freddy would not come back to them, would
not redeem them, would not compensate them for their
various losses, including the loss of Freddy himself. Yet in
that young handsome face of his twenty-year-old father
Herz could see no foreknowledge, no doom. He had never
known his father in that guise, with an unknown future
before him. He remembered him as a haggard figure,
obliged to sleep a lot, remembered with a dreadful pity his
father's grateful relinquishing of the daytime hours as he
went heavily up the stairs to the flat above the shop in Edgware Road for his nap, to reappear some two or three
hours later, dishevelled and unkempt, the very image of a
failure. Yet here was a photograph of his parents at some
sort of function, presumably that same annual dinner for
which his mother composed her appearance so carefully.
They looked worldly, even complicit, his father's eager
smile setting off his mother's beauty, captured in a rare
mood of pleasure, soon to be lost forever, and hardly remembered in the maelstrom of their changing fortunes.

Here were his mother's parents, the grim couple who put their faith in every religious prohibition and who observed even more rules than were theirs by inheritance. They had an appearance of worthiness which was fallacious, a photographer's compliment, the formally dressed man standing respectfully behind his wife's chair, and that wife, monumental in black, staring forward without the trace of a smile, never once, in the lifetime that Herz dimly remembered, ever showing an instinctive affection towards any member of her family, yet undoubtedly mourning the defection of one daughter while grappling the other to her side. It had somehow been decreed that this remaining daughter should never leave home. Had his grandfather not taken pity on her and introduced the so appropriate young man into his household she would have remained unmarried for the rest of her days. Herz examined the two rebarbative faces, acknowledged the repugnance he felt, yet was grateful that they had died naturally, in their own home, a fate denied to so many of their kind. Looking at them from this distance he could discern what had made them so disagreeable: they had never known pleasure. Under those stiff formal clothes were stiff formal bodies, which had learned to keep their distance from one another, coming together only for certain regimented purposes, and resuming their forbidding demeanour immediately afterwards, and no doubt with relief.

Here was the Baden-Baden photograph, the most precious of all, and here at last was one of himself as a child, in short check trousers, with his hand to his heart, as it so often was these days, but in the photograph without a hint of weakness. He too was solemn, but with a wide mouth that was prone to move into a smile, even then. That smile had become one of protection, as his family's destiny unfolded, of propitiation too. It had never left him, although his own destiny was obscure by any standards. The feeling that he had escaped still puzzled him. In Herz's particular cosmology there were no lucky escapes; all good fortune had to be elaborately justified, and above all nothing taken for granted. To be sitting in his own flat, with no obligations, seemed to him more precarious than it might appear. He knew that it was luck that had brought him to this pass, and he distrusted luck as fervently as his devout grandparents might have done. Maybe it was from that unlovely couple that he had inherited his conviction of God's irritability, and with it the likelihood that undeserved good fortune might incur the strictest of penalties.

Their later lives were not recorded, apart from a photograph of a deserted Hilltop Road which he had taken with his own camera, somehow brought intact from Germany, and one of Freddy in shabby grinning retirement, all traces of his mother's ambition eliminated, as if by will alone. Taken by someone unknown, it showed him sitting on Brighton beach, his trousers rolled above his ankles, shirt sleeves protruding from an ancient pullover, wearing a smile that Herz thought unlike his own in that it implied an absence of memory that was also deliberate. Freddy was happy! Herz had only to contrast this photograph with one of Freddy in full concert-platform fig to understand what a burden his former life had been to him, and to sympathize. He had somehow escaped blame: the move to England had effaced his nascent reputation, after which he had lapsed into an illness that was sufficiently unspecific to allow him a breathing space. He had also escaped his parents' disappointment, since they were so anxious to believe him on the verge of a miraculous cure, a new maturity that would raise them all to eminence, would wipe away their tears. It was in order to nurture this illusion that they visited him so little, delegating the task to their younger son, who saw, early on, that there would be no renaissance of their former way of life, and none at all of Freddy. The illusion was shared only by his parents, a *folie à deux,* in which the husband was implicated largely by fear of his wife. That later photograph of Freddy, looking like a daytripper, was all that remained of his life as a man. So improbable was it that Herz gazed at it in wonder before reluctantly laying it aside.

The other photographs were of lesser interest, mainly postcards of his travels, souvenirs from which the original attraction had faded, and reproductions of favourite paintings, only some of which he had seen: a bird from the catacomb of Priscilla in Rome; a portrait of an English lady wearing a large hat, from the Jacquemart-André Collection in Paris, bought because of the hilarious yet touching contrast between her clumsy appearance and the elegant surroundings of the museum; a stylish back view of a woman by Manet, barely sketched in and evocative of further nudity; an almost illegible sculpture frieze from Parma Cathedral; an arresting image from the National Portrait Gallery of a dressmaker pinning the skirt of an impassive client who resembled Fanny Bauer (black hair, dark eyes, prominent crimson mouth, and bad-tempered expression); and a Fayum portrait head which he cherished because Josie had sent it to him and which he could imagine her

choosing carefully in an effort to adapt to him. That postcard had moved him unbearably. He had read into it a desire to please which she was normally determined not to
show, and perhaps a glimpse of a response to beauty that he
had longed to cherish. It had been in the early days of their
relationship; he had taken her to the Wallace Collection,
he remembered she had been bored; the visit was not a
success. But two days later she had enclosed the Fayum reproduction in a note thanking him for a pleasant afternoon. He had thought it a charming gesture, a tribute of
sorts to something she did not share but which she acknowledged as being part of his dreaming mind, and which,
puzzled, she respected.

As a record of a life it lacked consistency, hinting at
grandeur, hinting at tragedy, but subsiding at the end into
that grinning figure on Brighton beach. And it was a
record from which Herz himself was virtually absent, his
life after boyhood unwitnessed. There was a prehistory that
had vanished, schooldays, holidays completely absent. There
must have been other photographs that had been left behind, only these few selected to present a picture of family
life that was intended flatteringly to obscure the banal existence that his mother deplored. It was she, he saw, who
had made this selection, ruthlessly excluding those aspects
of life with which she was impatient. At least she had left
some kind of representation which she might produce for
public consumption. For she too had required an audience.
As she had turned so gracefully at the piano she too had
imagined some sort of public. He had inherited this from
her, only in his case the public was reduced to those who
might serve as fascinated observers, or as the friends he no

longer had, or as an impossible lover whose only interest was himself. This had never come about, which was why there were no further photographs. No one had said, 'Over here! Smile!'; he was as absent from other lives as he was from his own. What he was looking at was what had been laid down for him: a life of patient attendance and no less patient study. He had inherited his father's sadness, as that father had made his dutiful way to work every day, returning every evening to his myth-making wife. Yet he, Herz, had schooled himself into pragmatism, and in so doing had acceded to a condition which was not quite enviable though no doubt necessary. The absence of photographs of himself had made him appear and feel invisible, and so, he supposed, he truly was as he went about his self-appointed business of staying alive, diverting himself as best he could, showing only a licensed eagerness, a permitted receptivity, yet knowing that at any moment desire might resurface, might prompt him into making a rash move, such as he had not made when it might have been possible to do so. The boy in the check trousers, with his hand held so poetically to his heart, foreshadowed the ardent lover he was willing to become, foreshadowed Nyon and his absurd adventure. These days his hand went to his heart for other reasons, to make sure that his pills were still in his breast pocket. To date he had never used them. They were there as protection against the rash move that even now might undo him, precipitate him into a condition from which there might be no recovery, the next big thing to which Ostrovski had alluded. In due course that mystery might be solved. Or not, as he supposed.

A knock at the door startled him. Hastily he shovelled

the photographs into a drawer of his desk, where he imagined they would remain until he decided to dispose of them. He did not think he would look at them again.

'Laura! How nice. Do come in. A glass of wine?'

Mrs Beddington was not a frequent visitor, not even a particularly welcome one, since she usually asked him to perform some service for her, to regulate the burglar alarm, or to take in and store in his flat a bulky and inconvenient package if the postman called before she had left her home in St John's Wood. Although Herz, like most men, craved a female presence, he would have liked to design that female presence for himself, would have chosen something sweet-natured and indulgent, whereas after an initial meeting he had recognized Mrs Beddington as entirely self-centred. This was borne out by her conversation, which was one-sided. She had many complaints, most of which were directed against people he did not know, but he recognized the tone: anyone who failed to satisfy her demands was demonized. He supposed she had employed this technique against her two husbands, 'both scoundrels', she had affirmed, though with a reminiscent smile. She was a handsome woman, with a powerful presence. He supposed that she had been even more handsome as a girl. Now her darkly dyed hair added harshness to an expression which was always less than accommodating.

He was normally acquiescent to her demands, having nothing better to do. He was aware that she saw him as something less than a man, but useful for her purposes, which were far-reaching. As far as he knew she was a successful businesswoman, although he had seen few people in the shop, few customers, that is, since her sister seemed to be there every morning, engaging her in leisurely conversation, in the course of which both wore identical expressions of disgust. The absence of customers did not surprise him. This he put down to what was on offer in the window, two or three confections of alarming formality, silk trousers and embroidered tunics in violent shades of turquoise or viridian, unlikely to appeal to any woman under sixty, and designed to ensnare a younger lover, one impressed by the only asset such a woman would have to offer: opulence. He had to concede that the girls in the workroom did a highly professional job with the embellishments, though these tended to glitter in the morning sun and looked somewhat out of place in the mild surroundings of Chiltern Street. He could not imagine any woman of his acquaintance being tempted to make such a purchase. Even trying on one of these outfits would be burdensome.

'What can I do for you, Laura?' he asked. His hand stole to his breast pocket; the photographs had upset him. At the same time he knew he was not quite ready to throw them away.

'I've come to warn you, Julius, I'm retiring.'

Though this did not in the least concern him, as she obviously thought it should, he felt a certain unease. He did not welcome change.

'Retiring? What made you decide? You're hardly of an age . . .'

'Oh, I know I still look pretty good—you have to in this business. But I'm tired, Julius. I've worked hard all my life, survived two divorces; I deserve a bit of a break. I've sold the shop, by the way, and the workroom. That's already let, to a young woman. So you'll have a new neighbour.'

'Come to think of it I haven't heard the girls recently. I assumed they were on holiday.'

She laughed. 'Girls like that don't go on holiday. Most of them are here illegally anyway. They were only too glad to find a job. And I think you'll agree that their working conditions were pleasant.'

'What will happen to them?'

'I've no idea. I did what I could for them. Now they're on their own.'

'And the shop?'

'Well, that might concern you. I've sold it to an outfit selling radios and televisions. Part of a chain.' She mentioned a series of initials which meant nothing to him. 'So it might not be as quiet as you've been used to. But there you are; I had the offer and I took it. I'm treating myself to a cruise, treating my sister as well. She's been having a few problems with her marriage, so I'm taking her to the Bahamas. Have you been? No, I suppose not. Just the two of us. We should have a whale of a time.'

'Will this changeover affect me? Apart from the noise, that is?' He imagined an open street door, different programmes on different television sets, mesmerized assistants indifferent to the building's tenants, principally to himself, and passers-by agglomerating outside the window to watch five minutes of a football match. He fancied he could already hear the roar of the crowd.

'You've got a lease, haven't you?'

'It has only three years left to run,' he said, with a feeling of dread. He had been here, he realized, for five peaceful years. The flat had represented a new beginning when he had first seen it. That new beginning had not materialized, or rather it had materialized into an eventless existence which he had had to fashion for himself. This had not been entirely unrewarding, although without the kind of passionate engagement that he found he still desired. Now that it might be threatened he felt his latent attachment to the place ready to burst forth, to proclaim his right to remain in exactly the same circumstances that had appealed to him at the outset of this particular adventure.

'I expect you can negotiate a new lease. Who's your solicitor?'

'A friend.'

'Mind you, it'll cost you something. A new lease is bound to cost more than the old one. I wonder you don't move a bit further out, find somewhere with a bit of a garden.' She picked up her keys and her bag. 'You'll work something out,' she said vaguely. 'Life's too short to worry about what might happen in the next few years.'

'Don't go, Laura. Tell me more about this new tenant. My neighbour.'

'Young woman. Calls herself a consultant. Rather an offhand manner. Good-looking, if you like that style.' In her eyes bloomed a sudden hatred for any woman younger than herself. It was easy to imagine her on her cruise, getting changed in the evenings into one of the harem outfits that had not made the shop's fortune. She would carry off the lot, and devise a way of life to suit them. He did not quite see what this would be like, but was able to imagine far-flung holidays in ever more exotic surroundings. She would acquire a bronze patina, lighten her hair; her voice would darken, her nails grow longer. She would devote her time to her appearance, yet gradually lose the air of hauteur that she had worn in the shop, would acquire cronies like herself, laugh heartily and scornfully at everyone and everything. She would be on the lookout for a man, would not much care if he drank too much, since she might drink too much herself. Herz sincerely regretted the dignified, even forbidding presence he was used to seeing through the windows of the shop.

Women aged as best they could, he supposed. He had not given the matter much thought. But age was a grievous business for everyone. The only woman he knew who had survived it with indifference was Josie, yet the years of her greatest anxiety were still to come. Fanny he imagined unchanged since girlhood, since her fifteenth year. Even in Nyon, pale and compact, she had retained something of her youth, or that was how he saw her. She was iconic, as some women seemed to be; that was their abiding attraction. It was an uncommon distinction, and one not easily come by, conferred on them by others, by popular approval, so that they need do little to justify it. It was precisely Fanny's unaltered opinion of herself that made her impervious to the opinions of others. It was an enviable capacity, or rather incapacity. What had been in her heart he had never known.

'A consultant, did you say? A doctor?'

'No. Some sort of new job they all seem to have these days. Name of Clay. She might advise you. I'm not leaving till the end of the month, so you'll see me around. After that, who knows? Who knows about anything, come to that?'

After he had shown her out he sat once more at his desk, with his head in his hands. There was no way in which he would relinquish this flat, although it no longer gratified him. He supposed that he could find another, which at

this stage of his life would probably do as well. But if he decided to stay his peace would be shattered by the noise from
the shop and the comings and goings of a stranger. What
disturbed him was the prospect of turning once more into
a suppliant, a petitioner. And he suspected arrangements
over which he might have no control. The new tenant
would have a more advantageous lease. The world might
once again turn into a conspiracy, as perhaps it always had
been. He had three years left to him. The thought that he
might die in the meantime was no longer a threat. It now
presented itself as a guarantee of his safekeeping.

# 10

'I'm glad you phoned,' he said. 'I should have phoned you anyway sooner or later, booked you for lunch . . .'

'I didn't want lunch,' she said. 'I haven't got much time. That's why I suggested we meet here.'

'Here' was the Bluebird café in the King's Road, less distance for her to come from Wandsworth, and less crowded than their usual restaurant.

'I didn't bring the car,' she said. 'I walked.'

'Walked? It's quite a distance.'

'I needed time to think. I've got a lot on my mind, Julius.'

She did indeed look newly thoughtful. She had made an effort to smarten up her appearance, wore a tweed suit which might have been fashionable some fifteen years previously. On the lapel of her jacket he was pleased yet somewhat surprised to see the garnet brooch he had given her on their wedding day. This added to a new impression of maturity, as if she had studied how other women looked when they wanted to give an impression of seriousness. Even her hair was disciplined into some kind of order. She gazed beyond him, as if lost in thoughts of her own, ignoring her coffee.

'Is anything wrong, Josie?'

'In a way. Changed, certainly. I'm leaving, Julius. I'm leaving London.'

'Where are you going to?'

'I'm going home to Maidstone. To my mother. She's not well. She's eighty-six, Julius, and she lives alone. Apart from a neighbour there's no one to look after her. And I'm all she's got. So I'm going home to take care of her.'

'But your work? Tom?'

She sighed. 'I'm too old for any of it. I'll miss the work, but I'm probably past my best. In due course I may start up something of my own. But I doubt it somehow.'

'What does Tom say to all of this?'

'He'll replace me, of course. Both at home and at work. Tom is still a good-looking man. You knew he was younger than me?'

'I didn't know that, no.'

'Seven years. They don't matter at the beginning, but as you get on . . . And I wasn't happy.'

'I thought . . .'

'No,' she said fiercely. 'I wanted what other women had A home of my own. I wanted children. Did you know that? Not that there was any possibility in your set-up.'

'I'm sorry.'

'Oh, it's too late for any of that now. Mother will leave me the house when she dies. At least I'll have that. A woman without assets is in a hopeless position.'

'I suppose it's always a good idea to be independent. That's what other women seem to want these days. Isn't that the feminist position?'

'I don't go along with all they say. It makes sense, that's all I know. But there's more to it than that. Women aren't good on their own. It's easier for men.'

'I don't think it is, you know. Men are vulnerable.'

'I've seen them at it. They make up their minds pretty quickly when they want something.'

This he knew to be true, and was anxious to change the subject. He would have liked a brief interval in which to contemplate the matter. With the ruthlessness of a man in the grip of a new obsession he would have welcomed an opportunity to discuss his feelings, which were unexplained and almost unwelcome, but enlivening, fascinating. He felt for them as fondly as a parent, knowing that if he were to turn his back on them he would be forgoing something in the nature of a gift. After a lifetime of fidelity he glimpsed the ravishing possibility of abandoning his high standards and surrendering to the spirit of improvidence, of subversion, the spirit which he supposed moved most men and which, he now saw, he had been unwise to ignore.

'What will you do for money?' he asked.

'I've made Tom agree to give me an allowance until . . . Well, Mother might have a bit put by.' She paused.

'If I can help . . .'

'Thank you, Julius. I knew you'd say that. You were always very good about money. It's just until I find my feet, work out how much I'll have to live on.'

'Yes, of course. I'll do what I can. Although I should warn you that I may not be able to do this for more than a couple of years. My lease is running out; I shall have to negotiate a new one. If I stay, that is.' But he knew that he would, that there were now compelling reasons for staying.

'You don't want to move at your age. I don't much want to move myself.'

'I still like the flat, although I took it in a hurry, didn't much care where I was as long as I was on my own. But it's beginning to change. There's a new business on the ground floor, and it threatens to become noisy. And I have a new neighbour, though I don't know her very well. Sophie Clay,' he said, for the pleasure of pronouncing her name. 'I'll let you have a new address, of course. You'd better give me yours. When will I see you again? You'll come up to town, I suppose?'

'I don't know that I will. There comes a time in a woman's life when she no longer wants to make an effort, wants to let her hair go, wear comfortable shoes, stop trying to attract men. And yet there's a sadness in this. You lose a future. I've noticed this in women who give up. Men seem to go on for longer. You see quite old men looking at younger women as if they still had something to offer. The men, I mean.'

'Women have been known to take advantage of this.'

'Only the clever ones. Most women want love.'

'I loved you, Josie.'

'I know you did. It made me happy at first. But . . .'

'I know, I know. The past makes me angry too. I'm only glad we can meet like this from time to time. We seem to get on better now. I can't bring myself to think I shan't see you.'

'I'll miss you too.'

He saw that she would, would miss the status he had once conferred on her, the assurance that she had fulfilled a destiny no less precious for being entirely ordinary, would miss the public advertisement that she had succeeded, when there were times of doubt, of failing nerve, even of loneliness. As a young woman she had seemed determined, practical. Above all, practical. He had thought she had approached their marriage in a spirit of pragmatism, tired as she was of being condemned to the society of women in that small shared flat. Now he saw that although this was undoubtedly the case she was not entirely immune to self-questioning, had pondered the tedious mantras in the women's magazines, had filled in the questionnaires, and had found that she was largely in agreement with the majority view, that it was all a matter of striving, of trying very hard, and sometimes without success, until that day when personal triumph could be confirmed and proclaimed to the world. That this view had probably been shared by his mother, and even by his grandmother, he did not doubt. That disappointment could follow that moment of triumph he also knew. But the moment was essential. Even he could see that.

Men, he thought, married for different reasons, weighed up similar backgrounds, looked for someone suitable, or were driven by the need to establish themselves. Yet he was willing to believe that men fell in love more often, and sometimes more disruptively. His own case, which a lingering sense of decency prevented him from making clear, was evidence of that. He was chivalrous enough to know that he must not discuss it, and had been alone too long not to be aware of the drastic loss of dignity involved were he to do so. Yet other men were no good for this purpose, and the lack of a proper confidant could lead to foolish indiscretions. He was not to be allowed the luxury of displaying his feelings for another woman to the woman who had once been his wife, with all that that signified. There was even a certain self-righteousness in knowing that he had not given way to this particular impulse. At the same time he would have liked to examine his emotional state in a rather more permissive setting than this half-empty café on a bleak mid-morning in weather that was growing colder by the day. This was not easy for either of them, but he thought he had the better part. He would hand Josie all his worldly goods, and think the price worth paying, if in exchange he could enjoy this new perspective without censure. He was sufficiently alert to know that censure would be forthcoming, and not from Josie alone. If that audience he had once craved knew of his disposition the mockery would be unending. He was honour bound to conceal it. Disclosure was not an option.

His most precious secret, and one that he must keep to himself, was that after years of inanition he was able once again to feel desire. He doubted whether any woman could appreciate this fact, this unexpected gift. He understood for the first time that the world was not a well-ordered place in which one was bidden to do one's best, but an arena of anarchy, of impulses that ran counter to the public good, and that men and women were divided into those who shared this knowledge and those who merely failed the test. He looked with distaste at religious precepts designed to impose shackles, to curb freedoms which were an inherent part of the human personality. He marvelled at the fact of being able once more to appreciate physical beauty, so that the face of a stranger would give him pleasure, as if he might partake of that same pleasure with another. That there was as yet no recipient for these new untethered feelings did not greatly disturb him. It was enough to know that there was an agent to reassure him that they were not mere fantasy.

He saw Josie looking at him speculatively. He laughed, blushed, drank his cold coffee. 'Sorry, was I woolgathering? I've had a lot on my mind. This business of the lease . . .'

'What's the problem? You can afford it, can't you?'

'I don't know. That precisely is the problem, as you call it. I get a bit anxious sometimes. I don't want to move, probably shan't. But I'm not proof against changes. No one is. Oh, I daresay I'll manage. But what about you? How will you live?'

'Well, I'll have a house of my own eventually. I'll probably find some work.'

'Anything in mind?'

'Ideally I'd like to start a nursing-home. I am a nurse, after all.'

'That would take a great deal of money,' he said gently.

'Oh, don't worry, I'm not looking to you. It's good of you to offer to tide me over.'

'If anything happens to me get in touch with Bernard Simmonds. He's living in the Hilltop Road flat. Funny how that place never seems to go out of the family. He's my solicitor. He'll know where to find me. If I move, that is.'

There was a silence. Idly he watched waiters laying the tables for lunch. At the back of his mind was a suspicion that he had not done Josie full justice, and that she was aware of this. She had come to their meeting prepared for a serious discussion about money, and had instead met with speedy, even careless acquiescence. Nor could he give her his full attention. He had mislaid his earlier desire to make things better, had done what was required of him, and was prepared to leave it at that. He could see that Josie was not entirely happy with his reactions. He could also see that she was unhappy on a more general level, and that he should endeavour to discover the reason. Her decision to leave had conferred on her a certain dignity. Yet that dignity had more to do with renunciation than with the immediate cause of her mother's failing health.

'What is it, Josie?' he asked quietly.

She smiled sadly. 'It never goes away, does it?'

'I'm sorry?'

'That longing to be with another person.'

'Not with me, I take it.'

'No, no, not with you. Not even with Tom. There's a man who comes into the office. We have a drink from time to time. Married, of course. Yet we get on so well . . .' She broke off. 'You don't want to hear this.'

'Why not stand your ground? See what comes of it?'

'Look at me, Julius. I'm old. I might as well accept it. What surprises me is that I could still feel hope, look forward to seeing him, perhaps no more than that. I couldn't undress for any man now. As I say, I accept it. Mother's illness may have been the jolt I needed. Once the decision was made I realized that it had saved me from a lot of uncertainty. Humiliation, perhaps. I still have my dignity.'

'I admire you for it. I know how unwelcome one's dignity can be.'

'So you think I'm right?'

'Probably. I also know what you mean. Keeping one's dignity is a lonely business. And how one longs to let it go.' This was perhaps unwise. 'When shall I see you again?'

'I don't know. I'll give you a ring from time to time, just to make contact.'

'When will you leave?'

'Next weekend. And there'll be plenty to do before then.'

She picked up her bag. 'I won't say goodbye, though that is probably what it is. Take care. Think of me sometimes.'

'You're part of my life, Josie, always will be.' He knew this to be true, was affected, as she was. They embraced with more warmth than they were accustomed to show. He watched her walk away, saw her bent head, then turned resolutely in the opposite direction.

She was right: dignity was important. But so was the impulse to get rid of it, as he knew from his recent awakening. This fugitive vision of what he thought of as a pagan world was both liberating and disturbing. It had to do with sex, even with the contemplation of sex, and yet he preferred to think of it as love, as pictured in ancient times, or perhaps simply as free will, though will had little enough to do with it. He knew that he was in danger of losing his head, may have already lost it, but submitted to the experience, even welcomed it. He felt newly re-admitted to the world of men, though his position was more properly that of eunuch or palace servant. Ever since the monotony of his days had been miraculously lightened by the advent of Sophie Clay he had been newly made aware of phenomena which he had hitherto taken for granted: movement, sights and sounds, the weather, faces to which he had grown accustomed and into which he read a new friendliness. He told himself that his interest in her was entirely innocent, that he was being given the chance of living life vicariously as a young person. That this young person was a woman did not particularly matter, since it was the power of her youth that beguiled him: the life force, he told himself, still this side of reassurance. Her arrival had been as spectacular as an apparition. A crash on the stairs had sent him out of his flat, thinking that someone had broken in. He had found a heavy bag barring his way, followed by the entrance of two young people, a man and a woman. He had time to notice that both were extremely good-looking and more than a little alike: he put them down as brother and sister, but a brother and sister from some legend or other, vaguely incestuous. He had offered his help, had dragged the bag into the down-stairs flat, had straightened himself, trying not to notice his breathlessness, had put out his hand and introduced him-self. Julius Herz, he had said; we are neighbours, I believe. Sophie Clay, she had replied. And this is Jamie. Your brother? he had asked. They had both laughed.

Well, he had said, in some confusion, I'll leave you time to get settled. If you would like some coffee I'm just above you. Coffee would be great, said Sophie Clay. He had time to notice that her flat contained very little in the way of furniture apart from a large bed and an oversized television. We ought to get acquainted, he had said, as we're living at such close quarters. She had looked up, surprised. I don't suppose I'll be here much, she said, but thanks, I will have that coffee. I'll expect you both then. Not Jamie, she said; Jamie's got to get to work. She had kissed the young man passionately before sending him out of the door. Nice to have met you, said Herz politely to the departing figure, whose heavy tread sounded all the way down to the street. Moments later he heard a car door slam, and then a car drive off. He noticed that more bags had been added to the one he had already taken in, and manhandled these as best he could. Normally after such exertions he would have sat down quietly until his heart returned to its regular rhythm. Instead, with only slightly shaking hands, he went into his kitchen to prepare coffee. On a tray he thoughtfully placed a plate of biscuits, hoping for no more than what he thought of as an agreeable diversion. He could buy his newspaper later in the morning.

When they were seated, with the tray and the un-touched biscuits between them, he had time to notice that she was beautiful, in a severe and unadorned way that he immediately found attractive. He told himself that any man would have had the same intense admiration for her pale regular features and scraped-back hair. She looked as if she had just got up, and would go through the day in just such a negligent manner, which was quite different from that of the women he had known, all of whom had seemed anxious to present themselves in a favourable light. Even Josie, in the early days of their marriage, had spent time in front of her mirror, had brushed her unruly hair, applied lipstick. It was this girl's pale lips that he found par-ticularly beguiling, especially when they parted to reveal faultless teeth. She had introduced herself, had handed him a card which read, 'Sophie Clay. Independent Financial Consultant'. Oh, he had said, how very opportune; you may be able to advise me. She had looked up at him un-smiling, said that she worked in the City, for companies, on a freelance basis; she did not do private work. Oh, how disappointing, he had said, wondering at the note of joviality in his voice; I should have enjoyed consulting you. She had lifted one eyebrow. Since you are so near at hand, he had added, feeling foolish. As for the arrangements here, do feel free to call on me. I am usually at home in the evenings, and of course in the early mornings.

He liked to think of her, in her black trouser suit, moving among the sort of men who worked in financial institutions and who would look up from their desks to appraise her slight neat figure before returning to their calculations. He liked to think of her setting out each morning with her briefcase and returning in the evenings to their common home. He did not quite time his outings to coincide with hers but was pleased when they did. In addition he was glad to be of service, to take care of her spare keys, to sign for a registered letter, to pay Ted Bishop. Her severe demeanour, which was her most attractive feature, broke down somewhat in the late evenings, and, regrettably, at night, when he supposed Jamie to be in residence. This he found much more annoying than the laughter and conversation on the patio, which was now furnished with a table and chairs, and sometimes a radio tuned to a foreign station. He did not really object to the friends she invited back for the evening and whose shouts of laughter were clearly audible. They did not seem to feel the cold; sometimes they were still there after he had gone to bed. This he found quite acceptable, welcoming the sounds of life into what had for so long been sadly lifeless. Rather less acceptable were the disturbances from the bedroom directly below his. Yet in the morning she would appear businesslike, even repressive, as she went off to work with her briefcase and her copy of the *Financial Times*. He could hear her heels, surprisingly loud, on the pavement before they faded away into the distance.

He told himself that his interest in her was paternal, although he was alive to her beauty, as any man would be. He had no children, no grandchildren, and this girl, in her late twenties or early thirties, might have been a grandchild. This reflection aroused others: regret for his past blamelessness, together with a fierce desire for some sort of reward before it was too late. What this could be he had no idea, nor was he foolish enough to fantasize. He felt as if for the first time a longing for love such as he knew should only be felt by the young. He shied away from the evidence of his own physical decline, his tall sparse body, his large red hands, the thick veins that marked his dry sapless arms. The presence of a young creature, so nearly under his roof, kept his thoughts chaste, yet when he went out into the street he was amused to find himself entertaining notions that were almost lubricious. These were not confined to the person of Sophie Clay: he saw women everywhere who offered some almost forgotten possibility of pleasure. This was a welcome reaction; this was when he most felt like a man. He raised a hand in greeting to the woman behind the counter at the dry-cleaners, and was gratified to see her smile and nod, as if responding to an entirely welcome invitation. The same went for the girls in the supermarket, whom he now felt inclined to tease. All this was new and delightful. Only occasionally did he become aware of the absurdity of the situation. It was then that he lambasted himself: an old man trying to be flirtatious was as ridiculous as the cuckold in the cruel dramas he had studied at school and which he remembered with uncomfortable vividness. It was then that melancholy made surreptitious inroads. He welcomed it back as a familiar, while making determined efforts to remain urbane, detached, even diverted by his own condition. He would turn himself into an object of study, and spend not entirely fruitless evenings dissecting his own behaviour. This restored his objectivity, but did not quite remove an awareness of potential damage.

In all this welter of new or unaccustomed feelings it was important to keep Sophie Clay inviolate. He thought that what he felt would be understood by anyone who had lived as long as he had: the regret combined with the avidity, the libidinousness too. The old cherished the unmarked faces of the young, but resented them as well, even wanted to wreak some havoc on them before their own impulses died. That was the reason for so many of the spiteful remarks old people exchanged among themselves, condemning behaviour of which they were now deprived. Those who had been led along the paths of righteousness were the most bitter of judges. He had not been of that number, but bore the marks of an earlier education which he now thought of as picturesque in its quaintness. Respect had been the keynote, showing it, deferring to it at all times. That he had gained any experience at all was a marvel to him, but he observed that life had a way of breaching the most jealously guarded of strongholds, introducing that note of anarchy which some found unbearable, and others, himself included, a blessing, an endowment. From his reading he knew that nature was merciless, would not condemn a mismatch, would even encourage one for its comedic potential, such as enjoyed by the gods of antiquity who held mortals in such derision that they were only mildly diverted by the foolishness they exhibited. Yet it was enlivening to share for a brief moment the standpoint of those same gods, to adopt a callousness that had been absent from his sentimental education, to let all principles recede into an inhabitual limbo, and to obliterate the careful hierarchy of obligations that society is all too willing to impose. It was all wonderfully welcome, a last moment of blitheness before consciousness was finally extinguished.

Yet when he stood at the window to watch for Sophie's return he was not entirely comfortable. Why else would he dodge out of sight when he saw her waiting to cross the road? Why did he find Jamie, her intermittent companion, so objectionable? When he was in bed and aware of the intimate noises he wondered how he could tactfully allude to this. To remind her, with excusable jauntiness, that the house was badly insulated would not quite do. He would have liked to convey complicity, which was even more ridiculous. And she would not modify her behaviour, for he suspected a cruelty in her which in fact she had never manifested. All she had ever shown was indifference, regarding him as a fussy neighbour who was useful in tedious minor ways, and in whom she otherwise took not the slightest interest. He slept badly, waking several times, shamefully alert for signs of life. It was almost a relief when she was away for the weekend.

Even then he would find himself standing at the window, waiting for her return.

11

As his longing grew Herz rose earlier and earlier in the morning. Only in the dark streets, the empty unresonant air, could his inchoate feelings reach a precarious point of equilibrium. As he walked he wondered for how long he could sustain this pitch of tension, in which the past mocked him for his foolishness. He was still sufficiently aware to understand that in allowing himself this brief interlude for aberration he would be able to live out the rest of the day with a semblance of self-mastery. Occasionally he was able to mock himself for the old fool that he undoubtedly was, more usually he regained fragments of the excitement that had originally urged him towards expansion, liberation. He knew, confusedly, that something had been denied him, that he was worth more than the pale simulacrum of the life he had inherited, though that life had been based on the most sensible of precepts. He had not neglected his duty, or duties: he had made the best of what had been on offer. He had never considered himself free enough to choose. That, he saw, was the problem underlying his present dilemma. A life of observing the rules does not predispose one to reckless happiness.

Realistically he knew that he could expect nothing but the pleasant stimulus of watching a young life at close quarters, such as might be enjoyed by any parent, or rather grandparent. Unrealistically he desired pleasure for his own sake, or perhaps for its own sake, some measure of reward for all the careful years. Unsuitable images presented themselves, and were briefly but furtively enjoyed. At such moments he was grateful for the entirely ordinary aspect of the streets, undisturbed at this hour apart from mysterious young men cleaning the windows of sleeping shops. Turning once more towards home he was able to re-inhabit his usual self, and, with the aid of physical fatigue, become once more a nondescript pedestrian, at one with those others now emerging from their private unsupervised lives, and assuming the normality of those bidden to join the crowd. Even now cars were starting up, buses filling with workers; soon the business of the day would be engaged, and he would be back in his ordinary disguise. Routine would help, and he saw that routine must keep him sane. For what had threatened was surely insanity. He had never been given to feelings of such intensity. Yet even now, sober once more, he caught an echo of what had inspired them: the pure unthinking demands of the self.

A persistent admirer of Freud, Herz had a deep respect for the unconscious and its promptings and was even adept at bringing higher considerations into play. These, however, tended now to be fugitive. On approaching the house he simply wondered whether he would be likely to encounter Sophie on the stairs, or whether he was still too early for her. He was sufficiently rational to know that he must not contrive a meeting, must not linger, must not offer greetings, or an explanation for his presence where none was required, must not even stroll along the same stretch of pavement in the evenings when she might be expected to return home. The most he could hope for was something in the nature of the accidental, the unexpected, such as the times, fairly frequent, when she ran out of milk or bread or some other life-saving commodity with which he was always well supplied. Although he held her spare keys he had never committed the indiscretion of entering her flat, nor would he: the very idea was distasteful to him as a fellow property owner. Jamie did not bother him. If anything he considered him an unworthy adversary, no match for his own towering preoccupations. These made him a little more brusque than usual, though sometimes he looked up startled, as if woken from a sleep. When asked a question, however mundane—*The Times* was late today, would he take a *Telegraph* instead?—a second would elapse before he was able to reply. He supposed that in this he conformed to an acceptable stereotype, harmless, absent-minded, getting a bit forgetful. At such times a sadness overcame him. He no longer wanted to confide, was indeed grateful that there was no longer any opportunity for doing so. Briefly he thought of Josie, in her mother's little house, keeping her thoughts to herself. It was ironic that at a moment of almost identical regret there was no possibility that they might discuss such matters, might sympathize, might ruefully recognize a pattern in their otherwise distant solitudes, might once more find themselves intimates.

He let himself into the flat, preparing to spend the greater part of the day there until the evening released him for another excursion. That this was predicated on Sophie's return was no longer hidden from him: he took care only to raise his hand in greeting if he saw her, fearing the rush of words that might ensue. This evening walk calmed him and did something to prepare him for the night. It was the morning that found him in disarray, as if he were still young and in thrall to his body, or as if he were still younger and dismayed by that body's evidence. By contrast the days were almost peaceful. He would go through the papers in his desk—old records, letters received or not sent—as if preparing for a journey, an absence. At the back of his mind was the suspicion that he might need to move on if his future in the flat proved to be untenable. There was as yet no indication that he might not be able to afford a new lease; no demands had been made, no documents delivered. In fact nobody seemed to know that he was there. Yet he was sufficiently familiar with dispossession, such as that which had affected his early years, and of makeshift arrangements such as Edgware Road, or, worse, Freddy's hostel in Brighton, to sense uncertainty and to be once more ready to confront it. Yet while pausing to scrutinize a newspaper cutting which for some reason he had thought to file he could not imagine time spent in any more urgent fashion, and was almost bewildered when the darkness of late afternoon reminded him that days like these might be threatened by change. It was then that the prospect of a further late walk, but, more than that, the anonymous company of strangers, returned him to himself, so that by the evening he was sufficiently appeased to have forgotten the disruptions of the early morning, those unreal dawn hours, in which a more primitive and feral twin might break cover and destroy the whole structure of his life.

It was not that he wanted to appropriate Sophie Clay for

his own purposes, whether these be interested or disinterested. He wanted the image of a lover, an almost abstract lover, to keep him company. He did not know whether this illusion was permissible, whether it was anything more than a fantasy which should have been confined to youth and the troubled days of adolescence. Yet he had read enough to know that infinite longing was the stuff not merely of romance but of the most rigorous of classical fictions, and that although it was almost certainly a weakness it conferred a sort of heroism. He felt more closely in touch with other men during those disturbing early mornings than when he was peacefully seated at his desk sorting through the inconsequential papers that he could not bring himself to discard. Once again he was tempted to examine the photographs, and in doing so found in them a new pathos which disarmed him. For all its unruliness his early-morning self was preferable, more brutal, but also more honest. His daytime life was already that of a man sinking into senescence. When he awoke he was almost reassured by the lawlessness of his thoughts. This, he knew, was how men's minds had always operated. He did not deceive himself that he was a danger to others, not even to himself, though that was not so certain. He thought that he managed well enough. The only difference was that he no longer felt euphoric. There was no sensation of excitement, such as he might have welcomed, only an increasingly grim acquaintance with the further reaches of his mind.

When the postman called with a parcel for Sophie Clay he took it in automatically, hardly caring that this would give him a pretext for seeing her in the evening, but grateful that this event would give the day some shape. The intervening time could thus be spent peaceably doing nothing very much, trying to subdue anticipation of a meeting. He even admitted to a certain weariness with his changing moods, thought back almost fondly to his afternoons at the National Gallery which were now closed off from these latter days, and bathed in a sort of false harmonious reminiscence, though he had occasionally failed to respond to the familiar images. He knew that such afternoons were irrecoverable, that if he were to retrace his steps, pretend to be the man he had once been, the pictures would have lost their power to move. Unthinkably, they would present a blank surface to his unseeing eye. This would be against the natural order; his reactions would be circumscribed, deadened, or if not deadened, impatient. He would be like Freddy, thankfully laying aside his higher nature in order to accommodate impulses that he considered nearer to home. He was not as brave as Freddy had been in opting for the temporary, the unsuitably restrictive. He still cherished his small comforts, felt disturbed at the thought of having to uproot himself once more. At the same time he knew that his restlessness would enable him to deal with new demands if they should present themselves. The entirely unforeseen benefit of his more or less intolerable situation was an ability to live in the present, to calculate the advantages of turmoil over peace and quiet, and in doing so to be ready, prepared, active, even impatient.

Sophie's package was large and blocklike. He manoeuvred it into his flat, briefly wondering what this was doing to his heart. By mid-morning he was drained, seemingly incapable of future movement. The arrival of Ted Bishop, accompanied by his infant grandson, roused him from what may have been a brief trance.

'You don't mind Teddy, do you? Only I couldn't find anyone to leave him with.'

'Delighted,' said Herz, grateful for the presence of a real child after so many phantoms. 'Would you like to do some drawing, Teddy?' A pause, and then a nod. 'I'll just make the tea. Not much to do today, Ted,' he said over his shoulder as he went into the kitchen. 'Just give it a quick tidy-up. Perhaps the windows? Or not, if you're not up to it.'

'No, you keep it pretty clean, I must say. Not like downstairs. The stuff she's got down there.' He made headshaking sounds of disapproval.

'Come, Teddy,' said Herz, picking up the heavy little body and settling it in a chair at his desk. 'Here's a nice red pencil.' He closed his hand over the small fist and guided it into making a rough circle. 'Now see if you can do it.' But the wavering movements were too weak; the pencil failed to make contact with the paper. Fortunately the pencil itself was sufficiently distracting; passes were made with it over the paper, until the rage of the artist, or something like it, sent both pencil and paper to the floor. Behind him Ted Bishop exhaled smoke, coughed noisily, stubbed out his cigarette, and finally engaged in more or less efficient activity. Herz removed the ashtray, washed it, and put it away in the kitchen drawer where it belonged. He was burdened by the knowledge that he should be entertaining them both, but could not bring himself to do so. He wanted them out of the flat, could not give them his usual attention, though the child, quite at home, was stamping round the living-room, on his way, as Herz knew, to pulling the books in the bedroom from the shelves and using them as building blocks.

'Crafty little bugger, isn't he?' said Ted. 'Well, if you're sure. I'll do a bit more next week. Truth to tell, my back's not too good.' The recital of symptoms, which Herz normally appreciated, was perhaps shorter than usual, and less interesting. He was strangely absentminded, could not concentrate on what was being said; in any event he had heard it all before. He took out his wallet, his usual signal that the morning's work had been concluded to his satisfaction, whether or not this was the case. He gave the child the red pencil, ruffled his hair, and led him firmly to the door.

'I'll see you on Wednesday, then,' they both said at once, as they invariably did. Then Herz was free to close his door, to repel interruptions, and to give himself to the brief interval of calm which he usually enjoyed in the early afternoon, before the light began to fade, and the day with it, leaving behind only the shadow of a lost peace.

He got up with a sigh, washed his face, brushed his hair, and went out for his second walk of the day, somewhat restored by the life of the street, the normality of the home-going traffic. What dismayed him more than his futile obsession was this seeming descent into clandestinity, his absences calculated to coincide with those of Sophie Clay, his presences reduced to a form of spying. Nature had played her usual trick on him: after the exaltation the shame, and worse, the consciousness of his own absurdity. Worse even than this was the level of tension that it provoked, the suspicion that it must reach, was reaching, some sort of climax, that he would be driven to further folly by the sheer need for a resolution, and that sooner or later he would bring this about. With his rational mind he saw her for what she was, no more, no less: an attractive girl in the contemporary mould, cool, businesslike, independent, indifferent to compliments and favours, making her own choices, clear as to her rights, shrugging off obligations, making use of unsolicited offers, seeing her future as uncomplicated, a straight progress towards whatever goal she had set herself.

Her mind was impenetrable: he simply did not know how her particular generation operated. He was now a member of the weaker sex, missing the signals to which he had previously responded, those slight alterations of attention, those more willing smiles and acknowledgements, those graceful signs of physical accessibility that he had been used to decode. Now all was arranged differently; men had to be on their guard against purely natural impulses, advances, even gestures. Opening a door, giving up a seat were looked on as patronage, a hand on the arm as an unwanted audacity. Or maybe they had moved on from this position into one of even more extreme solipsism, armoured against what they perceived as superfluity, distraction, a redundant need to show themselves accountable—to other standards, those not fashioned by themselves—to some mysteriously intuited common purpose. Inviolate, women dressed severely, invaded, even conquered male territory, made love without compunction, gave no hostages to fortune, would grow old differently, knowing that they had made no mistakes, had suffered no loss of pride, had not encumbered themselves with outworn methods or procedures, had remained free.

Whereas the women of his generation had been easier to read, as had the men. But their good manners, their acknowledgement of standards imposed by parents, had left an embarrassing legacy of neediness, of moments when their feelings betrayed them and led to indiscretions such as the one in which he was currently shipwrecked. His generation knew how to accept compromise, saw its wisdom, married, settled down, perhaps with a partner who fell below their fantasy of the ideal, whether lover or companion. In this way they achieved normality, acceded to the aspirations of the majority, as he and Josie had done. The drawback was that they were never fully emancipated, as his own case proved, so that in later life, at the most inconvenient moments, their stifled urge towards freedom—in the most general, the most undifferentiated sense—would break cover, landing them in complications for which they had no experience and which carried a danger, that of disrupting lives which had been conducted with good sense and propriety, so that duties were observed and carried out, care taken, standards upheld, and all plans expected to mature into fruition.

These dangers now threatened him on all sides. A lifetime of good behaviour had precipitated him into a folly from which he might not recover. His strongest suit was the ability to perceive it for what it was, an aberration, a departure from good sense. His greatest vulnerability was to lack the means with which to combat it. Why else would he have timed his movements to coincide with those of Sophie Clay, deriving a masochistic pleasure from his calculated absences, his even more calculated attentiveness, his hideous disguise of uncalled-for gallantry, behind which lurked a sad sense of betrayal, of decline, of loss of innocence? His days had been given a shape by his very obsession (for he accepted that it was nothing less than that); whereas previously he had pursued a more or less dignified path, he was now ludicrous. Even if his life had lacked overwhelming satisfactions, his lack of the more obvious triumphs had not left him resentful. Now he was conscious of one thing, and one thing only: pleasure, and its lack. In its narrowest sense it made inroads into his every preoccupation, so that his hand would go out involuntarily as if to grasp another, his arm curve round an imaginary shoulder. The absence of reciprocity did not even greatly trouble him. What was of greater importance was the instinct that impelled his own hand, his own arm, as if even now, at this late stage, he might liberate desires that should have dwindled into inanition along with his youth, his looks, even his health. Such signs, such frustrated gestures, were surely evidence of a cruel joke, perpetrated on him by his own unlived life.

Back in Chiltern Street he switched on lights, saw them come on in the houses opposite, prepared some food, half-listened to the news, became aware that no book, no spectacle could breach this mood which, in the course of the day, had somehow reached critical mass. At eight he picked up the telephone. 'Sophie?' he said. 'There's a parcel for you. Do you want to collect it or shall I bring it down?'

'Could you bring it down? I'm just out of the shower.'

She no longer used his name. That had hurt him almost more than anything, increasing his perception of himself as a mere factotum. He picked up the parcel and made his way cautiously, sideways, down the stairs. The door to her flat was open, a radio was playing, smells of coffee and bath essence wafting out onto the small landing where he stood awkwardly, trying to balance the heavy parcel onto one uplifted knee. 'Sophie?' he called. 'I'll leave it just inside your door.' He was suddenly sick of the whole enterprise. She appeared from the bathroom in a white towelling robe with loose sleeves, her hair newly washed, her face given some unaccustomed animation from the heat of the shower. She looked as he had never seen her before: naked. His eyes penetrated the ample folds of the bathrobe to what he imagined he knew was underneath.

'Sorry to come at an inconvenient time,' he said, still with that twinkling note of insincerity.

'Tomorrow would have done,' she said. 'But thanks, anyway.'

With the towel she carried she rubbed her hair. Her sleeve fell away from a wrist which he perceived as unusually fine. Without thought, without volition, his hand reached out to grasp it, then slid up her arm to the soft crook of her elbow where it lingered. She stared at him, unsmiling; shamefaced, he removed his hand, prepared to make some small joke to cover his confusion, but could think of none. 'Such soft skin,' he mumbled, making things worse. Her expression was stony. 'I've seen you looking at me,' she said. 'I've seen you at the window. You want to be careful. I could put in a word, you know.'

Nothing now could be worse. He did not know how he managed to get himself out of the door and back into his own flat. His heart filled his chest, moved into his throat. He sat immobile, waiting for it to subside, yet wishing for annihilation. He must have sat like this for some time, without the power to move. He did not see how he could ever recover from this humiliation. At a late hour, or what would have been a late hour in his well-regulated existence, his doorbell rang. 'Sophie's keys, if you don't mind,' said Jamie. Wordlessly he handed them over. Then, but only as if from memory, he went to bed.

The brief illness that overtook him was almost welcome. He did not account it a physical malaise, although it produced the physical symptoms associated with an infection. He diagnosed it as psychic shock, beyond the reach of doctors. Desire had imploded, sending him into a state of crisis. This he accepted. In intervals of lucidity he reflected that his amorous inheritance had been shaped by the past: it had no relevance in the present. It was as absurd to improvise love as to improvise learning. He had made a significant error which could only attract contempt. But anger? But the cold distaste that still made him wince? At the same time he experienced some anger on his own behalf. A mature woman, such as he supposed her to be, would have known how to deal with an unwanted advance. Such knowledge should have been part of her repertoire. A mature woman would simply have smiled and moved away, would have behaved as if the incident had not taken place, would certainly not have threatened reprisals. For that was what she had done, had so meaningfully mentioned that she would 'put in a word'. He saw himself arraigned before some sort of moral tribunal, consisting no doubt of potential landlords to whom he might apply in vain for an extension of his lease. This seemed to him entirely probable. He did not doubt that she had had dealings with such people in acquiring her own flat; for all he knew they (a still nebulous 'they') were on the best of terms. In such a context her word would be inevitably preferred to his own. No man could summon a defence against an accusation of sexual harassment. For the gesture, his poor gesture, would be amplified, would attain considerable weight in the telling, at best would be deemed undesirable. His blameless record would count for nothing, his activities be dismissed as worthless. He did indeed consider them to be worthless. Had he led a more reprehensible life he would have known how to deal with such counter-harassment, for that surely was what it was? She had the right to despise him, however crudely she did so, but not to dispossess him. She must know as well as he did that no further imprudence would be forthcoming. He would take care never to encounter her in the future, would once more calculate his exits and entrances on her comings and goings, but this time to avoid her. If he were so unlucky as to meet her on the stairs he would merely nod and smile. There would be no need for words. He would remain urbane, fearsomely urbane, as if deprecating her youth from the summit of his experience. This, in fact, he was prepared to do. He had no difficulty thinking himself into the part. It already felt authentic.

But something even more serious must be taken into account: his desire had gone, leaving behind only a taste of bitter weariness. He would no longer look at a woman with appreciation, with approval. He did not adduce blame here, merely knew that he had persistently, and so mistakenly, cast the present, and indeed the future, in terms of the past, when he had been young and viable. He was now paying the price for being an anomaly, an old man in love.

For it had been love of a sort, though self-generating and unrequited. Perhaps that was love in its pure state. He had never envisaged any sort of recognition: that must, he thought, exonerate him to some degree. What he had done wrong was to expect the kind of courtesy he had always observed in such situations, but that, evidently, was to expect too much. Having never met with hostility in his relations with women he must now accept the facts of a changed situation, even of a changed historical situation. Although he still burned with shame, it was shame for his ignorance rather than for his impropriety. He had not understood how guilty he must appear when facing that tribunal, which, he knew, would be composed of women. He imagined the courtroom: rows of women with briefcases, and in the public gallery a solitary man, ostentatiously tearing up his lease.

On the Wednesday Ted Bishop, always at his best when faced with decrepitude, brought him a cup of tea. There was a biscuit in the saucer. This small token moved Herz to tears, which he managed to conceal until he was alone. On the Thursday he got up, albeit shakily, bathed and dressed. He was aware, from the evidence of his clothes, that he had lost weight. He did not feel well. He supposed that he did not look well, but this was difficult to evaluate, for glancing in the mirror he saw only his mother's disdain, his father's bitter mouth.

## 12

The relative silence that followed this episode was very welcome to Herz, although he knew it to be fallacious. There had been no reprisals. When he encountered Sophie Clay on the stairs he merely made the gesture of tipping a non-existent hat and passed on without a word. She pretended not to see him, which suited him well enough, though he thought he detected the vestige of a response in her inexpressive eyes. He felt for her now a coldness, a disaffection, although in fact she had done him a service: she had separated him from his softer feelings and turned him into what he should have been, a man in whom the main life-giving impulses had died, so that he was now the ghost of himself. Consciously, conscientiously, he played his part, smiling, harmless, an obedient good citizen. He no longer feared any kind of exposure, for the man he was now had no connection with the man he had so briefly been.

Yet he knew that a fundamental change had taken place. He was distanced, estranged from his former affections. He no longer sought companions, accepting his solitude as the reality he had tried to escape. But he knew that this was not the sort of stasis to which all old people were subject. This was more radical, more fundamental. This was a state over which irony ruled, a mocking acquiescence totally divorced from the reality of desire. At the same time he knew he must cultivate this posthumous condition, and within its confines he was sometimes lucky enough to find a distant contempt, which enabled him to view the eventless present with something like grim amusement. So it has come to this, he told himself: a life of misplaced enthusiasms petering out into indifference, women who turned out to be the wrong women, duties which were always unsought, a conformity which passed unnoticed because the gigantic efforts to conform were of interest to no one but himself. That audience he had once longed for had been persistently absent. Even now he knew few people, yet this was something of a relief to him. Acquaintances were acknowledged by simple gestures of recognition, so that a code governed his relations with the rest of the world: a smile, a raised hand, a nod, were all that were now required of him.

The winter was mild, so mild that people shook their heads and predicted floods, a cold spring, a summer even more intemperate than the previous one. He was able to spend his days in the public garden, well wrapped up in coat and scarf, immobile on his bench, with an unread newspaper beside him. Frequently he had the place to himself, except for a few children at lunchtime whom he was careful not to watch. They would, he knew, afflict him with a revival of feeling. Their appearance was his signal to repair to a café in Paddington Street, where the other customers, some known, some unknown, made the same gestures of recognition. Even this simulacrum of company was burdensome to him, and when he judged that the children would have returned to school he went back to his seat and renewed his concentration on phenomena near at hand: a crumpled leaf shifting sluggishly across the path, or, more welcome because a sign of spring, the imprint on damp ground of a crushed petal from one of the municipal flowerbeds, now almost denuded. In a habitually misty milky November it did not strike him as unbearably eccentric to spend his time in this way: this was after all a sort of holiday, quite in line with the holidays he had taken in the past, holidays mainly given over to the sort of passivity he now enjoyed, or, if not enjoyed, accepted.

He did not even regret those wider horizons, although he would have welcomed some kind of prospect other than the sparse vegetation he was obliged to contemplate. Ideally there should have been a broad path filled with strolling couples, for whose intimacy he would have felt affection. These passed across his inner eye in some sort of resort, an entirely notional place filled with figures from the past, none of whom he knew but all familiar from his reading. Instead of this November haze he envisaged a mild sun, not the sun of the south but something that softened the edges of a reality which bore little resemblance to this small permitted space with its wooden seats and its rubbish bins and its silence, uninterrupted apart from the children and the occasional young man with a briefcase who sat on an opposite seat, made a few indistinct calls on his mobile phone, then got up again, presumably to go to an office. Herz would have liked to ask him what work he did, but realized that this interest too belonged to the obedient past. The answer would reach him now only through a miasma of indifference. Much better to return his attention to that last fluttering leaf hanging forlornly from a spindly nearby tree, or those damp footprints left by a person who was no longer there. Nature he loved now, and no longer art. The signs of life that were presented to him impressed him by their isolated discrete character: the leaf had no connection with the footprints, and yet in their very humility both were utterly absorbing.

Dusk came early, and in its benevolence compensated him for the absent sun. It was then that he rose stiffly, picked up his now humid newspaper, and, summoning his courage, turned towards home. A light rain usually fell at about this time, and he was able to appreciate certain urban signs: the fall of lamplight onto damp pavements or its reflection in shallow puddles, the animation of the supermarket, where he was obliged to buy the elements of a simple meal, the distant splash of a car manoeuvring too close to a wet gutter. His street, still empty, impressed him with its abstract red-brick strangeness, its absence of curves, its remorseless symmetry. As he fitted his key into the lock he gestured to the young men in the shop, Mike and Tony, one of whom held up a mug as an invitation to join them for tea: with an equivalent gesture he smiled and refused. He was fond of these young men, and so was careful not to embarrass them with his company. He performed small services for them, taking in their milk and storing it until they arrived to open the shop, keeping a set of spare keys, as he had once kept a set for Sophie Clay. It was a peculiar blessing—unhoped for in the present circumstances—that the shop troubled him so little. Television sets were switched on as soon as Mike and Tony arrived, but the sound reached him only as a distant booming, rather like the sea, and was only distinguishable in brief bursts when a cus-

tomer asked for a demonstration. He appreciated the young
men as workers, even as fellow workers, remembering his
days in the record shop, and understanding how unwelcome was the advent of a customer too close to five
o'clock, how familiar the sound of locking up . . . Back in
the flat he drank his own tea in fellow feeling, often standing at the window to ease his back after the long day spent
sitting in the damp garden. He would stand there until he
saw Mike and Tony leave. Sometimes one of them looked
up and waved. As soon as he heard the clip of familiar heels
he retreated into the further dusk of his sitting-room. He
took care to be nowhere near either the front or back windows when his lights went on, drew curtains, as he had
never done before, completing his concealment, signalling
his unapproachability. Then the evening would begin,
lengthy prelude to a night which might or might not usher
in sleep. Rarely did the nights bring dreams, a cause of particular disappointment. He, who had once dreamed so
vividly, took this absence as a sign of vanished life.

There was one more ritual to be observed before he
could count the day as finished. His lease, removed from
the second drawer of his desk, where it kept company with
an outline of the will he intended to hand over to Bernard
Simmonds, had to be re-examined, in case the word 'Renewable' had previously escaped his notice. It had not.
Both documents, the lease and the will, were deceptive,
since he had nowhere to go and nothing to leave. He
would have willed the flat to Josie if it promised to belong
to him, but he felt it slipping away from him, as if his hold
on it were physically weakening. There had been no re-
minders, no signs of activity, but he knew from the young
men in the shop that the building had changed hands, had

been put in the charge of managing agents, and that these
people were even now gathering their strength for an all-
out assault. This no longer frightened him as it had once
done: the flat had lost its virtue for him as soon as he
understood that all places were henceforth to be more or
less alien. Yet his income was restricted; the flat was his
only asset. Only if he sold the flat would he have more
capital. He had almost come to the conclusion that he
might pay rent rather than buy, but it was by no means certain that he would be given the choice. Only by disappearing altogether would there be anything left for Josie; only
if he sold the flat and died promptly afterwards would she
inherit any money that was left. These reflections moved
in on him at roughly the same time every evening and
were still unresolved several hours later. Only in the damp
silence of the garden did he feel physically removed from
them; the relief was limited by the amount of time he
spent there, and dwindled progressively as he reached Chiltern Street. Inside the flat it vanished altogether.

On the evening of what he dimly remembered was his
birthday he telephoned Bernard Simmonds and invited
him to dinner. It always gratified him that this invitation
was cordially welcomed. This cordiality, this geniality was
no doubt a semi-professional attribute, much appreciated
by Simmonds's clients, although Herz suspected that the
younger man felt something a little more personal, had
fashioned Herz into the sort of elderly friend who might
offer sage advice and yet so tactfully refrained from doing
so. And then their money flowed from the same source, to
which each obscurely felt he had no right, though profit-
ing from it without further regard to the donor. This was
rarely alluded to but acted like something of a common

legacy. In the absence of anything more straightforward it constituted a link, one of those mysterious links which was felt rather than explicitly acknowledged. The shadowy godfather, having brought them together, functioned as an ancestor, without whom their relations would have remained more formal. They arranged to meet in town, at the restaurant to which Herz habitually invited Josie. Herz had warned Simmonds that this would be in the nature of a consultation, indicating that he would expect to be charged for it. Simmonds's fee, enormous as it usually was, would not be referred to in the course of dinner, a small civility which Herz appreciated. The bill would arrive in due course without comment, and without comment, be wordlessly paid.

'You're looking well,' he said, as both unfurled their napkins.

'You, on the other hand, are not, Julius. Are you sure you're quite all right?'

'At my age no one is quite all right.'

'Oh, I'm sorry.'

'It's nothing. I had some kind of flu.'

'Have you seen your doctor?'

'No, of course not. In any event I have no faith in doctors. No, it was Josie I wanted to talk to you about. I wrote to you about making her a small allowance.'

'That has been seen to. But are you sure? You are under no obligation, you know.'

'Quite sure. But that's not all. I want to leave her some money. It's all in this will I've drafted.' He handed over his two documents. 'As you will see there may be no money left. My lease is not, apparently, renewable. Josie's money depends on my having any. And my money depends on my staying in the flat. If I have to buy something else—at a no doubt extortionate price—there will be nothing left.'

'You could always rent when the lease expires.'

'Surely that would be a problem?'

'Not at all. Or you could sell now.'

'Who would buy a three-year lease? Surely no one would be foolish enough.'

'You'd be surprised. Firms are always looking for places for their executives. It's all short-term contracts now, a year, two years. You'd have no difficulty at all.'

'But where would I go?'

'A client of mine—I shouldn't be telling you this— faced the same problem when her husband died. She moved into an hotel in the south of France, came to an arrangement with the management, paid them a fixed sum every month, and after that was more or less independent. They—she and the manager—were on excellent terms: he appreciated the advantages of a client who occupied the suite in both the high and low seasons. When she died he even arranged the funeral.'

'I see.' A pause. 'I've never been very happy in hotels. They make me feel like a fugitive.'

'Or there's residential accommodation.'

'Some sort of home, you mean? An even more charming prospect.'

'You could always purchase another lease on your present flat. Would you like me to make a few enquiries? I believe your building has changed hands recently. Up for development, I imagine.'

'Could you do that? I really don't want to move. The thing is, I did want to leave something for Josie.'

'I'm afraid that might not be possible.'

'Yes, I see that.' He thought of his poor girl, stranded, like himself, with the future dependent solely on his resources. Then, reluctantly, he abandoned her to her fate. After all, her position would be no more perilous than his own. 'It's just that I should have liked to have made things better before I died. Making things better was what I always tried to do. I made a poor job of it.'

'Come, come, Julius.'

'Had we stayed in Germany, I should have studied, enjoyed a professional life, become a gentleman, as my father was originally. I can't help thinking of my landlords as dispossessors: the shadow of the past, I suppose. And yet this country has been good to me. It's just that I never quite manage to feel at home. That's why I'm so hesitant now: the small matter of a permanent address seems immeasurably problematic. Not that anything could be really permanent at my age. And of course I should be grateful if you would take this on for me. I'd be happy to leave everything in your hands. If you're not too busy, that is.'

'I'll see what I can do. Don't be surprised if you don't hear from me immediately. I've got a few things on my mind at the moment.' His face took on a look that was half-scared, half-complacent. 'Two problems, actually. The first is that Helen wants us to get married. The second is that I've been seeing someone else.'

'Oh, dear.' This was so heartfelt that he was obliged to add, 'Can't you do both?'

'Not really. Both are very keen on commitment, as they call it.'

'It sounds so legalistic.'

'And I want a bit of freedom,' Simmonds burst out. 'I thought we had an understanding, Helen and I . . .'

'Are you sure you want freedom? Freedom is sometimes a mixed blessing. Without obligations one frequently does less rather than more.'

'I have obligations,' protested Simmonds. 'I'm a professional man.'

'I should get married, if I were you. It's important to have someone to go home to in the evenings.'

'In fact my evenings have been well taken care of. I think I can say that without fear of contradiction.'

Herz was alarmed by the combative tone of this last remark. 'You are in love, of course. Love and freedom are incompatible, although freedom seems to beckon with each new enthusiasm. It is an illusion, Bernard, freedom, I mean. There is no such thing. In theory I am free. Yet if I were to change my name, move to another country—both of which I could do—I should not be free, any freer than I am now. You, on the other hand, are free to marry, as you have always been. One does not always possess the choice. And freedom, after all, consists in having a choice. I can see that falling in love has upset you, but then it always does. Sometimes it's the emotions that go with the new person that are so enlivening. And so misleading. One's own affections gradually take precedence. Does your new friend really care for you?'

'I think so, yes.'

'I rather imagine loyalty counts in these matters. It is so much more important than fidelity. Sexual fidelity, that is. Perhaps you owe Helen that loyalty?'

'She's not making it easy for me.'

'Why should she? Women seem to want permanence more than men do. Books are published on the subject; a whole industry has grown up in America. I picked up somebody's discarded newspaper the other day and read an article on this very subject. "To be continued", it said.' (In fact he had devoured the article, as he sat, unobserved, in the public garden, and had almost determined to buy the following day's instalment before being restored to his senses by the arrival of the children at lunchtime.) 'There seems to be a genuine incompatibility. More coffee?' He wondered how he could tactfully bring the discussion back to his own affairs. He was aware that he had given offence. 'No, no, let me. I insist,' he said, as the bill was presented.

Simmonds brooded, then roused himself. 'I'll be in touch,' he promised. 'Just be patient. My advice to you would be to take a holiday.' (It was what everyone said.) 'Or have a check-up. See your doctor; get yourself fighting fit. You're looking very thin, you know.'

'Only the flu. I'm quite all right, really.' But he knew this to be untrue. He was frequently breathless these days, which was one of his reasons for spending his time so quietly. In the misty deserted garden there was no one to see him put a hand to his heart to check its rapid and sometimes irregular beat. He put this down to his recent disturbance, which had assumed a physical disguise as if to mock him further. Even now he was anxious to get home in case his mounting distress should become apparent. Calmly he paid the bill, added his usual large tip, hoped he would find a taxi without delay. 'How will you get home?' he asked politely.

'Underground. Oh, by the way, this letter came for you. Obviously from someone who thought you were still in Hilltop Road. I should have forwarded it. You're right, I've been neglecting my duties.' He looked so crestfallen that

Herz felt like embracing him. Instead he patted his arm, and said, 'I'm so grateful, Bernard. As always. Let us meet again soon.' He put the letter, unexamined, into his pocket. The relief of getting home was so great that he left it there, until the slight rustle, as he removed his coat, prompted him to put it on his desk. Then the far more important business of getting himself to bed took precedence. The letter could wait. In any case there was no urgency. A letter sent to Hilltop Road could have little relevance in his present, unstable situation. Not for the first time he regretted that almost ancestral flat, so very different from the gimcrack lodgings that had succeeded their time there, and of which Chiltern Street was merely the latest avatar.

The sound of rain woke him from a brief but profound sleep. He looked at his clock: two-thirty. He knew from experience that his night was over, and in that instant decided to go back to that unsympathetic doctor and ask him for sleeping-pills. These dark hours were too conducive to unwelcome reflections. He felt unusually wakeful, and also uneasy. This unease was the result of his dinner with Bernard Simmonds, and their conversation, principally his part in it. He had been both flippant and didactic, the very mark of an inattentive listener. Yet he had not been inattentive: he had been wary, reluctant to engage in a discussion of the other's amorous dealings, or indeed of anyone else's. Such matters were no longer for him, and yet he had recognized Bernard's excited awareness of his own predicament, the slight heat that came from him as he deployed his credentials: not one woman but two! Even through the weariness and distaste he felt Herz had silently congratulated him. And this lent his pious moralizing an ambiguity.

If he had been able to break through the restraint that was usually the tone set for these meetings he would have urged Simmonds to obey his instincts, relegate good behaviour to the past, and impose his will on both his long-term companion and his new lover. In so doing he might have attained that ideal freedom which Herz's judicious reflections had done so much to spoil.

Herz's own notions of freedom, based on the highest precepts, had recently been undermined by that brief illumination. He recognized the signs in Simmonds but thought that he should give no authority to what was so eagerly awaiting his sympathetic response. It was sympathy that had been required of him. He should have been politely respectful of this confession; instead he had taken refuge in an old man's farrago in which cynicism vied with irrelevance. His very expression, he thought, might have betrayed reluctance to hear more, yet he knew that he had remained as gravely attentive as always, and only a little less self-possessed than he would have wished. His main reaction had been one of impatience, an impatience that now enveloped the dark room, the clock, and all the other accoutrements of his so careful and now threatened surroundings. He would have liked to write Simmonds a note, apologizing for having been so preoccupied, but knew that he would not do so, for to do so would merely compound the offence. He would also like, in this same unwritten note, to remind Simmonds that the matter of his lease must take priority over any emotional troubles that might be brought into the discussion, but knew that he would not do this either. He would remain silent and await developments, since that was what was expected of him. He would suggest another dinner early in the New Year, during which he would remain on his guard against his own indiscretions, while allowing Simmonds full licence to indulge his own. That too was what was expected of him.

Rain was falling when, on the following day, he set out for the surgery in Paddington Street, conveniently close to the public garden which he supposed would be out of bounds for the rest of this dark morning and no doubt the dark mornings that were to follow. Christmas would mark the nadir of the year, after which would begin the very slow ascent towards the light. Briefly he entertained fantasies of evasion: the prospect of that notional resort, populated by leisurely walkers, passed once more before his mind's eye, although he knew that it was his own creation. He also had a brief, quite isolated memory of a fluted glass dish on which his mother used to serve a chocolate cake on Saturday afternoons. These flashes of memory, which came quite unannounced, delighted him, and diverted him from his usual monotonous broodings. They came in the daytime, in the full light, rather than at night, when his wakefulness was mysteriously given over to unremittingly rational thought. For this reason he deduced that the night hours were of some service, and decided to forgo his visit to the doctor: sleeping-pills could wait. In any event the nights were less problematic than the days, which could be ruined by bad weather. He retraced his steps, entertained by the memory of that glass dish and of those remote weekends in Berlin when friends would visit. He now realized that his mother's attachment to Bijou Frank had been an attempt to revive that custom, of which nothing now remained. In the flat he resigned himself to a day at home, a prospect which normally filled him with dismay. On his desk he saw the letter which Simmonds had handed to him as they parted the previous evening, but instead took up his volume of Thomas Mann once more, and sank gratefully into the landscape, so well remembered, so totally familiar, of the bourgeois past.

# 13

The letter, which was inadequately stamped, had taken some time to reach Hilltop Road, longer still to reach Chiltern Street by way of Bernard Simmonds. Before settling down to read it Herz glanced at the signature: Fanny Schneider (Bauer). This he had somehow anticipated from the ladylike handwriting on the numerous sheets of flimsy paper. It was the handwriting of someone given to an expansive account of her own dealings with the world, not too attentive to the world's responses. Having no longer waited for this letter, which would have spared him many anxieties and disappointments, Herz found himself curiously unemotional at actually reading it. Like all messages which arrive too late it had missed its mark, lost its point. He held the thin pages for several seconds, wondering why they left him so indifferent. The contents were somehow irrelevant. The reality of Fanny Bauer had been dissipated by years of absence, of separation. He could still summon up that feeling of separation, which must have lain dormant since their last meeting. That had been abortive, leaving him with a sense of shame and confusion, his marriage proposal unhesitatingly rejected, against the unlikely backdrop of the Beau Rivage. Even as she refused him Fanny had taken up her bag and reminded her mother that it was time to change for dinner. Her mother, whom he had difficulty in recognizing as his dashing aunt Anna, had followed her without a word, sparing Herz only a look which might have been approving, accepting his homage as nothing less than her daughter's due, but informing him at the same time that such homage was no longer necessary, that he was no longer an eager boy, that he had outgrown the eagerness without gaining much in the way of worldly success. Perhaps that eagerness had surfaced in his proposal, which seemed so unsuitable in this setting, in this high-ceilinged room, in which he had suddenly felt entirely alone.

Or perhaps the separation had lasted longer even than that, since the children's birthday party at which he had gazed worshipfully at his cousin, admiring her haughtiness, her flightiness, wishing that they were for him alone. In time he came to recognize her behaviour as meretricious, but did not blame her for that. Quite simply she was better prepared for life in the world than he was. He saw that she would be demanding, easily bored, that she would not conceal her boredom, so that others would exert themselves to amuse her, and later to tease her in return, so that a heartfelt avowal of love or loyalty would be anomalous, as if phrased in a different language. He had known even then, at that same children's party, that she was cruel and that he was doomed to be faithful. Had she not snubbed him dreadfully when he had not understood a game they were playing and that she had instigated? The game consisted of truths and dares and forfeits, one of those humiliating games which need to be played with a maximum of artifice so as not to lose face. He had failed miserably, and had been deemed to be so inept that Fanny had dismissed him, relegating him to a corner where he sat with a puzzled smile on his face as the game continued without him.

That sense of exclusion had stayed with him and informed his every subsequent action. Across the years he could still recall, in sad detail, his misery, which at the time he had not understood for the adult emotion it was to become. And in Nyon he had recognized her dismissal of him as inevitable, had simply wished that she would allow him more time to contemplate her, to understand the changes that had taken place in her appearance, to discuss their lives, and if possible their feelings. That had not been allowed: the years had wrought too many changes to be described, even if there had been time to describe them, as he so vainly wished. Instead his aunt had invited him to join them for dinner. On learning that he would be leaving on the following morning Fanny had smiled, but had confined her conversation to the most banal of remarks, most of them addressed to her mother.

He had covertly studied the now buxom figure seated opposite him, had thought her still beautiful, though she was now paler than she had been as a girl: her eyes were as lustrous as he remembered them, her hair as dark. Only her hands were the plump hands of a woman who did no work and who spent days in pampered idleness. He had had no difficulty in remembering that she was a widow, for she had the unawakened look of one no longer troubled by her senses. He even wondered whether she had loved her husband, Claude Mellerio, or whether her marriage had been a practical arrangement on her part, brought about by her mother. Faced with her strange equanimity he had assumed her physical nature to be passive, giving pleasure by virtue of that same passivity but receiving none in return. He saw that although lacking in that one vital sexual attribute she would nevertheless continue to intrigue. Her self-possession alone would present a challenge. He doubted whether any man had or would deprive her of it.

Walking by the lake in the very early morning of the following day he reflected that this marked the difference between them, his own assiduity meeting her own impassive calm, and saw that this quality was directed not at himself alone but at men in general. He saw that she would never quite understand a man's yearning, or even his physical impulses, that she would be happier in female company, and most of all in the company of her mother. The transformation of the spirited girl at the party into this dignified and untroubled woman was not altogether surprising: she had never understood that others could be moved by their feelings, had mistaken her own caprices for sentiments, had never broken out of the chrysalis of her girlhood, and had remained monstrously unfamiliar with adult emotions, at home only with those that suited her purpose. That her purpose had been to be looked after in advantageous circumstances had no doubt been the reason for her marriage. Practical considerations would have been uppermost in both women: Mellerio had promised an easy way of life and would respect their closeness. Widowhood, however, to judge from their expressions, suited both Fanny and her mother much better. Their attachment to the hotel, which seemed so much their natural setting, was in fact an expression of true feeling: this was their due. Widowhood was Fanny's version of honourable retirement.

What impression could he have made, with the dust of Edgware Road still figuratively clinging to his heels? How could he imagine this delicate creature consenting to remove herself from this setting? His own humility, his consciousness of the enormity of what he was asking, had done something to prepare him for her refusal, but he was nevertheless chilled by her negligent way of dismissing him. She had kept her superior manners; her smooth mouth concealed a stinging tongue. Thus had she ruled, through a mixture of detachment and an ability to defend herself which would confound those in search of deeper feelings, even when deeper feelings were appropriate. She might annoy a man but she would also baffle him. What did she want, that man might ask. Simply to be left alone would have been the answer, had she been minded to give one.

Thus partly exonerated, Herz had watched the sun rise over the lake, had at length castigated himself for a fool, then turned back to the hotel to collect his overnight bag before taking a taxi to the station. What compounded his feeling of helplessness was the fact that he had not been able to pay for the dinner. His instinct was always to do so, but they had waved away his attempts, as if he were still the poor relation they had always considered him to be. That this had not been exactly the case in Berlin was in fact true enough of him in London; he provided for his diminished family but this alone condemned him: he was obliged to earn his living, while Fanny and her mother were cushioned by Mellerio's will and need never work or think in terms of working. So perfectly did Fanny fit the profile of a kept woman that he supposed that this might add to her appeal for a man. He would be purchasing the genuine article, albeit a stereotype. Maybe the genuine article was indistinguishable from a stereotype, a stereotype rather than an archetype, such as would appeal to the romantic Herz supposed he had been. He had longed to encompass the sheer otherness of Fanny, and she, with a lifted eyebrow, had once again condemned his expectations. Peaceful Nyon, with its unhurried strolling population, served as an ironic backdrop to his recognition of defeat. What had been an incompatibility at that children's party was no less an incompatibility in these new changed circumstances. And yet the sense of loss had never entirely disappeared.

In stark contrast to the humiliation of the experience, Nyon was mild, tentative, the sky a compromise between grey and blue, the old men playing chess in the café near the station as grave as senators. He could understand the appeal of the place for Fanny and her mother: it was an oubliette into which the cares of the world vanished. Their routine would be soporific, reassuring. Even he was seduced by the quiet rhythm of the place, the very sparseness of the streets, the unhurried pace of the few passers-by abroad at this early hour, the stone doorways leading to dark interiors, the scarlet of a geranium in a window box prudently restrained by an iron grille . . . By contrast the London to which he was returning was coarsened by work, by the harsh effort of earning money, by the absence of just those features that made Nyon seem benign, if a little unreal. He imagined a tranquil way of life such as that enjoyed by Fanny and her mother: the leisurely dressing, the adornment, the preparations made for a day of inactivity, in which the most daring excursion would be to the local *pâtisserie* for coffee and cake. Both were plumper, as they could not fail to be in this protected environment. The added weight had made them both appear voluptuous, yet their conversation, what he had heard of it, had been unremittingly practical, a sharp reminder to the waiter that their usual bottle of wine was missing, a comparison of the prices charged by two or more hairdressers . . . Few remarks had been addressed to him, for which he had been grateful, aware of how awkward his presence must be in this dining-room, through the large plate-glass windows of which he could just see the lake promenade, and beyond that, tideless waters stretching to a smudged horizon. The ladies had eaten delicately, but with appetite. He had thought of his mother and her valiant pretensions, of his father, struggling back to consciousness after one of his characteristically obliterating naps, of his brother, a failure who had found failure to be his proper element. Lastly he thought of himself and all his misplaced efforts, his short-lived marriage and the blame that had accrued from it. He longed to jettison the lot and simply walk out of the hotel into an unknown landscape, an unknown future. In that so unattainable future he would not be accompanied. Even in fantasy he could not see Fanny clinging to his arm. Fanny was married to her mother, who acted as her agent, her manager. If Fanny were to marry again it would be to someone who would make her mother part of the bargain. In this evolutionary struggle he could barely qualify.

He smoothed out the pages of the letter with some reluctance, so distinct was the memory of what had been less than a forty-eight-hour absence from work. 'My dear Julius,' he read. 'No doubt you will be surprised to hear from me across this distance of space and time. I found your address in a letter from your mother to mine; it was tucked between pages 123 and 124 of *Buddenbrooks* which Mother was reading before she died. I have been unable to read the book since that awful day, but I recently took it down when I asked Doris, my maid, to dust the shelves. The letter fell out, and it was a great relief to know how to contact you, for I am in need of friends, and I remember how faithfully you used to visit our house in Dahlem all those years ago. When I say I am in need of friends you will understand that life has not been kind to me. I have lost two husbands, but I confess that the greatest loss has been Mother, who lived with us until her death. We had never been apart from each other and I miss her dreadfully. Since her death everything has gone wrong. I am sure that if she were still here she would know what I should do. You and I are now the only members of our family: I say this although I do not know whether this letter will find you, or indeed whether you are still alive. We are now very old and only one thing can happen to people of our age. It seems particularly hard that I should be subjected to added misfortune at this stage of my life, and I write to ask you whether you can advise me.

'Let me explain. I met my second husband, Alois, in Nyon, where he was taking a holiday. He and Mother got talking, and it transpired that he was from Bonn, where he had a small printing works. We had dinner together, the three of us, and I found him agreeable. Mother thought it a good match, since he appeared to be a man of property, and we married shortly afterwards. I have to say that he was very smitten with me, and, as I say, I found him agreeable.

At first all went well; we had a beautiful house in Poppels-dorf, a suburb of Bonn, and Alois's sister, Margot, was very welcoming and attentive. The surroundings were pleasant and there were servants who looked after everything, so that it was quite easy to adjust after life in the hotel. Un-fortunately Alois was not a well man; he suffered from asthma and various other complaints, and although I tried to cheer him up, and, indeed, bolster him up, he remained something of an invalid. Margot was a frequent visitor, too frequent I sometimes thought, and we did not always agree. I think she was jealous of me; she was a widow, not par-ticularly attractive, and very possessive towards her brother. In time Alois's health deteriorated, and with it his business. To cut a long story short we were obliged to sell the house and invest the proceeds in his company. Worse, we had to move to a flat in Bonn, which I found intolerable. The in-evitable happened, or it may not have been inevitable in other hands: Alois went bankrupt. Fortunately he had put what remained of his assets in my hands, but the shock more or less killed him. He lingered on for a year, getting more and more depressed, and died quite suddenly, not of his assorted ailments, but of a heart attack.

'My sister-in-law blamed me for this, although I had looked after him to the best of my ability. Mother was afraid I was taxing my own health, and urged me to think of myself. But in fact this was impossible, as she was caus-ing me grave concern. I will not linger over this for it is too painful. She died of cancer of the stomach, since when I have been truly alone.

'But worse was to follow. Margot's daughter, Sabine, put it into her mother's head that as a direct family member she was more entitled to Alois's money than I was. She is much sharper than her mother, and said that I had no right to inherit what was left of the business, that it should have reverted to the family; in brief she has gone to court in an effort to dispossess me. She has even claimed that I should not be in the flat, though my lawyer says that here she is on shaky ground. So I am living alone, and threatened by this unpleasant woman (whom I never liked). Margot, of course, takes her daughter's side, and we rarely speak now. Fortunately Claude, my first husband, left me a small portion which I keep in the bank in Lausanne, but it is small, barely enough for the upkeep of this flat. And Bonn has become very expensive since so many government agencies have been set up here. I am told that I could get a good price for the flat, but where would I go?

'I have always relied on men in my life, and on Mother, of course, so I am hoping that you will be able to advise me. I am not happy in Bonn, though it is a pleasant town, and I find myself thinking back to Berlin, where I had such a happy childhood. Do you remember our marvellous children's parties, which Mother organized so beautifully? She of course is the greatest loss, for she always had my best interests at heart, and I am adrift without her advice. Naturally I shall do my best to win this case, but I feel uneasy with so much hostility around me, and whichever way it turns out I shall have made no friends. The man who bought the business has put it about that Alois could have managed his affairs in such a way as to have kept afloat; he seems to blame me for its decline. I must stress that Alois was perfectly agreeable to our arrangement. I have to say that after he was declared bankrupt he took no further interest in the proceedings. He said it was a matter of indifference to him that he was no longer an honourable citizen, as he put it. I thought this very selfish of him, but by that time his health was so poor that I did not have the heart to quarrel with him. And when Mother died I had no heart for anything.

'I wonder if you could suggest how I should proceed. I have no head for business but I can certainly fight for my rights and my conscience is clear. My one fear is that this letter may not reach you, but I know that if you are still as I remember you, you will do your utmost to help me. Of course you may have moved away, but if you are still as hale and hearty, and as gallant, as I remember you in that brief visit to Nyon, I know that you will do your best to help. Perhaps you could manage a visit to Bonn; my lawyer would almost certainly take more notice of a man than of my humble self, although he assures me that he is doing his best. I somehow doubt this, but I have always been too sensitive. And I have no one else to turn to.

'I also wonder how life has treated you since we last met. Mother remarked that you had become a handsome man, very different from the shy boy we knew in Berlin. She was greatly impressed by you, and thought you must have made her sister very proud. As you know the two did not get on, but they managed to exchange quite affectionate letters. It was hard for us to imagine you in London, and your mother gave the impression that there was more to tell than she actually told. In any event the letters petered out, and Mother kept none of them, apart from the one she used as a bookmark. Have you read *Buddenbrooks*? I must confess I never got beyond a few pages. Hilltop Road sounds very pretty.

'I do hope you are in good health, and that you will be

188 | ANITA BROOKNER

able to visit me in Bonn. We shall have much to talk about, and I look forward to hearing your news. Until we meet again, I remain your affectionate cousin, Fanny Schneider (Bauer).'

Herz laid the letter on his desk with a low whistle of admiration. She would marry the lawyer, of course, if he were available. She might even have thoughts of an alliance between the two of them. He would spirit her out of her difficulties and they would live happily ever after, in Hilltop Road. He marvelled at her magnificent self-regard, or rather self-deception. But was that not the quality that characterized the entire family? Only Freddy had been free of it, but then Freddy had been free of everything. None, however, had attained the peak from which Fanny regarded the rest of the world. Clearly supreme selfishness was the recipe for a successful life. She had, as the letter confirmed, dropped out of history, had regarded the menacing years that preceded their exile in terms of pretty houses and children's parties. He did not delude himself that she was interested in him as anything other than a further agent, deduced that her husband had not pulled his weight on her behalf, and had thereby proved himself a broken reed, even worse than that, a failure, a wastrel. She would not have shared his shame over the bankruptcy, would in fact have separated herself from it as successfully as she had divorced herself from the terror that had afflicted their kind, and of which no trace was evident in the complacency—the indignant complacency—so undisguised in her letter. He felt for her the same gratitude that he had briefly felt for Sophie Clay: she had put an end to his fantasies of love, something that she had not quite managed to do in Nyon. Like most fundamentally inert people she had immense power over others. He had loved her, or had thought that he had loved her, for many years, ignoring the facts of their long divorce (for it was nothing less) and maintaining a fiction that had satisfied his unassuaged longing. In all that time Fanny had not spared him a thought. She remained as she had always been, a woman who viewed others in terms of their potential service or support. He could not even feel anger, for he could not accuse her of calculation, only of entirely natural egotism. A lawyer would be better placed to settle her affairs. Or she would settle them herself, with some of the steeliness she must have inherited from her mother. He could see her issuing from the lawyer's office, having stated her requirements, and proceeding to the hairdresser or the dressmaker or the *Konditorei,* her mind as unruffled by speculation or anxiety as it had been in the Berlin of her youth.

Except that she was old. Her hair, if not white, would be the result of the hairdresser's artifice; her body would require the ever more expert attentions of the dressmaker. And even if she were as free of reflection as he knew her to be she would not be able to ignore these signs, or even the knowledge possessed by people of their age that the most valuable part of their lives was over, irrecoverable. Maybe she would even regret her vanished youth, which she had always seen in terms of marketability. Desire would not trouble her, but only because it had never troubled her; she would be spared that rage, that hunger for a last encounter that could go so disastrously wrong, leaving a legacy of shame and disaffection. He owed her perhaps a meeting, since she seemed to want one, although entirely for her own purposes. But he would be in no hurry to suggest this. His own affairs must take precedence; his own health required some care, perhaps some investigation. Fanny's mother's demise ushered in melancholy reflections; maybe the same was true in Fanny's case. In that sense she deserved his respect. Her care for her mother would have been heartfelt, unstinting, unlike his own dutiful attentions, during which his mind had often wandered, and his eyes sought the liberty that surely existed beyond the window of the hospital room.

The thought of Fanny's unequal struggle, not with her late husband's family, for he had no doubt that she would win that particular contest, but with mortality, moved him in spite of himself. It seemed unfitting that she who had never known uncertainty should be confronted with the battle that no one can win. And she would be alone, having alienated the very people who might help her, the sister-in-law, the litigious niece. He was better placed than she was to face the depredations to come, if they were not already under way, as he suspected. In his humble admiration of her affectless unattainability he had always been the petitioner for her favours. His masochism had done the rest. To be a petitioner herself had altered the balance of their relationship in a way that he did not altogether appreciate. He would have preferred to think of her as she was in his memory, impermeable, even unsympathetic. To change places now implied a lack of symmetry which he found almost physically disturbing.

The memory of their original connection, established when they were both young, surprised him once again with its force. And there was this quasi-mystical concept of family to be reckoned with. He had never been aware of overt family feeling, had indeed entertained thoughts of the most flagrant disloyalty, but had somehow managed to survive in a unit that was neither supportive nor companionable. He had certainly longed for a family of his own, even admired the families of others. Why else had he clung to those wisps of conversation that had reached him on his solitary perambulations? Those holidays, when he had sat in cafés, in restaurants, on solitary benches, hidden by a newspaper, were in fact full of signals that he alone could decipher. That husband, that father, that grandmother, that beautiful child, had all been sustenance for an imagination that hungered for fulfilment, even for surfeit. The irony was that with this powerful need he had managed to live his life in the strictest isolation. The family that he might have had resided in the murmurs that reached him from other lives. And now, near the end, as he was, that fantasy obstinately re-created those early days in Berlin, when he had sat waiting for a fifteen-year-old Fanny to rush carelessly into a sun-filled room, and, just as carelessly, to rush out again.

He went out into the cold Sunday streets, deaf now to what he might hear. He would not go to Bonn. This decision had been made without his active participation. He would write back, not with reassurance but with fellow feeling. He would offer advice, though what she wanted was practical help, and even more than that, partisanship. But in Chiltern Street, in Paddington Street, in Nottingham Place, in Spanish Place, in George Street, where he had walked so many times, the mournful emptiness reminded him of a long-desired companionship, no less sweet for being the construct of his own faltering heart.

# 14

'Dearest Fanny,' he wrote, 'My former wife, a nice woman, recently told me that she had formed an attachment to a man, whom, I surmised, she hardly knew. She told me this prudently, but her eyes were sad, from which I deduced that she had fallen in love, one of those unforeseen episodes that are so disastrous at our age. I could easily sympathize for I know the symptoms, that eagerness which reawakens the eagerness that lies dormant in each of us and which we remember from our youth. It is that eagerness that sends us out so willingly in the morning and which furnishes our dreams at night. I imagined her, living her rather boring days in the anticipation of a meeting, never scheduled, deliciously postponed, until the reappearance of this man, framed in her doorway, would let her know that she had not been mistaken, that there was something there that existed in reality, and not just in her imagination.

'In the end she did a brave and dignified thing: she went away. I thought that I was doing such a brave and dignified thing when I left you in Nyon, although in fact I had little choice. I remember urging Josie, my wife, to stand her ground, and now I see that I was talking to myself. I should not have left matters as they stood in Nyon. I should have insisted, if not at that particular moment, then later. I should have defied you (and your mother) and returned time and time again to argue my case. Even a woman such as yourself, quiescent, must have been bored without male companionship, or if not companionship, for you had that of a kind, the homage and protection that only a man can give. You would have respected me if I had insisted on the rights of my claim, even if I failed to interest you as a man.

'I doubt that you were ever in danger of losing your dignity, as Josie, my wife, was. She explained to me that she thought herself beyond the age of physical love, not because such impulses had left her—on the contrary—but because she was aware that she stood to lose too much by revealing herself as an ageing woman to a man who was, she said, attractive. Her decision was heroic, but I think wrong. I now see that dignity has little to do with the affections, which are all too often inappropriate. I made the same mistake, which proves, bizarrely, that once again Josie and I thought along similar lines. I never really had thoughts of making love to you, for that would have been beyond my expectations. I should have fared better by treating you as I would any other woman; instead I lavished respect on your so complacent person, thinking you too fine to entertain any gross feelings. Who knows? You might have enjoyed a rather more undisguised approach, though somehow I doubt that you would have appreciated it for what it was.

'I had always thought you a rare creature, so beautiful and so confident that you could make your own choices. Now I see you rather more clearly. Others made choices for you, and you accepted them, reserving your will for whatever actions might be demanded of you in the name of survival. It should not be forgotten that we were both exiles at this stage, and that this condition presupposes a certain caution, a certain good behaviour. I thought that I had behaved well, as well as I could in the circumstances. I was, as always, humbled by your assurance, so very different from my own anxieties. Quite simply, I did not see how I could ever be good enough for you. All this, you remember, against a background of teacups and the first aperitifs, with people coming and going, in an atmosphere of easy living, the unreal ambience fostered by hoteliers all the world over. I am ashamed to say that I felt humbled by this too, but most of all by the fact that you seemed to belong so naturally in this particular setting. I had in mind, you see, my own particular circumstances, which at that time were uncomfortable: cramped living quarters, parents for whom I was responsible, the sort of employment you would have found unacceptable in anyone you knew, let alone a husband. But with hindsight I see that none of this was irreversible. I should have left home, sought other work, allowed my parents to sort out their own destiny without my help. I believe that your own parents disliked my mother, and even I can see that they were partly justified in their dislike, which I came to inherit. It was the imprinting of those early attitudes that led to our perceptions of each other, as, on the one hand, superior, and on the other so markedly inferior as not to be taken into consideration. This is the curse that families hand on to their offspring. I regret most bitterly that I was not able to overcome this particular constraint, to overturn this particular verdict. But neither were you. You had simply never exercised your judgement, and now I think, and indeed see, that your judgement has always been in default. The letter you recently wrote me supplies proof of that, if additional proof were needed.

'I returned to London believing that I had done all that could be done. I was all too ready to concede the charms of your life in Nyon, which I could appreciate for myself, in that brief interval before catching my train to Geneva. The air was softer than London air could ever have been, the simple gestures of greeting that even I encountered were more benign than any I had ever experienced. Since leaving you there my life has been dull, for I knew that I had avoided the supreme emotional challenge: that of getting my will to conquer yours. I now see that this need not have been as difficult as I thought it was then. Your letter makes clear that you are still enough of a woman to seek a man's support, though what you ask of me now is ludicrous. I cannot, I think, come to Bonn. What would I do there? My German is now rusty, and somehow I do not see myself making representations to a German lawyer. And I do not know that I want to see you as you must be now. I would rather remember you as that lovely girl, whose dark beauty aroused suspicions in easily influenced minds. You are now as old as I am, within a year or two. Josie, my wife, told me that women have more to fear from age than men do, but this I doubt. From middle age onwards all is loss, unless one has children. This, I believe, is where we both failed. With only our own welfare to preoccupy us how could we not go wrong?

'I understand now the tricks that Nature plays, how we can be awakened in spite of ourselves, and to our very great detriment. Love can strike at any time, as Josie, my wife, made plain. I find myself thinking of her so much these days, rather more so, in fact, than I think of you. Yet you remain an image in my mind, an icon, if you like, indistinguishable from the buoyant Berlin air, or the soft penumbra surrounding the lake in Nyon. You will always be young to me, and perhaps I prefer to keep you that way. I am shocked to say that as an elderly German lady you have little interest for me. I can imagine you all too clearly, for I have an ancestral memory of such women, as you have. You may even have lost your looks, and I should find that too cruel to contemplate. No doubt you have only the haziest memory of myself, and as little interest in my life as I have in yours. And yet my imagination—and your letter—furnish certain details which I am obliged to consider. The house in Poppelsdorf I can picture easily. It is far more difficult to come to terms with the decline in your fortunes, for which you make your husband responsible. I would wish you to be cocooned in your original arrogance, and I dare say you have managed to retain a good part of that, just as you have managed to retain your assets. Yet you are anxious lest these should be taken away from you; you even invoke my help after so many years of absence. Your letter reflects anxiety on your own behalf, not on anyone else's. That too I find entirely characteristic.

'Let me explain to you how I live. I have a very small flat in central London, in a district which no longer interests me. I have an old person's preoccupations: my health, my ability to endure the general uncertainty that life today generates. Sooner or later, and I think sooner rather than later, I must look for somewhere else to live. My days are spent in decorous pursuits, or perhaps they merely used to be: I read a lot (and you really should try *Buddenbrooks* again), sometimes go and look at pictures. Such harmless activities do not preclude the promptings of utter folly, to which one somehow succumbs. This is where I come back to Josie, my wife, and her wisdom in removing herself from such temptations. And yet I still see this as the greater of two evils. I believe—I am even ready to concede—that Nature knows best, however much we are humiliated in her remorseless process. I have never doubted that we were put on earth to provide amusement for the gods, for there is too much proof of this cruel joke to be ignored. In this sense you are no worse off than I am. Of course I appreciated your letter, on many levels, I may say. But you should know, dear, that I am no longer susceptible. What moves me now is that same Nature that has deprived us, you and I, of our beauty. I can respond to a flower, a child, to the all too rare sun, as I can no longer respond to a woman. This is all loss, for memory persists in providing the details. But I must accept this, as you must. Let me hear from you again. As a persistent reader I long to know the rest of the story. And in spite of everything I still love you. I always shall. You are part of my life. If I came to you now I should not come as a stranger (I could never be that) but as a man who has known many defeats and who has somehow survived them. I shall advise you as best I can, of course, but do not be surprised by my apparent coldness. As is stated in one of the many great books you have not read, if I were to see you again no good would come of it. Despite my defences, acquired with such difficulty, through such hardship, I might fall in love with you all over again. It is better that I remain your affectionate cousin, Julius Herz.'

He read his letter through, tore it up, and started again. 'My dear Fanny,' he wrote. 'How delightful to hear from you and to have an address for you at last. You will see that I too have moved, but may not be here much longer. Should we not meet to discuss these and other matters? Unfortunately I cannot come to Bonn, but we can choose some halfway house where we can be at our ease. What about the Beau Rivage? I remember that you found this comfortable, and I was favourably impressed during the brief time I spent there. The weather here is harsh, as it always is in the early days of spring. Of course it will still be cold in Nyon, but we should be well looked after in the hotel. Let me know when you would be free to meet me there, the sooner the better, I think, as unfortunately our time is not unlimited. You can leave everything to me: all you have to do is buy your ticket. You have my telephone number now. I expect a call from you when you receive this letter. It will be good to see you again after this long time. Your affectionate cousin, Julius Herz.'

This suggestion had come into his mind quite involuntarily, but once accepted bloomed magically into something like action. He and she would meet at the Beau Rivage, for an unspecified length of time. He could see no reason why they should ever leave. Would that not be an answer to his problem, if not to hers? When and if their sojourn came to an end he would send her back to Bonn and her machinations with a clear conscience, having done his best to advise her, if this were possible. And he would also do his best to steer her off the subject, trying once more, and no doubt in vain, to establish an intimacy which he had always imagined would be possible, given the right circumstances. In the hushed and discreet atmosphere of the hotel she would surely lose her sense of grievance, while he, having recovered a long-lost equanimity, would walk by the lake, with no plans for the day ahead, no tedious routines which he would be obliged to observe, no halfhearted contacts with people he hardly knew, no careful preparations for meals he no longer wanted to eat. He disliked hotels, but this was not the kind of functional establishment he was used to, the normal background to his wistful holidays. This was a luxury pit-stop for wealthy transients, mild businessmen, divorcées, contented tourists of the type he had never found it possible to emulate. Why, in fact, should he ever leave? This idea, equally involuntary, possessed him with a brief excitement. An unlikely answer to his present problems, which he had taken no steps to resolve, he envisaged, if not permanence, at least a long absence. Once there, and becalmed, as he somehow knew he should be, he would allow himself to be absorbed into the surroundings, would recover his dignity, would realize his destiny as an exile, and perhaps acknowledge the rightness of the solution. He would wean Fanny from her preoccupations, fashion her into the companion of his dreams. Memory and increasing familiarity would make this easy. And there would be a face opposite his at the tea-table, the dinner-table, mild remarks of no consequence to be exchanged, excursions to be undertaken, an illusion of symbiosis, the symbiosis he had always sought. They would be regarded as a couple, yet be spared intimacy and the embarrassments of physical closeness. He could clearly see rooms on the same corridor, but not adjacent. Thus dignity would be maintained, the kind of dignity that had so recently deserted him. He would be retired at last, would attract respect, if only of the kind that could be adequately remunerated. And his home would dwindle into something he had once known, while the lake shore would take its place, as if he had always had it in reserve as a suitable setting for his last years. Here he might find peace, certainly a degree of amusement, for Fanny would just as certainly supply that. She took her place in his mental landscape, no longer prominent, as he had always fashioned her, but as just another acquaintance, whom it would interest him to rediscover. She too would dwindle, for the girl, the woman he had loved, would be no more important than himself. After this long parenthesis he would at last occupy his proper place.

Since the whole project appeared to have been encoded somewhere in his consciousness, without the active participation of his will, he accepted it as inevitable. Seized with a sudden excitement he began to make plans that would have been inconceivable only a few hours earlier. He would let the flat, would come back to it only to make arrangements for its ultimate disposal. Or he would return to it in a few weeks, knowing that he had the power of choice. He would give Bernard Simmonds power of attorney, instructing him to defray his expenses from funds he would leave in his account. In time, if that moment were to be reached, Simmonds could liberate the flat and its contents. As if acting on this assumption he opened all the drawers of his desk, pulled out the sheaves of accumulated papers, and destroyed them, leaving only the photographs as relics of a life that was no longer relevant. He was not even surprised that he felt so little attachment to his previous existence, though he knew that at the moment of departure mute objects would exert an appeal that he might find it difficult to withstand. He felt a physical lightness, as if he had shed a burden. Only one more thing, or rather one real thing, remained to be done. He took up his pen again. 'Dearest Josie,' he wrote. 'I may be going away for a little while. Don't be alarmed if you cannot reach me. Bernard Simmonds will have your affairs in hand, and your allowance will be paid for as long as you need it. This is a somewhat unexpected departure, but I feel the need of a change. I hope you are well, and not too lonely so far from London. I find it difficult to imagine your life, just as I find it difficult to imagine your courage. Such heroism would now be beyond me. I wonder why we are called upon to make such efforts of will, when a little moral laxity might achieve a much more agreeable outcome. But I always admired your sense of purpose, which was in fact superior to my own. You always thought me impractical, poured scorn on my efforts to make those around me comfortable, and you were right to do so, for my efforts have always been based on a misreading of character. One cannot always make things better; my one remaining regret is that I did not make things better for you. But you were always clear-sighted; maybe you did not love me more than you were able, prudently keeping some feeling in reserve for another man you might eventually meet. I loved you, perhaps unrealistically, as is my wont. My one hope now is that you will not be lonely, for you always had such a cheerful disposition. Do not let your mother occupy all your time. Forgive me for offering such pitiful advice; you will of course do as you think fit. I hope you will not let the past encroach too much on the present. That is the mistake I always made. I find it easy to tell you that I love you. Think of me sometimes. Ever, Julius.'

He sealed and stamped his letters, emptied his waste-paper basket, realized that the day was nearly over. There was no food in the house, but this did not bother him: in the future food would appear without his having to think about it. His excitement had given way to a sense of purpose, for which he was dependent on no one but himself. It felt good to have entered into this new autonomy, which, he thought, could be endlessly implemented. But not here, not in his flat, with all the difficulties that might ensue, the endless obstacles that would be put in his path by those faceless others who, even now, were planning to uproot him. He made a note to telephone Bernard Simmonds as soon as he got back from the post office, the supermarket, the dry-cleaners, and all the other places he no longer recognized as anything other than petty accompaniments to a life soon to be transformed.

He seized his letters, wound his scarf round his throat, and prepared to leave the flat. On the stairs he heard the surprisingly noisy footsteps of Sophie Clay. 'Ah, Sophie,' he said, without prevarication, as they came face-to-face. 'Just the person I wanted to see. I'm thinking of letting my flat. Do you know anyone who might want to rent it?'

Her eyes widened appreciably. 'Sure, no problem. I know one or two people who might be interested. Are you going away, then?'

'Yes,' he said genially. 'I'm going away for a bit. The flat had better be let on a monthly basis, renewable, of course. Tell your people to get in touch with me. I'll need refer-

ences, of course. And I'll give you the address of my solicitor. He'll take care of everything.'

'Where will you be?'

'Oh, that's quite undecided at the moment.' For some
reason he preferred to keep his intentions secret, and with
them his destination. In a moment of dizziness, both mental and physical, he saw himself moving on, the Beau Rivage another home to which he might or might not
return. 'It might be nice for you to have a friend here.'

'Yes, right. I'll get going on it tomorrow.'

'Thank you,' he said absently. 'I'll wait to hear from you.'

'It's raining,' she warned him.

'Just the post office,' he said. 'These letters must go this
evening.' He would have kissed her goodbye had reality
not intervened in the shape of a blast of music from one of
the televisions in the shop. A late customer, he thought.
Poor boys; they must be longing to get away.

In the street the rain was little more than a fine mist
which softened the outlines of the houses and even lent a
touch of poetry to a neighbourhood unlikely to evoke
tender emotions. He raised his eyes to a roofline bristling
with television aerials, lowered them again to windows still
blank before the evening lights were lit. The sky was already darkening; signs of spring were absent, and yet the
chilly damp held a promise of greenness, of new life only
just in abeyance. It was even possible to appreciate that sky;
its opaque blue reminded him of certain pictures, though
no picture could compete with this strange sense of immi-
nence, with the crust of the earth ready to break into life,
the roots expanding to disclose flowers, the trees graciously
putting forth leaves. The impassivity of nature never ceased

to amaze him. This awakening process was surely superior to anything captured on canvas, yet art made all phenomena its province. In its unceasing war with the effort of capturing moments of time art won this unequal contest, but only just. The majestic indifference of nature was there to remind one of one's place, and no doubt to serve as a corrective to the artist's ambition. When the canvas was finished it was already a relic, outside change. And surely change was primordial; all must obey it. To ignore the process was to ignore the evidence of one's own evolutionary cycle.

Herz wondered how he had ever imagined a state of permanence. Renewal was an altogether wider prospect, one that affected his future rather than his timid present. He thought of himself in new surroundings, without a history, benign, gentlemanly, an agreeable acquaintance. This ideal condition, though it had lost, and indeed was losing, some of its sharpness of contour, contained the rapt enchantment of a dream, and like a dream was infinitely more persuasive than what reality had to offer. Logic had transferred itself to another realm, and he knew the fleeting satisfaction of the artist: this was his creation, brought into being by a process that was almost entirely involuntary. It was this unknown faculty and its promptings that impressed him most. The speed with which the day had taken shape was almost frightening.

He lost a little of his confidence in the course of his walk. The walk itself was valedictory, round the little public garden before it closed for the night. He would not sit there again, would not spend his time brooding over the past. The past would be, if not dismissed, then at least re-

solved into this almost unknown woman, this unreal landscape, this undreamed-of future. Already the prospect was
inducing a sort of languor; he felt his steps becoming
slower, was reminded of the weight of his body. And yet
he did not want to go home. Home was in a sense irrelevant to the day's events. He remembered, almost with impatience, the humble gratitude he had felt when he first
took possession of the flat, the amazed delight with which
he had furnished it, added to it, his timid pride at being a
householder. Now that very timidity saddened him. He
saw that he had lived his life as if it were under threat, as if
he still bore the marks of that original menace and of the
enormity of the fate that might have been his. This, he was
convinced, made transience the only option, exile, imper-
manence, the route indicated for him so long ago. And it
had taken a lifetime for him to understand this! At last he
would take his place in history. In making his home in a
country famed for its neutrality he would be obeying ancestral impulses. In that direction lay the safety he might
yet come to desire.

He reached the flat at six, unwound his damp scarf from
his throat, and sank down heavily into one of the chairs he
was soon to abandon. He ran his fingers over the little table
that had come down to him indirectly from Ostrovski's
mother, and reflected that this was the hardest of all the
challenges he had to face, this disjunction between rash
optimism and the pessimism that was his natural condition.
His euphoria had ebbed away in the course of his walk,
during which he had been beguiled, in spite of himself, by
the cold streets, by the dim poetry of familiar surroundings. To abandon one life for another, and that other quite

unknown, seemed to him suddenly an impossibility, the burden of Fanny a task that he had brought on himself almost unawares. The illusion of a past love, constructed almost entirely from memory, had paled in comparison with the unlikely alliance he had forged with Josie, whose brisk cheerfulness had kept him afloat for the duration of his brief marriage, and which even now he missed, most of all since he knew he would never see her again. Had he been brave enough to telephone her he knew that she would have rallied him, dispelled his fears (for now he knew a certain fear), but instinct told him to avoid the contact. He might have caught her at an unguarded moment, when her own fears had turned into a melancholy not unlike his own. He wanted her to be unchanged, once again compared her honesty with Fanny's complaints, knew which of the two women was worthy of his respect. And yet worth and respect had so little to do with love. One loved in spite of one's judgement, one's better nature, and even now, though more fitfully, the image of Fanny as she had been was sufficient to displace the all too probable reality of Fanny as he might find her again, in a baroque setting which might not, in the long run, be to his taste, the idle company soon to be his, an ironic footnote to his strenuous thoughtful days.

But those days too were past. He sat at his desk to write his last letter, after which there would be none more to write. 'Dear Bernard, I am going away for a while and should be grateful if you would look after my affairs during an absence which might be prolonged. You have my will and the lease of my flat; please execute both when necessary, and draw the appropriate fees and expenses from my bank account, of which you will find the details in my will. My movements are still uncertain; it is entirely possible that I may take up residence abroad. Today's Europe is not the Europe I once left: the natives are now quite friendly. Truth to tell this is quite an unsettling decision, but as you implied the time has come for decisions to be made. You will find all necessary details in the enclosed paper, which also gives you power of attorney. I am grateful to you for our past friendship; you were always a delightful companion. My thanks to you too for carrying out these somewhat nebulous instructions. I expect to be gone within a week or two, and will let you have an address when I have one myself. With every possible good wish, and my thanks for your kindness. Ever yours, Julius Herz'

He went into the kitchen and made a cup of tea, stood at the window while he drank it. He had forgotten to buy food; tea would have to do. Suddenly, shockingly, he choked, fought for breath, felt his heart surge up into his throat. When the attack subsided he was limp and gasping. He made his way back to his chair, and, almost as an experiment, retrieved his pills from his breast pocket, slipped one under his tongue, and within minutes felt his chest expand, and with it his head. So the pills did work. That was good to know. The tiny rattle of the enamel box in which they were kept, and which he was so used to ignoring, might prove to be a comfort. Breathing now steadily but carefully, he undressed and got into bed. His last conscious thought was that he must recover sufficiently for his plans to work themselves out. Then he let his mind slip its moorings, had a memory, for some reason, of his mother, and abandoned himself to sleep.

## 15

Instinct had told him to act swiftly, even precipitately, to leave with a flourish, letting others resolve the details. Rational consideration, to which he still had occasional access, dictated an interval before plans could be implemented. This proved once again that instinct was the better, if easier guide. Arrangements still had to be made for the disposal of the flat, and he had yet to hear from Fanny. Fanny, however, in the cooling light of reason, was proving as evanescent as she had always been. He discovered, with something like genuine interest, that if Fanny were not moved to be as impulsive as he had originally been, she was of less interest, certainly of less value. He remembered the startling dream he had had in which she commanded his actions, had been her old wilful self, had deprived him of his coat and in so doing had somehow denuded him. This had stimulated a whole spectrum of sensations, chief among which had been the perverse gratification he had always experienced in waiting for her, indeed waiting on her, never really disappointed when she failed to meet his expectations, always postponing some hoped-for fulfilment to a future in which, finally, he would be accepted as her equal.

He now saw this process as a disastrous waste of energy.

Fulfilment was more important than anticipation. That was the reason why he had recognized his instinctive haste and insistence as correct, as the engine which might have resulted in his own immediate gratification. It was his ego which had sought some acknowledgement, his own will which must be obeyed. He also saw that there was no one to obey his will but himself. This opened up a more tragic perspective, that of his past life, in which his will had been too effectively suppressed, leading to a sadness that was life-long. But if this explanation satisfied him, the realization that he had failed the one important test that a man must pass was terrible. His will had been at the service of others, to use as they thought fit, and in allowing this, in the fallacious enterprise of making things better, he had surrendered the part of himself that others could not and would not supply, and in so doing had forgone his right to respect. He saw that the instinct that had prompted him to surrender his life, if only for a sequence of fantasies that might prove incapable of realization, had been the entirely correct prompting of an under-used faculty which might have saved that life, or turned it into something more forceful, more inventive, certainly more successful. Yet by dint of good behaviour, by attention to duty, and entirely in the interests of conformity, he had ended up respectable, but not respected. That was the lesson he had learned in the course of an uneasy night, in which the image of that final retirement on the lake shore had retreated into that same lake's mists, leaving him still hungry for another life, for other company, and no more iconoclastic than he had ever been.

He had had a brief dream, all too brief, which teased

him like an enigma. He had dreamed that he was on the pavement of a busy thoroughfare in the middle of an ordinary day, feeling some slight anticipation of a meeting. On the other side of the street, on the opposite pavement, he had seen the person whom he hoped to meet. It was a woman, dressed formally in a coat and skirt and a wide-brimmed hat. From these clothes he had deduced that this woman was middle-aged, or perhaps a throwback to an earlier time. She had raised her arm in greeting and he had done the same, yet he had known that he should do no more, should not cross the road, now busy with traffic, to join her. The dream ended on this note, not of hesitation but of caution, as if in going to join her he might lose all dignity, all discretion. He had known that if he had made that move he would have relinquished authority, that the severest prudence had held his raised arm in check. Thus might two mild acquaintances greet each other, yet more had been at stake. It was as if love had been involved at some stage, a love he was determined to keep within recognizable bounds. The woman had appeared to be waiting for him, but that had not quickened his actions, stimulated him into some kind of activity. The entire dream thus consisted of this one image, of his own raised arm, and, less distinctly, of hers, and with it the awareness of a prohibition that he had adopted, even fostered, in the interest of not losing face.

From this he gradually deduced that his relations with women were still inchoate, that good manners had, time and time again, disguised desire, and in disguising it, or in keeping it in its place, had denatured it. Whatever had arrested his movements in the dream turned out, in the light of morning, to have another explanation: instinct had been corrected by a need to avoid confrontation. He now saw this as a grave loss, just as his love of women had been tempered by a wish not to harm them. As a lover he had been too kind. Those afternoons waiting for Fanny had been wasted; even now he was prepared to wait for her. Some dim knowledge of this had propelled him on a course of action that had argued the superior wisdom of unilateral action, of speed, careless of the consequences, pure instinct reacting to years of considerate behaviour. Selfishness, even brutality, might have procured him delights other than those he had known in marriage, though those had been appreciable, but that there was liberation to be experienced above and beyond such delights was now quite clear. So that his flight, elaborated in the course of a few hours, was in fact no more than a metaphor, one so beautifully envisaged as to hide the darker truth.

He regretted the letter to Fanny he had torn up, for in writing it he had expressed something of that darker truth. Once again he had shielded her from that darker truth, and by his very action of destroying the letter had failed to come to terms with it himself. For the letter had revealed bitterness for a failed love affair, in which she was not entirely at fault, in fact not at all at fault by his present reckoning. Certainly her scornful manners had been unattractive, but no doubt women felt scorn for men who respected them to the point at which self-sacrifice became inanition. His fantasies concerning her had been so beguiling that he had not seen them to be a substitute, an inferior product which would, in the long run, prove deceptive. The great advantage of his so practical wife consisted in her being the sort of woman about whom no man could possibly fantasize; hence his unequivocal enjoyment of her, and also his acceptance of their incompatibility. The rest was poetry, art, but with art came artifice, contrivance, a willed ignorance of things as they are. He had built the greater part of his life on the artist's assumptions: as a lover, and specifically as a lover of Fanny, he had thought to offer nothing less than a poet's homage. And she, an all too ordinary woman, had looked on it as something that could be endlessly renewed, a resource of which she might avail herself when other resources were lacking. Hence his restraint, in the dream. Quite literally, with these thoughts now coming into the forefront of his mind, he would not cross the street for her.

Yet somehow, hazily, he had accepted her presence in his life yet again. Her letters, together with her complaints, had disclosed another truth: she was friendless. And he was lonely. In no sense could these be compelling reasons for seeking each other's company. As against this they were eminently sensible. Her letter had suggested a course of action which, on the surface, had a good deal to recommend it, chiefly an alternative to their isolated lives. He had no doubt that the plan had been hers. He, as ever, had responded with some of that eagerness which had always characterized his dealings with her.

The main attraction of that plan, for him, had been escape, flight, his will recklessly seeking its own satisfaction, if only in the destruction of his so careful life. For that was how the plan had appeared to him. Overwhelmingly sensible though it might seem, indeed was, it took second place to that glimpsed abandonment of all caution, all

good and careful continuation of things as they stood in his
so respectable present state. The fact that his life gave him
no pleasure was indictment enough. Here he began to
look more kindly on his brief but authentic passion for Sophie Clay. That, he saw, had been love: he had fallen in
love with her. And he had no need to point out to himself
how ludicrous a late love would always be. He had watched
for her, studied her movements, listened for her footsteps
like a lunatic; he had felt for her like a young man. That
was his tragedy. He had survived it in the only way he
knew, by further confinement. This had been partly successful; he was now able to speak to her quite naturally. He
had not then been tempted to run away, had once again
had recourse to good behaviour. Yet the ardour that would
once have gone into the conquest of such a woman (of any
woman) had taken the not quite logical shape of a late idyll
with yet another woman, to whom, he now discovered, he
was almost indifferent. This would be like an arranged marriage, of the kind that used to be endured in closed soci-
eties. It would be detached, unimpassioned: each would
remain conscious of the other's defects, would strive hu-
morously to excuse them, and in so doing act as an example to all other right-thinking and unhappily married
spectators. And he—and she—had brought this into being!
For it was such a rational proposition that there could be
no possible reason to turn it down. They were two lonely
people who had been given a chance of companionship at
an age when companionship was largely in default. Nevertheless he regretted that he had not gone ahead, all guns
blazing, regardless of whether Fanny joined him or not.
He would have had the brief satisfaction of acting on im-

pulse, whatever the result. Not ever to have done so cast his past life into a history of failure that made him so breathless, constricted his chest. It was this sense of failure that had moved him to slip a pill under his tongue every night since his plans had degenerated into confusion. The momentary ease that it produced went some way to deceiving him that all was not lost, that it might be possible to contrive a delay, to proceed, certainly, but at his own pace, and in accordance with his own wishes. Those wishes would, alas, be appropriate to one whose will had always proved defective. He might, in the end, be as dependent on Fanny as she promised to be on himself.

He could of course defer the whole plan indefinitely. There were a dozen excuses available to him. He could plead the unseasonably cold weather, although in fact it was growing appreciably warmer. He could plead the necessity of finalizing business arrangements, though in fact he had none. But he owed explanations to no one, for the world had proved itself indifferent. The letters had perhaps been imprudent, the one to Bernard Simmonds slightly too valedictory. That might arouse suspicions in that eminently sensible mind. The letter to Josie he dismissed as irrelevant; she would disregard it, as she had disregarded most of his outpourings. Fanny was mistress of her own plans and would not be likely to defer to his. There was however the question of the flat. He had entrusted this problem to Sophie, who would be more prompt, might produce a solution in a matter of weeks, if not days. But he doubted that he would accept any of the candidates she might propose, and even if they were all suitable he could prevaricate. In truth he no longer wanted a stranger in his flat, which once again asserted its right to be inalienably his. He could simply say that he had changed his mind. This would annoy her, but she was used to being annoyed by him. Once again the prospect of his unchanging days exerted an appeal. Yet the profile of that curious illumination he had had, of himself undergoing change, of bringing about change for its own sake, had a kind of inevitability. It had come to him in the guise of a solution, and although he knew that there were in fact no ideal solutions he still retained a memory of that exhilaration, that almost aesthetic exhilaration that had brought his fantasy so near to a conclusion, or, if not a conclusion, to the beauty of enactment. He might have been writing a book, the book of his own life, or of someone infinitely more decisive. He had had a sense of being his own hero: this was the plot he would have devised. At the same time he doubted whether he were brave enough to be that hero. He knew himself to be lacking in heroic qualities. Even the sensible aspects of the plan no longer appealed. It was his right to take his own hesitations into consideration. The further sense of failure would be his own business, mercifully invisible to the rest of the world.

A knock on the door brought him back to present-day reality, to three o'clock on a Friday afternoon, with an unaccustomed sun pouring through his windows. He had a guest, or if not a guest, a caller. On the landing stood Sophie Clay with a young man by her side.

'Why, Sophie,' he said. 'You're home early.'

'It's about the flat. I thought this was more important. This is Matt Henderson. He's looking for a place, and he's going to New York next week, so he's in a bit of a hurry . . .'

'Come in, come in. Is it too early for tea?'

'Oh, we don't want tea,' she said.

'Oh, but I do. And anyway there's quite a bit to discuss. Come in, Mr Henderson. Do sit down. You're off to New York next week, I gather. Then you must want to get things settled. Though I have to warn you that there might be some delay on my part. My plans are not quite mature.'

Mr Henderson, who had not said a word, leaving his life in Sophie's hands, entered the living-room with a polite and amiable smile, having ushered Sophie in before him. His unusually striking face had no doubt let this smile speak for him on all formal occasions. 'I hope this isn't too much of an intrusion,' he said.

'Oh, you're American.'

'Half. My mother is American, my father English. I grew up here and in the States. And I work here mostly, though I do go home quite a lot. This looks great.' He cast around pleasantly, expressing no undue anxiety that Herz might not fit in with his plans. His fine head, framed in dark curling hair, was no doubt the reason why Sophie had lent herself so promptly to the project. And the carelessly impressive lines of the body spoke for themselves. Sophie, Herz noted, had not taken her eyes off him, and the look she had given Herz, as they had both stood on the landing, had been meaningful, so meaningful that Herz had detected a plea. She had set her sights on this Henderson, who seemed quite impervious to her concentrated gaze, but Herz saw that if not yet in love with him she had him in mind for a future partner. Herz could see his attraction for her, not yet hers for him. Here was a young man who would need no help from the gods: his impressive looks, and his politely detached manner would achieve his ends, whatever they might be. He was, as yet, Hippolytus to any woman's Phaedra, untouched by female calculations, able to proceed innocently on his own unawakened path. He must be conscious of his good fortune in possessing such attributes, sufficiently well-bred to ignore them. No doubt he too made his own arrangements. Knowing that he had the means to implement them would no doubt explain his relaxed self-assurance.

Not so in Sophie's case. Herz saw with some amusement, but also with some sadness, that this man, now looking closely at what he saw around him, had affected Sophie, had indeed altered her, reduced her to a supplicant. How else could she explain the almost pointed looks she exchanged with Herz, as if admitting him to her intentions? Whatever difficulty she had ever had in expressing her feelings—and Herz saw that this must always have been the case—her eyes on this occasion spoke for her. Her obdurate little face was as closed as ever, but he detected tension in her posture. He regretted, as much for himself as for her, this loss of autonomy, hoping that she was woman enough to denounce it. This he doubted. Men were better fitted for this exercise than women. And Sophie, whose own emotions seemed so unavailable, would experience any undue tenderness on her part as a fall from grace. As indeed it was. Mr Henderson's attention was claimed entirely by the flat, his eyes expertly ranging into corners, his mien agreeable. When he passed her he touched her arm with kind camaraderie. Herz mentally sighed. This was the way to conquer a woman, not by appeals, not even by attack, but by sheer indifference. Herz found himself unable to address the young man by his Christian name, some acknowledgement surely that respect on his part was due to both beauty and self-possession. There was no doubt that if he so wished he would move in straight away.

'I think I will make tea, if you don't mind. Do look round, Mr Henderson. As I said, my plans are still rather shapeless. I had intended to leave in the near future, but in fact there may be one or two impediments, quite a considerable delay, in fact. That might not suit you.'

'Tea would be great,' said Mr Henderson. 'I'll be in New York for the best part of a month, anyway. And I wouldn't want to rush you. I think Sophie told you that I'm looking for a permanent address? If I found the right thing—and I think this may be it—I'd be prepared to wait.'

'I see. So you think this might be suitable?'

'Sure. Good location, good communications, and so on. Is there a garage?'

'No,' said Herz, hoping that this would deter him. 'But we are quite near the Underground. Baker Street and Marble Arch are within walking distance.'

'I could give you a lift in the mornings,' intercepted Sophie, a slight flush now apparent on her normally colourless cheeks.

'Do you work together?' enquired Herz.

'We met through work. We're both in the City. Sophie works in my firm, but only from time to time.'

'Ah. Short-term contracts.'

'Exactly. She knew I was looking for a place, and she mentioned that there might be something going in her building . . .'

'Yes,' said Herz, tired. 'How do you like your tea?'

He was almost won over, not by the young man's amiable lack of persistence but by his conviction that his needs would be met. So must he have proceeded throughout his life. The large sum of money he mentioned brought Herz out of his trance. 'The flat is not for sale,' he said severely. 'Although it may become for sale eventually. I had in mind an absence of a month or two. But as I said I may be gone for longer, even for good. That rather depends on another person. No doubt this makes the proposition less attractive for you.'

'No, that's fine. I like the place. I'd be prepared to fit in with your plans.'

'I'll need references, of course.'

'Sure.'

'Sophie will tell me when you return from New York. We can talk again then.' But Sophie, whose eyes were fixed on the large hand lifting the teacup, murmured only abstractedly, 'Of course.' Herz felt for her an unwelcome pity. So she too was destined to be a victim. The thought gave him no pleasure.

They parted on mutually complimentary terms. Herz shut his front door with a sense of relief, though the flat felt strangely quiet. It was not the quiet of his solitary days, but a quiet that signified the departure of youth. To his surprise he had enjoyed their visit, though it had disastrous implications for himself. He saw that they were entitled to make demands, to be fully conscious of their own advantages, to pay only halfhearted attention to those who stood in their way. What impressed him was their physical ease, a faculty of which he had long lost sight. How could their

assurance let them down? Though the decision was theoretically his, Herz found himself in danger of being disregarded. What were his plans in comparison with theirs?

Later that evening the telephone rang. 'I've got Matt
here,' said Sophie. 'Would you like to join us for a drink?'
A kind of mutual sympathy seemed to have sprung up between them, for which Herz was grateful. The fact that he
seemed to be aware of her feelings had predisposed Sophie
in his favour. The fact that no acknowledgement had been
made was acceptable to her mute way of conducting her
affairs. He felt protective, as he always should have done,
and he suspected that she sensed this as well. He sighed. It
was a role the old were forced to play, sometimes against
their will. Nevertheless he accepted the invitation with
something like alacrity. He was, in spite of himself, genu-
inely interested. Who would win, vanquish the other? He
was entitled to take some pleasure in the spectacle. He
brushed his hair, armed himself with a clean handkerchief,
as if he were leaving for the theatre. His own role would be
as a member of the audience. Their youth had seen to that.

He seemed to have arrived just before the interval, for
during his very real absence something extraordinary had
taken place. Though the expressions of mutual accord
were offered, and indeed received, these lacked commitment on the young man's part. The look he gave Herz was
abstracted, almost haggard, the gaze he returned to Sophie
markedly less so. Herz watched, fascinated, as this wordless
exchange took place. Mr Henderson, it seemed, had been
woken from his neutralizing affability. From the look of
dawning astonishment in his eyes, from the momentary
abandon in Sophie's answering smile, Herz knew that this

was a sacred moment, the descent of the gods, perhaps. He had been present at this strange conjunction, which rarely affects two people simultaneously. When it does the future is irrelevant. His future as well, Herz reflected. Whatever discussions would now take place would be dazed, abstracted. He was moved, as he could not fail to be. Earthy practical considerations were swept aside. Tactfully he signalled his departure to Sophie, who acknowledged it with an almost languorous smile, such as he had never seen before on her face. It was an act of the purest discretion to leave them alone together. What happened next needed no witnesses, for the outcome, as their almost ritualized expressions denoted, was not for his eyes, not for anyone's. Love, once again, asserted its exclusivity, its so triumphant right to possession. Herz was relieved that he had left so discreetly, glad that he had not shown undue interest. His own thoughts would be entertained in the appropriately sylvan setting of the public garden, thus promoted to classical glade or grove. He was also relieved that his own plans had been halted by an unexpected delay, that no further mention had been made of references. The beauty made manifest in their recognition of each other, and of the significance of the moment, was its own recommendation. No further acknowledgement would be required.

Their obvious enchantment—quite literally, as if they had been put under a spell—threw his own proposed merger, his marriage of convenience, into unwelcome relief. What he had witnessed had been the mystic moment before desire had taken hold and released their movements, and yet it was desire, or a knowledge of desire, that was imprinted in their wide-open eyes, in the colour that had crept into their cheeks and lips. This was the stuff of myth, of legend; it seemed almost possible to think not of Cupid, but of Pan, of Apollo, who favoured ravishment and turned reluctant partners into trees. Yet there had been no cruelty in their gaze; they were too humbled by this apparent compulsion either to question it or to take it further. Their dramatic conjunction was, if anything, a cause for wonder, an understanding that it could take place in ordinary circumstances, between quite ordinary people, all calculations of the outcome, or even the next move, quite absent. The world would reclaim them at some point, but for one extraordinary interval each had known the other as if some ideal were being enacted. It was even possible for onlookers to be drawn into the drama of the moment, and in the following moment to feel bereft, deprived of that glimpse of another dimension, and all too sadly understanding their own unregenerate because earthbound condition.

On returning to his own flat he had the impression that a film of dust overlay his belongings. This too was metaphorical, since Ted Bishop had cleaned everything only two days previously. As a place of safety it had served its purpose and now appeared illusory. It would be taken over by somebody else, while his own absurd merger would go ahead. It seemed appropriate to think in terms of merger, of appropriation, business terms which had nothing to do with his own modest preoccupations. The moment of felicity which he had witnessed made even his fantasies seem tedious, for without some benevolent supernatural agency how could his own life be rewarded? It was impossible not to be moved by what had taken place, that charged look . . . It had been brought about involuntarily; that was the beauty of it. Even the knowledge that it would eventually descend to the level of the banal, the everyday, made no appreciable difference. By comparison his proposed flight to Nyon and to Fanny, though it had once made eminent sense, seemed ludicrous. It had made sense because he had not put it to the test, had not translated it into the process of lived life, had seen it continuing into a not yet problematic eternity. He thought of Fanny's letter, of her complaints. He had no doubt that these would be renewed. And how would he fare as a witness to her dissatisfaction? For he did not doubt that he would be cast in a supporting role. His next task would be to convince her of the necessity of returning to Bonn to settle her affairs. And yet, still, there might be a longed-for dignity in the proposed arrangement. He thought with pity and contempt of the excitement he had experienced in watching and waiting for Sophie Clay. It had been possible to be in love even at that remove, and now he knew that life without love would be a desert, and moreover a desert that would reclaim him for its own, bringing the past back into the present, even into the future, and with it the dead whose absence he almost envied.

When the telephone rang he assumed that it was Fanny, even felt a sense of relief that she was responding to his letter with plans of her own, but it was Bernard Simmonds, his voice tired and a little tetchy.

'Julius? I got your letter, but I think we should meet to discuss matters further. It seems to me that you have been a touch precipitate.'

'It seems to me that way too. I appear to have let the flat.'

'You haven't signed anything?'

'No.'

'I'm not quite sure . . .'

'Bernard. Can we meet? I think I need some advice with this.'

'Of course. I take it that you don't want to come to the office?'

'No. Have dinner with me at the usual place.' He waited while a diary was being consulted, then agreed to the Tuesday of the following week. Fanny receded into the distance. If he were fortunate she would take an age to make up her mind, giving him one last chance to make up his own.

## 16

Bernard's advice had been terse but cogent: insist on a monthly agreement, to be terminated, if necessary, at short notice. Having delivered himself of this verdict he attacked his ravioli in a zestful manner which Herz found disquieting. His mind was not really attuned to this interview. The morning had brought a postcard from Bad Homburg. The message, in Fanny's butterfly hand, had read, 'Enjoying a brief respite from my troubles. Letter follows.' From this he gathered that she was in funds, was looking forward to a successful outcome to her lawsuit, and had forgotten him altogether.

This left him with the obligation—it was no less—to repair to the Beau Rivage for at least a month, probably on his own, in order to satisfy Mr Henderson's ever polite but pressing enquiries about the future of the flat, which, Herz reflected, had somehow passed out of his ownership. If he vacated it, even for the shortest period of time, it was less in his own interest, rather more in that of Mr Henderson, for whom he felt an absurd sympathy. The young man, whom he met frequently on the stairs or on Sophie's landing, appeared flushed with love and determination, but still clear-headed enough to pursue his own plans.

Herz felt as tenderly for him as he would have done for

a child proceeding unsupervised into a busy road, not because he was in love, but because he so obviously thought that he had all aspects of the situation under control. He would have liked to take him on one side to explain to him the difficulties that lay ahead. Look at my case, he would have said: a mistaken early love for a woman I find I no longer care for has led me into a sequence of muddled intentions for which there seems to be no resolution. A memory of early euphoria, or even very real euphoria, seems to have condemned me to a form of exile. And in your case that same euphoria, of which I had proof, may fade; your initial conjunction may break down into a conflict of interests. Sophie is no innocent maiden waiting in her bower, whereas you, I think, are rather more unprotected.

As for myself I seem to be on your side, even prepared to go away, to give up my home, simply because your own wishes are so much stronger than my own. I too had elected a companion of sorts, though I now see that I had misjudged her. No doubt at this very moment she is conducting her own affairs without reference to mine. That is my point: how could she know what spurred my actions? How could she appreciate my situation when her own mind is so completely filled with her own preoccupations that she could hardly be expected to give her full attention to what I have become: a virtual stranger, whose life is almost at an end and who relies on further fantasies—of escape—to prolong that life and to bring it into some sort of focus, if only to restore a dignity which is so impaired that it may no longer be within his own control? You see the problem, he would have said. You too may find that you have entered into something which prudence should have warned you against. The dangers implicit in a love affair, whether real or imaginary, are incalculable.

'I was against the letting of the flat,' Bernard Simmonds was saying, 'although of course you have every right to take a holiday. But you could simply have gone away for a month or two without coming to this sort of arrangement.'

'I had in mind a longer absence,' murmured Herz. 'At one point I thought it might be a solution to my problems.'

Again he had a brief glimpse of the original image of himself as a sort of boulevardier, taking his walks along the lake shore, smiling appreciatively at women, becoming a favoured companion, or if not a companion some sort of ideal escort. All this was so far from the truth that all that remained of it was amazement that he could have departed so radically from the facts. But there had been that other impulse, the strength of which was not to be denied: the need for a rash act. That act alone was out of character. He knew himself to be cautious, even knew the need for caution, as he proceeded carefully along familiar streets, his hand pressed protectively to the rattle of his pills in their little enamel box. And there were few pills left, which meant another visit to the doctor. This was not to be avoided; he had been converted to his pills. One placed under his tongue at night ensured a painless transition into sleep. He hardly knew or cared what made them effective. His mother had taken one pill for all her ailments, while his brother Freddy's array of remedies had merely resulted in the suppression of every appetite he had originally possessed. Herz was content to surrender to this need for as long as the need remained. He was in no sense dependent on the pills, he told himself; he regarded them less as a necessity than as some sort of treat. They enabled him to look forward to an untroubled night, and that advantage alone was immeasurable.

'You've insisted on references, of course,' Simmonds was saying. 'Are they satisfactory?'

'Oh, yes.' They were in fact more than satisfactory; they were ideal. If anything they inclined Herz to further indulgence. They presented the candidate (for so Herz thought of him) as an honourable employee, successful in his profession, and amply rewarded in the course of his duties. These references, if anything, added to Mr Henderson's peculiar lustre, which in fact did contain some element of the ideal. In addition to his splendid appearance he seemed, if the references were anything to go by, to possess a noble character. This merely confirmed Herz's wish to protect him, even though this militated against his own interests. At the same time his own interests seemed to take second place to Mr Henderson's prospects and indeed his entire future. Herz had no difficulty in acceding to the laws of nature: the young must be preferred to the old, whom they would eventually replace. The onerous duties that lay ahead for them must be palliated by the pleasures accorded to them—again by nature—throughout their early years. And Mr Henderson was so splendidly in love that Herz felt he should be denied nothing, that no obstacle should be put in his path. The only obstacle at the moment was his own inconvenient self. It was therefore somehow ordained that he must tactfully disappear. In this mysterious way his own nebulous imaginings had been implemented by necessity. That was what he should have liked to point out in one of those imaginary conversations that would never take place. Yet inferences could be drawn from it, and Herz had no doubt that they were valuable. One simple idea, one wish, could be overtaken by events, so that in the end compromise was inevitable. In his own case sympathy for this stranger would ensure his absence from the scene, when he would have enjoyed and appreciated his presence, if only as spectacle. He must therefore deprive himself of a legitimate interest, even a benevolent interest, simply in order to let the other exist in his place.

As for Fanny and his invitation to her, he no longer knew what to think, or indeed how to proceed. He could hardly withdraw it now, yet the need for her presence had diminished. The postcard from Bad Homburg seemed to confirm to him what he had always suspected, that she was frivolous, and moreover that she was in receipt of such invitations all the time. Bad Homburg was expensive, yet she had given the impression in her letter that she was in financial difficulties. His plans had taken no account of her situation, though to judge from her letter that situation was by no means clear. The fantasy of their proceeding comfortably into some kind of golden apotheosis thus received a further check. His own funds depended on the eventual sale of his flat, yet if he sold it he would be homeless. He had managed to persuade himself that Fanny would make similar arrangements, and that the two of them would settle down together in the comfortable knowledge that their well-being was assured.

Now he saw the folly of this assumption. There was no reason for Fanny to give up her present life, any more than he need give up his own. For that brief moment of reckless optimism he was now being made to pay heavily. This too he would point out, by means of the most delicate analogies, to Mr Henderson, in one of those conversations that would never take place. It was the conversation that he now craved, the confidences of the young, the company of the uncompromised. This too was a fantasy, but like his original fantasy rooted in some very real instinct, in this case the desire for a son whose own desire to replace him he would see as entirely legitimate. Instead of which he had condemned himself to further childlessness, since the residents of the Beau Rivage would not be young, would indeed be drawn together by the camaraderie of the impaired. In his so brief visit to Nyon he had had a glimpse of tinctures, of decoctions, of remedies on other tables, had even congratulated himself on being vulnerable only by nature of his own quest.

He had frequently wondered whether the outcome of that journey had not coloured his subsequent life, and was responsible for his latter-day resolution to return, to replace his failure by a revision of the original test, to recapture a modified version of Fanny, and by so doing to bring to a satisfactory conclusion a series of events that had always struck him as inconclusive, as if the director of this particular comedy or tragedy had made an error of taste in ordaining if not a happy ending then at least an ending which would somehow preclude that lasting regret that Herz had felt from that day to this, and which even now struck him as undeserved.

One's fantasies were out of character, he reflected: that was the reason for their being fantasies. One furnished oneself with an imaginary companion, with imaginary offspring, when all the time the unforgiving nature of real circumstances contrived to submerge one. And all the time that disjunction between fantasy and reality brought un-willing recognition of one's sad limitations. In fantasy he was free to be that dashing figure by the lake who was even now taking on the lineaments of someone entirely differ-ent, furnished with a moustache and a silver-topped cane, like an actor seen in some forgotten film. Only in such a disguise could he prove himself to be successful. To de-mand of his unemphatic self such a transformation was to demand the impossible, just as it was impossible to imagine Matthew Henderson as a respectful audience for his maun-derings. The reality consisted of Mr Henderson's footsteps on the stairs which always ended outside Sophie's front door. There was matter here for sadness, yet on the rare occasions when they had, all three of them, come face-to-face, he had felt a warmth of approval for their condition, had smiled unreservedly, and made no attempt to delay them. There were elements here too of an ideal situation, and he would do nothing to disturb it.

'You'd better send those references to me,' Simmonds was saying. 'That way I can see if there's any kind of loop-hole. Otherwise I'd say that you've left yourself rather vul-nerable.'

'I agree.'

'Mind you, a break would be pleasant. You might even enjoy it. Lovely part of Europe, lovely time of the year . . .'

'It just seems rather difficult to envisage it from here. I have a picture in my mind, but I have a suspicion that it is entirely misleading.'

That picture, though complete in every detail, was based

simply on a memory, of a blurred and peaceful blue dusk, of splendid appointments, of a discreet background to a conversation that had proved tame and unsatisfactory. It was true that on the morning of his departure he had been soothed by the strengthening sun, which had enabled him to postpone reflections on the disappointing days that lay ahead. Even now, in Chiltern Street, the sun was gaining strength, as if it had been brought into being by Mr Henderson's requests and desires, lighting up the whole flat and transforming it into something wider, larger than it was wont to appear. This again was a metaphor, but for once a metaphor that entirely fitted the occasion. The appearance on stage of the major actor, no longer himself, served to rearrange the cast, so that lesser characters fell into position in spite of themselves. The sun was democratic, could be enjoyed by everyone, even by exiles in distant parts. Herz knew that if given a choice he would have lingered by his window, looking out into the street, watching for the return of the young people, and smiling as he turned away, fearful of offending them by his presence.

He was conscious of the fact that this evening was proving something of a disappointment to both Simmonds and himself, that he must appear absentminded, forgetful, inattentive to his duties as a host. In fact his own interior drama took precedence. At least his absurd position might stimulate further reflections which might at some point prove useful. For some of those reflections he was indebted to Fanny's letter, and even more so to her postcard, prompting a reading of her character that was probably more accurate than any he had formed in the past. In the past the knowledge that their natures were different, even antithetical, had not deterred him. Now he was inclined to that loss of patience, that shrugging of the shoulders that should have been available to him as a young man, even as a middle-aged man. Her notional presence by his side was no longer of interest to him: rather the opposite. Together they would have presented a touching but fallacious picture of two former sweethearts reunited by that same passage of time that had robbed them of all their attractions. He had had too recent a sighting of the entitlements of those favoured by nature to think otherwise, and if this was unfair to Fanny that could not be helped. Unfairness was an argument advanced by children. The process by which one was disqualified despite one's best intentions was rather more arcane. Nor would it be revealed to him for as long as there were more immediate examples of felicity to hand. The secret smiles of lovers put all thoughts of dignified maturity to flight. There was little evidence that Fanny had advanced beyond the conviction that she was owed more than she had received and that this too was unfair. And he had volunteered to listen patiently, to sort out a labyrinthine muddle that was somehow shady, to restore her self-esteem, to express admiration for her resilience! Such was the part that he seemed to have written for himself. It was small wonder that he had envisaged a brutal recklessness that would have overturned all expectations, not least his own. Where this took place was no longer relevant. The important thing was that it should somehow be enacted, made manifest, if only to himself. Above all to himself. Such recklessness would have the beauty of an *acte gratuit,* without consequences. It is usually the consequences of one's actions, he would have told any young person who could be persuaded to listen, that spoil the fun.

'And your own plans, Bernard?' he enquired.

'Oh, I suppose we shall go away at some point. Next month, perhaps.'

'You and Helen?'

'Yes.'

'You're still living at home, then?'

'Oh, yes.' His expression was moody.

'And your other friend?'

'Well, she's at home too. Her husband's in Singapore on business. We could have seen each other, if Helen hadn't insisted on our being together all the time. As it is I don't see her nearly enough. Don't look at me like that, Julius. I see from your expression that you don't approve. As I remember you came down rather hard on me the last time we met.'

'Yes, I regretted that. It's just that I live more or less out of the world these days. How do you see your future?'

'I don't see it at all, that's the problem.'

'Well, I can sympathize there. The future is a problem for me too.'

'It need not be. I'll need an address for you, of course, and a telephone number. And I'll need to know your dates.'

'Dates?'

'For when you intend to return.'

'So you see me returning, then?'

'Almost certainly. I'm sorry, Julius. I shouldn't be discussing my own troubles with you.'

'I asked, you remember.'

'It's just that you were always such a good listener.'

So were you, Julius thought. Those benign meetings in the past, their shared experiences, were somehow too at an end. He felt the familiar discomfort, felt his breath getting shorter. 'Shall we go?' he suggested. 'You must be tired after your day's work.'

Simmonds looked up. 'Are you all right? You look a bit pale.'

'I'm fine.' He paid the bill with as much composure as he could muster. 'Don't wait, Bernard. I'll take my time here.'

'If you're sure.'

They parted with mutual expressions of regard in which genuine affection and a slight feeling of discontent played equal parts. Herz sat quietly until his breathing returned to normal.

'Will there be anything else, sir?'

'If you could just get me a cab.'

The elderly waiter guided him to the door, a hand under his elbow to steady him. 'We haven't seen the lady for some time,' he said. 'Such a pleasant person.'

'My wife? Yes, a very pleasant person.' He handed over a five pound note. 'Thank you.'

The night, or what he could see of it, was unusually serene. There were no sounds in Chiltern Street to disturb him. Sophie's windows were dark. He was aware of his awkwardness as he scrambled onto the pavement. This was now a humiliation to which he had become accustomed, together with many others. There was a flaw in the divine system, he reflected: the body, and its own inexorable processes. He longed only for bed. Yet the night hours, which usually consoled him, would on this occasion fail in their duty. He might ask the doctor for a sedative, since that was surely allowed. He made a note in his desk diary to book an appointment. I am going away on holiday, he would say, glumly aware that this was the truth. So kind of you to fit me in.

'Mr Herz,' said the doctor. 'An admirer of Freud, if I remember correctly.'

'Less so these days, perhaps. But I do agree with him about dreams. That they are about desire. Or the lack of it,' he said, reminded not quite comfortably of his most recent interpretation.

'Quite so. Just roll up your sleeve, would you?'

Herz sat obediently, his pale arm across the doctor's desk. From a distant room he could hear the high encouraging voice of the practice nurse, which reminded him of Josie. He noted that the watercolour he had so disliked had been replaced by a reproduction of Van Gogh's *Sunflowers,* as also supplied to his dentist's waiting-room. 'I wonder you don't have something more relevant,' he said. '*The Anatomy Lesson of Dr Tulp,* for example. That would give you an opportunity to mention the enormous technological improvements made since Rembrandt's time, the scanners, the keyhole surgery, the pills. It was about the pills that I came, as a matter of fact. I am going away, you see.'

'Just give me a moment,' said the doctor, rewinding the cuff round Herz's arm.

'Oh, I'm so sorry.'

'It's very high. Have you been taking your medication?'

'Well, not recently, perhaps.'

'You need to take it every day.'

'Oh, I will, I will. And if you could let me have some more of Dr Jordan's pills. I don't use them, but being away . . .'

'Have you been experiencing discomfort?'

'Just occasionally. A slight breathlessness, nothing more.'

'I had better examine you.'

The cold stethoscope was applied to his chest, to his back. He willed his poor unguarded heart into obedience.

'There is an irregularity. I'd like you to have a further investigation.'

'When I come back, certainly. Only, you see, I leave tomorrow.'

'Well, it would take some time to make an appointment. How long will you be away?'

'I'm not sure.'

'It doesn't do to neglect these things.'

But Herz knew that his heart was in some ways his ally, would prolong his life no longer than was necessary. His own endurance would see to the rest.

'Come and see me when you return. Avoid stress, that goes without saying. Perhaps it would be better if it did go without saying. Stress is unavoidable. Well, enjoy your holiday.'

'Oh, I will, I will.' Scot-free, he said to himself; no more questions than I expected. He thanked the doctor profusely, made a clumsy exit, aware that he was being watched. He had exhibited signs of morbidity, and had thus proved himself not to be a time-waster. But he longed for the outside world, as he had never longed for it before. To be on the street was to be delivered from the watchful detective he now knew the doctor to be. But this was always going to be difficult, he reminded himself. And at least he had his prescription. He felt as if he had been identified as a fraud, his cover blown. As it had been. He had escaped, but only just. The next time would be more difficult.

The sun was high as he left the surgery, though he knew it would soon decline into a beautiful greenish dusk. He was in no hurry to reach home. He lingered in the street for as long as he could, gazed unseeing into shop windows that he passed every day, was unable to fend off sad thoughts as the light faded. In the supermarket he bought his frugal supplies, smiling at the children, at the mothers, at the hovering manager. Few smiled back, too intent on the meals to be prepared, the business to be transacted before the day's end. The people he encountered in the mornings were more forthcoming. But then they were mostly old, and, like himself, had little else to do.

In the flat he made tea, disinclined to watch the news programme. At this juncture the outside world had little to say to him; his head could only encompass thoughts of his immediate dilemma. Even this bored him. He would have welcomed an opportunity to discuss it with someone on a purely human basis. Bernard Simmonds had been disapproving, had, though too polite to express his frank opinion, regarded Herz as woefully impractical, and worse, reprehensible, since he had not asked for advice at the appropriate time. There had been exasperation in the way he had expedited his food, had not asked permission before he lit his cigarette. Herz felt cast into the role that had been assigned to him. That another, and that other a friend, saw him as inept was a further cause for sadness. He drank his tea slowly, conscious of his slightly shaking hands. When his doorbell rang he reacted with a shock, would have expressed alarm were he not too schooled to do so. When he opened the door to Sophie his heart was still beating heavily. If he behaved like this when disturbed by a simple interruption how would he fare on a journey which would be all noise, all confusion?

'Come in, come in,' he said. 'Would you like a cup of tea?'

'That'd be nice.'

He watched her as she sat, politely drinking her tea. There were changes that were perhaps visible only to himself, used as he was to dwelling on her. Her hair had worked its way loose from its knot; a strand lay against her cheek. Her lips had lost that adventitious colour that had so enlivened them, and looked dry. From time to time she chewed the inside of her mouth.

'You're tired,' he said gently. He was filled with a protective love for her.

'Yes, well, plenty to do. I came about the flat.'

'Yes, I imagined you had. I thought Matthew was still in New York.'

'He rang me last night. He wondered if you had come to any decision.'

'We agreed that nothing would be decided until he got back. He said he was away for a month.'

'Only he's getting a bit anxious. Well, very anxious.'

'I wonder he doesn't move in with you.'

'No room. And he wants his own place. You can understand that.'

'Will he be ringing you again?'

'I suppose so.' She looked dejected, made an effort to sit up straight, as no doubt instructed long ago, and placed her teacup on the table.

'You're fond of him?' asked Herz, still gently, so as not to offend her.

'You could say that.'

'And he of you?'

'Maybe. I know he has a girlfriend in the States. They were engaged once, he told me, but she broke it off. They still see each other.'

'I shouldn't let that worry you. Nobody starts with a clean slate. It would be nice to think so, I know.' He thought back to that shock of recognition he had witnessed, wondered how the directness, the unavoidability of that moment had deteriorated into considerations of loyalty, of sentiment, all the baggage that had somehow obscured the earlier truth. He wanted to tell her that it was absurd to squander such moments, so rare in themselves, on notions left over from some catechism of the past. He had no doubt that there had been the usual discussions, the laying of cards on the table, the enquiry into both past and present relationships. And with every frank confession would come increased anxiety, such as was affecting Sophie now. It was apparent that she was more anxious than her lover, whose splendour might have armoured him against the suspicion that there were others in the field. Herz marvelled once again at the strain of obtuseness to be found in every classical hero, whose noble looks are left to profess his superiority to the world. In the theatre that was quite in order. In life that unawareness would provide grounds for suspicion.

Sophie was alert to her own misgivings, though perhaps not in a position to quantify them. The ease with which the young man had gone to New York, without acting on the moment, or perhaps without acknowledging the strength of this new tie, forged in a single encounter, would have acted against him, have opened the door to doubt. Sophie's pale mouth, her normally inexpressive eyes wide open as suspicions crowded in, indicated unhappiness. Her normal obduracy would have served her better, Herz thought. He could not say this, and in any case wondered if the same rules applied today as had applied in his youth. He was not there to give advice, was in any event thought incapable of giving advice, rendered insensible by age, with only a dim memory of former feelings. He could have told her, but would not, of the permanence of such feelings, of the longing for love that persisted beyond the canonical age, of those other appetites which made their inconvenient voices heard until death put an end to all feeling, all appetite. It would in any case have made no sense to her to hear this. She was young enough to be enormously sophisticated about relationships, as they called them these days, yet at the same time unused to this particular test. All this he wanted to say to her, knowing that she would regard it as presumptuous, would have bridled, would have retreated into the iciness he had provoked on one unfortunate occasion about which he preferred not to think. He tried to adopt an air of benevolence, but failed. The situation was too serious for that, too serious for Sophie to have estimated his own courage, his own forbearance.

'You must be guided by your feelings,' he said instead. 'If you waste your time in worry, which is probably needless in your case, you will lose something precious.'

What he did not say was already enshrined in any number of clichés, all of them to hand. It offended him to think of her sitting by the telephone like any other woman, she who had so much scorn at her disposal. Rather more powerful was his need to tell her of the multiple disappointments of those who stopped to evaluate their feelings, who wanted to be fair to others, who took a false pride in their sensitivity. Act only on the moment, he wanted to tell her; consult only your own wishes. The rest is poetry, and has no place in love.

'I should enjoy your friendship, without worrying your head about previous attachments,' he said. 'I'm sure it will be fine. Just don't waste too much time thinking. If you do you may spend the rest of your life regretting a lost moment. And you know it never pays to hang back in these matters. If you do you may find yourself truly unhappy.' He heard his voice break, hastily cleared his throat, manufactured a cough. 'Tell Matt,' he said, 'that I'll have an answer for him when he comes home. That's what we agreed, after all. Now, are you all right? No more worries?' But here he had gone too far, had overstepped the mark, and was punished with a guarded look from her once more closed face. 'Shall I make some more tea?' he enquired gaily. 'Or are you in a hurry to go out?'

'I'd better go,' she said. 'What shall I tell Matt if he rings?'

'What I've just told you. I'll let you know as soon as I can. Keep in touch, Sophie. Oh, and have a pleasant evening.'

When it was properly dark he tried to telephone Josie, thinking they might exchange some message that would see them both through the night, but there was no answer.

He tried again later, listened with painful concentration, as if it were a message in itself, as the telephone rang endlessly through an empty house, and would, he imagined, ring without response for as long as his efforts to reach out continued.

# 17

Fanny's second letter was as bulky as her first, but this time correctly addressed. Herz sat down at his desk to read it, as if dealing with some mildly disagreeable business matter. Before briefly scanning and counting the number of pages (five) he noted that the handwriting was becoming fainter, as if the writer were on the point of expiring, or, more probably, as if her pen were running out. This would be a complaint, he thought, along the lines of those sung by minstrels accompanying themselves on some early stringed instrument. He had once attended such a recital at the Wigmore Hall, and had not much appreciated it.

'My dear Julius,' he read. 'Your letter was most welcome, and it reached me at a time when I had need of kindness. I had just returned from Bad Homburg, and was so badly affected by my visit that I was obliged to stay at home for a couple of days until I felt well enough to go out and face the world. When Lotte Neumann invited me to join her party I accepted almost eagerly, though I have always found her a rather tiresome woman. What I did not realize was that I was expected to pay for myself. This led to what has become a routine humiliation. I had to promise to send a cheque from Bonn, which I managed to do, though it has led me to wonder how I shall face the future.

This fear has dogged me all my life, and it is one from which Mother tried to protect me. Now that she is gone and I am obliged to fend for myself I find that I lack the wisdom and the practical help on which I had come to rely. Yet I am forced to encounter this embarrassment day by day, and can only regret that I was not better trained to face hard times. This is strange, since hard times have been my lot since leaving Berlin, and even more since leaving Nyon.

'I relied on Mother's experience to guide me through, and for a time it was sufficient. We left Berlin with just enough money to tide us over, but when Father was killed it ran out altogether. It was Mother who encouraged Mellerio, who was in the habit of meeting business acquaintances at the Beau Rivage for dinner or a glass of champagne. It pains me to say this now but I disliked her way of showing me off, almost of proposing me. I had never needed a sponsor to attract men, and the looks that I intercepted from some of the people in the hotel offended me. Fortunately Mellerio, who was twenty years older than myself, was a courteous man and a gentleman: I believe he sincerely wished to put an end to my discomfiture. And of course I was very pretty. He was also pleasant to Mother, for which I was grateful. I could not blame her for her manoeuvres. She thought she was making provision for my future. I thought I was making provision for hers.

'When Mellerio died he left enough money for us to live quite comfortably at the Beau Rivage for a few years, though not enough to live there when Mother became unwell. I was older, and that was my tragedy. I had thought that my looks would last me all my life, and this is perhaps an illusion from which women suffer, until they look in the glass one day and see that some sort of fading has taken place, as if a veil had obscured the original brightness that no amount of added colour will restore. Your visit to Nyon occurred just before I had had such a revelation. I was still confident, you see, confident enough to wait for a better offer. Does that shock you? It shocks me too, though at the time I was thinking only in practical terms. I knew little of your circumstances; your mother's letters were full of false assurances that did not convince us. We remembered you as difficult people, who rarely shone in company. In our company, that is. And the antagonism between the two sisters was difficult to forget. As a small child I remember disputes which ended in noisy tears. I was for that reason somewhat prejudiced against you, despite your excellent appearance. Life at the Beau Rivage was endurable, even pleasurable. I knew that sooner or later something or someone would turn up. And so I sent you away. I have regretted it ever since.

'My second marriage was brought about in the same way as the first had been, but this time there were no alleviating circumstances. Alois Schneider was an unattractive man whom we both thought wealthier than he actually was. In fact although he had inherited a printing business from his father and grandfather he was something of a speculator and made a series of unwise decisions about the future of his firm. I came quite quickly to dislike him, but once again I had Mother to think of. At least I managed to look after her, but at a price. I hated my husband to touch me, which he did at every opportunity. I simply could not respond. Perhaps I never have. And yet I have always longed for love, romantic love, the kind of love that strengthens a woman against misfortune. I am convinced that with another man I would have had the courage to accept my situation. As a girl I was envious of those of my friends who became engaged, and who were nothing like as good-looking as I was. Perhaps that is why I have never enjoyed the company of women. As the only daughter of an adoring father I had got used to the idea that I should always be favoured. You were the one whose attitude most resembled his, but remember, I had so many choices in those days. Such choices ended pitiably, in two husbands who failed to bring me to life. As for you and me, we should have been lovers in Berlin, when we were young and perfect.

'Does it surprise you to hear me talking like this? It surprises me when I tell the truth, which I rarely do now that I have to keep up some sort of pretence. In fact I have been doing this for as long as I can remember. Now I am too tired to do so much longer. That episode at Bad Homburg convinced me that I must be wary of other women. I still attract enmity, notably that of my erstwhile sister-in-law and her terrible daughter. You may not know that women are natural competitors. Maybe you have never encountered women who will abruptly end friendships of long standing when a man is involved, not out of disloyalty but out of natural instinct. Perhaps I was not as lovable as I thought, though men found me so. But it is part of my sad inheritance to be loved only once, by Father, or perhaps twice, by you. If only you had been more forceful I might have relented, but that is what I tell myself today, when I am in such sad circumstances. Even the idea of seeing you again both tempts and frightens me. And the only way I could return to the Beau Rivage would be with a man at my side. Even then I know I might be subjected to side-long glances, for it seems that I still possess some elements of style. Or maybe I still have the manners and gestures of one who was once thought beautiful. You will find this too among women, a kind of natural confidence that causes envy, even resentment. And yet I never exploited my looks. It was Mother who did that for me.

'Julius, I have no money. There was no lawsuit, merely a consultation with a lawyer who explained to me that although Alois theoretically made his assets over to me the document which was to have been the formalization of such an agreement lacked a witness and was therefore invalid. He must have known this. Certainly his sister knew it. We have not spoken from that day to this, and I cannot help but suspect collusion between Alois and his family on this point. Of course I have no proof. It was the daughter who perceived their advantage in this matter. Much good it has done them; there was little left. I think I said that Alois was not even good as a businessman, let alone as a husband. I have no hesitation in saying that I was glad when he died.

'It seemed fated that I should end up with Mother as my only company, and now with no company at all. I wonder now at the cruel practicality of parents who seek to discharge their own duties onto a third party, or parties. I would guess that you, who were always faithful, were a faithful son, doing duty for your father, whom I remember as fatally mild, unable to sustain a household already riven by problems. There was a brother, I remember, whom I was not allowed to frequent. That was another maternal edict, on your side this time. It was thought that I would distract him from his music, but in fact your mother was jealous of anyone who approached him. What became of him? Did he marry? Somehow I think not.

'What I am trying to say is that I should love to meet you again at the Beau Rivage, as you suggest. But you will have gathered from this letter that I am in no position to pay for myself. You may imagine how humiliating it is for me to write these words. At least I will have repaid some of the debt I owe you—you who were willing once to marry and love me—to make this clear. So yet again we are divided by money. You do not tell me whether you have done well in life; in fact you tell me nothing about yourself. It may comfort you to know that I think back to the respect in which you once held me with genuine emotion. It would have given me great pleasure, enormous pleasure, to have seen you again. As matters stand you will not be surprised if I decline your invitation. I must accept the fact that the time for love is past, but this is very bitter. I can only end this letter by sending you my belated regards, not only for the compliment you pay me now in asking for a meeting, but for the compliment you paid me once before, in asking me to be your wife. No woman could ever forget such a compliment. Even now I am grateful. Fanny.'

Herz found himself so unsettled by this letter that he was obliged to go out, as if once again the company of strangers was the only panacea for his agitated feelings. So she had in some way cared for him, and did so even now, remembered his ardour as somehow precious, something of which she had never lost sight. That was the missing element in their relationship: her regard for him. He had acted and reflected like a jilted lover, so hurt that he had taken no account of the other, and in this way had lost all perspective. He had been ready to vilify her, to blame her retrospectively for disappointments in which she played no part, had seen her as the indifferent beauty whom he had failed to interest, whereas she was now changed from the girl whom he had once adored. What remained of her dazzling future was the bitterness of a woman who had been denied love, of the sort she had craved. Or had her mother denied it for her? There had been something perverse about those two sisters, his mother and his aunt; they were not given to sympathy, either towards each other or to their young and trusting progeny. There may even have been jealousy behind the iron closeness that united Fanny and her mother; neither was allowed to break their primitive agreement. He had even seen this in action in the course of his dinner at the Beau Rivage, the loving smiles that did not quite conceal Fanny's furrowed brow, the sort of flirtatiousness she was obliged to employ when some activity of her own, however anodyne, presented itself. Staying within the parameters of her mother's approval had become her only preoccupation. Without the need for that approval she might have had the courage to be free. Instead she had seen freedom as the most hazardous of enterprises, had sensed that without the chance to test that freedom she would never become fully adult, and, as her letter showed, had suffered from such an intuition but had borne the consequences of her choice because loss of the only love she knew was too tragic to be endured.

And she had thought of him, even when he had only noticed her indifference. She had retained memories not only of himself but of other family members, had shown discernment, had suspected something obscure in the attitude of his mother to his father, had detected the jealousy of other possible influences in her insane regard for his brother. Even now, even he had inherited the family trait of resentment, castigating Fanny for her hauteur, her self-regard, which, on examination, could be seen as a necessary disguise for ordinary frailty. He was cast into a terrible pity for her, although until he had read her letter he had been prepared to be disbelieving, sceptical, even unkind, dreading the prospect of seeing her again, or if not seeing her listening to her. But in fact her complaint had been that of common humanity: love, loneliness, regret. She had revealed herself, if only slightly, as a simple woman, one who was no longer sought after, who was in fact left alone to pay the price of the confidence that had once surrounded her and which other women so resented. She was being punished, or so it must seem to her, for her early endowments, for the teasing crowd of followers she had once attracted, for the atmosphere of security in which she had existed until exile put an end to all certainties. Though vigilance had certainly been in order, though practical arrangements had of necessity to be made, she would have sensed that she was being sacrificed. She might have stumbled on an even darker truth, namely that if all had been well and they had been able to stay in Germany she would still have been sacrificed by those who claimed to know her better, and who were, moreover, convinced of their good faith.

To go back further would be to enter the unknown world of those two sisters, whose lives, he now saw, had been entirely unmodified by the men they had chosen, or who had been chosen for them. A distrust of natural appetites would have been implanted in them from their earliest days, their inclinations to pleasure seen as a dereliction from family observance. They would therefore feel the same distrust for children, whose lives, they were so lately to realize, might lead them into wider expectations, even opportunities. Such mothers had thought their own narrow upbringing the only true guide. His aunt Anna was no less guilty than his mother, had regarded Fanny as her own creation, her own preserve. For all her hospitality, lavishly dispensed in her sunny salon, she was a martinet. Herz had always known this, had been dismissed too many times, not for any fault of his own but because he represented, or might be thought to represent, an incarnation of impulse, of instinct, from which Fanny must be guarded. She had succeeded in preserving this daughter throughout the uncertain years of exile, but largely for her own benefit. The husbands she had chosen for her had the advantage of compliance, could be persuaded to accept her as a necessary accompaniment. Perhaps Fanny had been presented as delicate, fragile, requiring her mother's care. This mythology had undoubtedly ensured their communal future. Herz saw with pity that Fanny had been denied access to her own desires, and, worse, may even have known this.

He walked into the public garden, sat on his usual bench, regretting that he had not brought the letter with him. Yet the news that it contained had seemed too troubling for a casual re-reading. There was matter here for intense regret, largely for what he now saw as Fanny's unhappy life. Over and above this, and indeed indistinguishable from it, was the knowledge that she had thought of him, had regretted him, a factor of which he had been entirely ignorant. She had even felt for him as a woman should feel for a man; why else had she said that they should have been lovers when they were little more than children? 'When we were young and perfect' had been her phrase, disconcertingly close to his own wistful approval of young lovers. That phrase had indeed established a kinship between their two selves; quite simply they had known each other all their lives. In revealing her regret that they had missed their chance Fanny had come closer to him. He had been deceived by the masks that adults are obliged to wear, whereas it was the girl, and his own wishes, that should have been addressed.

He shook himself out of his trance, got heavily to his feet, and made his way to a home that was now as fictional, as phantasmagorical, as the Beau Rivage. In that sense they were interchangeable, as they had appeared to him in his original, almost forgotten, vision of flight. He knew himself condemned to leave, not for any practical or impractical reason, whichever was the stronger, but because he had a role to fulfil, an investigation to undertake, a potential response to a need which had impressed him as being within his competence. Their reunion might, almost certainly would, prove a disappointment, but it might enlighten them. He was not quite able, however, to dispel uneasiness as to Fanny's motives. She was needy now, without support. Her letter had certainly revealed aspects of a character with which he was unfamiliar, but he was still subject to doubt. Crassly, he felt suspicious of her appeal for help. She had always been an expert at confusing him. Her letter was perhaps disingenuous; he had no means of assessing her sincerity. He shrugged. Perhaps this did not matter. The fact remained, however, that her apparent honesty was entirely out of character.

Meanwhile her letter required an answer. 'My dear Fanny,' he wrote. 'Your letter arrived this morning and I have been thinking about it ever since. I dare not re-read it in case it affects me adversely. This is what I mean. I agree that we should meet, if only to see what we have become, but such a meeting might, and almost certainly would, disillusion us. Now that I am at last free to cast a very cold eye on our family circumstances I see how helpless we were, in our original innocence, to fight against what had been laid down for us. We were possessions, no more, no less. I had the fate of my parents and my brother in my hands, and you were charged with the task of ensuring your own and your mother's survival. That we accomplished our respective duties made those duties no easier. I see now that we were given little freedom to grow, were forever imprisoned by family expectations. I do not blame you for your mercenary mother: at the same time I deplore her. I deplore my own. I deplore my father who provided so supine an example. I remember painfully, as if it were yesterday, your beauty, your confidence. In many ways it is almost easier to remember you as laughingly dismissive of my callow intentions than it is for me to think of you as dependent on the favours of others, as you now seem to be. I have too much wreckage on my own conscience to feel sorry for you. I merely recognize another victim.

'What help I can give I will of course give. That we should be in this position at all is almost laughable, but I

long ago came to the conclusion that those who are responsible for our evolution are indeed enjoying our discomfiture. There is a saying I have always enjoyed: if you
want to make God laugh tell Him your plans. Yet much as
I adopt this wisdom I still feel obliged to shoulder blame,
as indeed you should. We who should have been sceptical
have been revealed, by time, as naïf. Your letter shows that
you at least had some insight, perhaps more than I did. I
tried to content myself with little, thinking that I was acting for the best in suppressing my nature, thinking too that
I owed it to others to make rational decisions. One such
rational decision was my marriage, but I have been less rational in my latter-day dealings with the world. I now see
that all my affections were more or less imperfect, but as
you remind me I did once have my youth to guide me. I
see now the terrible errors, not of youth, which I am inclined to forgive, but of age, when the impulse to make
good what has turned out so badly forces one to adjust, to
compromise, to make do with less when one has always
longed for more. The people I see around me as I go about
my everyday business amaze me. How do you manage? I
want to ask them. Are you reasonably content, or do you
wish, as I do, to be liberated from your history? I once—
quite recently—had the painful illusion that I could so liberate myself, and that illusion was somehow connected
with early memory, or rather with early sensation. I wonder whether it was ever anything more than sensation, yet
I know that sensation is sometimes a better guide than es-
teem.

'I feel obliged to tell you this since you express little curiosity about myself. Maybe you think that you had me

summed up long ago, as someone to whom you could appeal for support if ever your usual conduct appeared puzzling or unsatisfactory. There was no reason for such an eager standby as I was to appeal to a woman who had a wide range of choices. It pains me that your choices proved so disastrous. There again I am forced back to thoughts of your mother and the choices she made for you. Even though I see that she harboured a certain primitive wisdom I think of her unkindly. And I am shocked to discover that some of that unkindness has come to be directed at yourself. There was the merest hint of opportunism in your letter and, although I am no cynic (another regrettable flaw in my character), a certain wariness grew in me as the day wore on. And it was such a lovely day, sunny and mild, a day meant for innocent pleasure, of the kind that you and I were never meant to enjoy. I lay the blame now on less than satisfactory parents, but that is what all children do, whatever their age. I cannot entirely exonerate our two selves. I am wary, you see, of easy answers. What gives me pause is that you appear to have little awareness of your own mistakes. You express a bitterness which I can understand: you express a hatred of your second husband whose touch defiled you. A more worldly woman would have arranged matters to her own advantage, would have taken a lover. If that had been the case I would almost have applauded. But you seem to have exhibited an alarming passivity, and I find it difficult to connect that passivity with your earlier self-regard. This is a matter which I would find interesting to discuss with you, yet I confess that the prospect wearies me. In some odd way I seem to have made you my life's work. And I see that that work is not yet finished.

'You almost loved me once, but decided against it. You were vain, justifiably so, and vanity is a heady commodity. I concede that you are prepared to love me now. This should be enough for me at my age, and of course at yours. If I feel bold enough to express dissatisfaction with this outcome you need not think that the dissatisfaction must be laid entirely at your door. It is lost opportunity that I crave, and in a sense the inexperience that allowed me for so long to live in hope. It seems from your letter that you have proved to be the more sophisticated of the two of us. Whatever your motives—and I must pay you the compliment of believing you to be unaware of them—I cannot help responding to the fact that you remember me so kindly. When I left Nyon that morning I felt I had disappeared from the face of the earth, never to be sighted again. You were still beautiful then, whatever you say. I knew that I had missed my chance. I am impressed by the fact that you knew this long ago. We were never mismatched, simply ill-advised.

'Let us meet then, but with no illusions on either side. We shall probably not like what we see, and may soon tire of discussing those matters we have in common. We owe it to ourselves, perhaps, to do what is necessary to maintain a fiction of family attachment, yet I must warn you that I am no longer indulgent on that score. If I return to Nyon it will be for the abject desire to be greeted by someone who knew me when I was young and hopeful, and who will not judge me too harshly for what I have become. The pleasure may last no longer than that initial greeting, but that pleasure will be rare. The prospect is not without its dangers, and we are at an age when so many brave efforts are required of us. Yet somehow we still long for love. This at least is a matter of interest to us both. Yours ever, Julius.'

This letter too he tore up. 'Dearest Fanny,' he wrote. 'Thank you for writing back so promptly. Let us agree to meet, perhaps at the beginning of next month. I assume that you will be happy to return to the Beau Rivage. I will of course make all the arrangements; you need have no worries on that score. I will telephone you in the next few days to make final plans. Needless to say I look forward to seeing you again. Ever yours, Julius.'

On another sheet of paper he wrote, 'Dear Sophie, if you are not back too late would you give me a call?', and went out to slip the letter under her door before he changed his mind.

Before sealing his letter to Fanny he had had to reassure himself that he was sending her the polite or revised version, and that his earlier words had been consigned to the wastepaper basket. Though it might have relieved him to stricture her, the discourtesy, he knew, would have shamed him for life. They came from an earlier age, when a suitable pathway had to be negotiated through thickets of unexpressed frustration: they were bound by that code. Yet he had a need to repeat those urgent words when they were face-to-face. It would be like a summit conference in a peaceful scenic setting, at the end of which they would have to issue a communiqué. The outcome would be inconclusive (here the analogy with a summit conference seemed apposite) but they would have made the necessary effort. He was even ready for a confrontation, and for the opportunity at last to stir her into some recognition of equality. He might even find in her that audience he had periodically desired: yes, that was it, for was she not the only person to whom he did not have to introduce himself, to set up an artificial preamble to a notional subject on which he might express notional opinions? And would she, might she find this acceptable, even diverting? Behind her complaints he had detected acute boredom, the boredom of a woman used to attention, and now condemned to live without it. Neither need lose face, for this would supply them with a much-needed stimulus, so that eventually their talk might stray into other regions, take in subjects other than themselves. The matters they thought they were meeting to discuss might be exhausted so much earlier than either of them had anticipated, for their position had been made clear in their letters, hers uncensored, his so prudent. Such prudence would soon be unnecessary. Once they were seated next to each other, and communing without difficulty, their separation would be forgotten, or, if not forgotten, irrelevant. Their years apart would be seen as a long parenthesis in an enduring relationship, one in which they both had a renewed interest.

'Sophie,' he said, when the telephone rang. 'Tell Matthew he can have the flat. For a month, initially. Then I'll let him know whether or not I've decided to sell. I don't think there's anything more to establish at this stage. I seem to have made up my mind quite easily. Strange, that. I thought it would be more difficult.'

# 18

Permission had been sought, and granted, for Matthew Henderson to move in certain of his possessions. Herz's sitting-room now housed a computer, a video recorder, two large speakers, and a couple of squash racquets. Since there seemed little room for him in which to pursue his ordinary occupations he took once more to leaving the building in the early morning, anxious to avoid his new tenant, who chose that time to deposit another discreet but bulky object outside his door. Once he returned to find a suitcase on the landing, which, with only a brief sigh, he transferred to his bedroom. He made no overt objection to this, preferred not to be present when the act of appropriation took place. Soon, he knew, sounds would reach him from Sophie's flat, and he thought it only tactful to make himself scarce. They would be gone by the time he returned, and then he would eat his breakfast, saving his newspaper to read in the public garden. This behaviour, fitting for a resort or some other temporary mode of existence, meant that a long day was at his disposal, most of it lived out of doors. But the weather was fine, and he took a restrained pleasure in his early mornings, though he knew that it was easier to leave the flat as a free man than to return to find it partly taken over, the stealthy progress in train even as he paced the known and familiar streets.

With a keen but indulgent eye he surveyed the landscape, seeing it now as benign, neutral, offering no comment
on his solitary progress, absorbing all eccentricities—men
gasping for breath on their morning run, old ladies looking
on protectively as dogs relieved themselves in the gutter
and regretting only that he could not intercept the odd
passer-by and engage in a little light conversation. This
would be meaningless, he knew, but similar to those remarks exchanged in the shops, comments on the weather
infused with a good will more noticeable at this hour than
at any other. With his decision to leave he seemed to have
moved into a wider frame of reference, one in which the
company of strangers was entirely acceptable, and saluta-
tions of the vaguest kind the agreed method of communication. With this mutual anonymity, as if each observed
some code in which a correct distance was recommended,
came an absence of pressure to explain oneself or one's
presence, and with it that freedom from history that was
what holidays promised but rarely delivered. The sheer
lack of intimacy, noticeable but not threatening, induced a
mood of some strangeness, as if the self were being dis-
persed into the mild air, leaving only the senses in place, to
admire, to appreciate, to enjoy, and for this brief interval to
function without impairment.

This might later break down, the capacity of the observer to absent himself from the scene being limited. At
this point Herz would return to the flat, already weightier,
as if recently reintroduced into the earth's atmosphere.
This was the less welcome aspect of the exercise, presaging
a day in which only an effort would do to reinstate that
early insouciance. If he were untimely enough to encounter either Matthew or Sophie, or usually both, on the

stairs, he would raise a friendly hand, smile, and move on, anxious not to disturb their easy progress into the life of a normal day. He was dependent on them to animate the house, which might otherwise have lapsed into an empty silence. This they did by way of signs—a window being pushed up, a remark called from one room to another, a burst of music from a radio, abruptly lowered, as if not to disturb him. They were, it seemed, aware of his presence, which he sought to make as elusive as possible. He in his turn was aware of theirs, as he had never been before, attentive to their comings and goings, and always to their footsteps on the stairs. Sometimes he saw them retreating down the street on their way to work. In this guise, formally dressed, professionally alert, they were all animation, their alternative selves, the personae they kept in readiness for the outside world, as briskly on display as if there were no hiatus between the life they lived together and those hours in which they were separate beings. At such times, watching them dwindle into the distance, he felt the onset of a slight panic, and with it a sense of estrangement or of advanced juvenility, wondering, like the exile from real life he knew himself to be, what it must be like to have entitlements in the realms of love and work. Such speculations were, he knew, invalid, and applicable only to his own powerlessness to create a context in which he might function efficiently and to some purpose. Any busyness he exhibited was for the sake of others, who might otherwise feel sufficiently obliged to enquire after his health, or whether he was going on holiday. His efforts were particularly successful in avoiding conversation with the young couple, whose impermeability he was anxious to preserve.

He hoped that they would read into his formal smile and his upraised hand whole areas of activity of which they knew nothing and in which he was furiously engaged.

In the interval between their leaving for work and their much later return he was able to think of them almost objectively, noting the changes he had managed to capture on his inner eye in those moments of meeting and greeting: Sophie's inward smile, Matthew's bland alertness. Of the two of them he appeared the less enlightened, accepting his good fortune as one to whom such advantages were commonplace. This could be seen as alarming, but Herz recognized that Sophie was vigilant enough for both of them. She had captured him, perhaps in that first glance, and both were content to live the aftermath, to cut it down to size, to reduce it to liveable dimensions. Neither now exhibited that capacity for extreme behaviour which, for a second or two, had made Herz hold his breath before absenting himself from the scene. Instead they exchanged cheerful talk as they manhandled Matthew's appurtenances from one landing to another. Their presence outside his front door proclaimed once again their ability to surround and absorb his diminishing space, but they were ignorant of any threat to his peace of mind, and indeed innocent of it, so that as often as not he obediently took in the heavy winter coat and the two pairs of shoes and stored them in his cupboards, which were now uncomfortably full. They knew that no acknowledgement would be necessary, that this painless exercise could only be accepted as a transfer of ownership, his own acquiescence guaranteed. There was therefore no basis for alarm on his part, for he had come quickly to understand the procedure, as if any objections

on his part would be an error of taste. He noted with respect the size of Matthew's shoes, and knew that he would
miss such details when he was no longer within their
range. He had a sense of what it must be like to house a
young person, reckoned that it might be both exciting
and exasperating, and returned with something like relief
to the half-life he had fashioned for himself and in which
he had striven to attain perfection. It was only in his more
habitual silence that he was able to gauge the distance he
had covered, the notional advances he had made. His
original letter to Fanny, the one he had not sent, had lightened him of a burden of accusations which he knew he
need never deliver. He could therefore meet her like one
newly risen from the dead, free of earthly corruption, pure
spirit. Whether he could ever get used to such incorpore-
ality was another matter. His instinct was to embrace the
world in its entirety, for better or for worse, like a marriage. Yet it seemed that another type of marriage was
being proposed, or at least offered, between two survivors
of disparate experiences, held together less by expectations
of the future than by a desire to understand the past.

Fanny's voice on the telephone had been tentative, as if
she dreaded interruptions. Once he had assumed a calm he
did not feel she responded in kind. She even recaptured
some of her original asperity, as if their original attitudes
had reclaimed them. This was almost a relief to Herz, who
had foreseen tearfulness of the sort he knew himself unable
to dispel. A crying woman would make him regret the
entire enterprise, which must be conducted with dignity,
however contentious their relations might turn out to be.
Indeed the greater the annoyance—for he knew there

would be claims and counter-claims—the greater the need for ever more extreme restraint, so that they might always give the appearance of repose if not of harmony. They had arranged to meet in Geneva: Herz had booked a car to drive them to Nyon. He hoped that such a gesture would appeal to Fanny, who might have missed courtesies of this kind in her present life. He had begged her not to bring too much luggage; she had told him not to be so silly. Surely, she had said severely, you expect me to be suitably dressed? There may even be dancing, she had added. The longing in her voice at this point had been audible, piercing the carapace of confidence that had been briefly in place. He felt he did not yet know her well enough to tell her how moved he had been by this sign of hope, of longing not for himself but for the sort of life she had once enjoyed as a girl. He knew that he must be careful not to show that he understood her too well, must accept as seriously as he could every account of her recent misfortunes, prepare to believe her when she referred to recent 'tiresomeness', for which once again she would blame others, as the version of the truth which she preferred. When he knew her better he might find this frustrating, but at that stage a certain degree of exasperation might protect them from sentimentality. Any undue emotion, assumed for the occasion, would strike them both as undesirable. It would be enough to know that they understood each other on this point to fall into a workable agreement, negotiated on each side with a care that might yet turn into love.

'What do you look like now?' she had asked him.

'Old,' he said.

She had laughed, but had contrived to leave him with

the impression that she herself was unchanged. The alter-
ation in her voice, from dull to alert, had managed to convince him of this. He was willing to make this concession.
Others might have to follow.

It flattered them both to know that they would be ar-
riving as a couple, their greetings to one another unobserved. He had given the matter some thought, but in fact
such potential problems were easily solved. The arrangements had been crowned with enviable success. A suite at
the Beau Rivage, overlooking the lake, had been available,
and all thoughts of physical embarrassment had disappeared. They would each have guarded the modesty of
those whose attributes were now less than flattering, and
would be scrupulous about keeping out of sight at times
when the reality might threaten the appearance that each
would be careful to maintain. His flight was booked, and
hers too. He trusted that so far he had given a good account of himself. Indeed all these procedures were accepted without question, so that for most of the time he
was able to forget them. He was rather more interested in
the life that he would leave behind him, and the lives that
would soon efface any imprint he might leave. He thought
it quite in order that this should be so, but was mildly re-
gretful that he would not be present to observe the un-
folding of the story that had started in so promising a
fashion. He knew that in moments of ennui his thoughts
might return to that bright prospect, and that if ever he
were to be homesick it would not be for a place but for the
sound of footsteps on the stairs, the front door opening
and closing, the murmur of voices, of sudden laughter. In
his so peaceful exile he would wonder how they were, as if
they, and not Fanny, formed part of his family. He would

send them a postcard, but not otherwise remind them either of his absence or of his former presence. In due course he would return for the space of a day to discuss his future plans, having warned them beforehand of his visit. He did not at this stage know what he would decide to do, knew only that a continuation of his life in Chiltern Street was unlikely, perhaps impossible. Only grave illness, or grave disaffection, would make it seem desirable, and he was determined not to succumb to either. Eternal vigilance was the price of liberty, and for that vigilance he had received more than adequate training.

His pursuits now had a valedictory air, though they had never been more wholehearted. He greeted every unobtrusive landmark: the streetlight outside his window, the muttering television sets in the shop, and, further afield, the postman's trolley, the supermarket, the garden. Such details now coalesced into a portrait of his life in this place, mute testimonies to his citizenship. He made no announcement of his departure, avoided conversations, left a note for Matthew giving details of his address and asking him to forward his mail. Ted Bishop had been provided for; they had shaken hands with extreme cordiality. This competence tended to desert him in the long evenings, when he would experience a brief failure of nerve. But this was to be expected and could be attributed to fatigue. He tended to stay out as long as possible, but this was self-defeating, since he had eventually to return. The street was more accommodating than the flat, which was now alien. He bathed as silently as possible. When he got into bed he noticed that his radio had been moved to accommodate a larger model.

On the day before he was due to leave he paid a last visit

to the National Gallery. He expected much from this even more valedictory act but found himself for once inattentive, even impatient, as if art were withholding its secrets, finding him unworthily busy on his own account. It was true that he was no longer capable of innocent contemplation, but this loss of faith troubled him. He paused briefly before many suffering saints, then passed into the main building and the more reassuring company of alternative deities: Mars and Venus, Venus and Adonis, Bacchus and Ariadne. This last image, a shock of blue, proclaimed its subversive message without the intervention of physical ageing. Ariadne, her arm flung out as if to push away the intervening air and impel herself forward, arrested by the charged glance that passes between Bacchus and herself, seemed by that very act to lose power, to be rendered uncertain, while Bacchus, his near nakedness easily outclassing her draped figure, demonstrates that he has no need to emphasize this act of possession. His companions, or collaborators, by their very indifference, proclaim that this is an everyday event, or, more probably, that they are excluded from the mystery. Herz felt suddenly faint, was obliged to sit on a bench. In the light of this extraordinary conjunction what comfort could he draw from his own conscientious intentions, from the prospect of two prudent survivors, each with safety in mind, each with a record of failed chances, of not even honourable defeats? How could they even mime a joyous reunion without a similar shock of recognition? What was reasonable, even pleasant company compared with the enactment of desire? He raised his eyes once more to the picture and lowered them again, reminding himself that Ariadne had much to lose from the affair and that Bacchus would grow into an obese and sozzled wreck whose fall from grace would be depicted by other painters less indulgent to his example. The story ended badly, but this was irrelevant, even unimportant. One could take the opposite view, that temperate companionship might, almost certainly would, outlast such dazzling preliminaries. Yet that companionship would also entail regret. Herz saw a girl lingering by the picture, recognizing it, perhaps for the first time, as the real thing, and willing such an apotheosis for herself. Quite simply, nothing could take its place. It would be acknowledged not by its presence but by its very absence, and would thereby leave an indelible mark. Even to see it, to hear about it at second hand, was enough to cause wonder. Or indeed dismay.

The faintness persisted. He remained seated, until warned that the gallery was about to close. He made his way to the exit, a warder walking slowly and watchfully behind him. His extreme physical discomfort was compounded by the suspicion that Fanny might expect him to make love to her, and he made a note to telephone the Beau Rivage as soon as he arrived home—if ever he arrived home—and book a single room for himself. Love was no longer a possibility: the blatantly blue image of Bacchus and Ariadne had finally completed its work, had convinced him that such imaginings were no longer appropriate, or rather were no longer available. Even at his late age he had failed to encompass reality, when the reality of the flesh was there to remind him of the truth. Out of reluctance, of fastidiousness, even out of modesty he averted his eyes daily from his changed appearance, and if he thought of himself as he

had once been it was as if he thought of some distant figure in a distant landscape, able to undertake any physical
act, meet any physical challenge. This almost mystical
memory of himself had something in common with the
beginning of the world, the belief in inviolability, in im-
mortality, which must return to haunt one as the days
began to shorten. Even then the prospect of death would
be unreal, its details hidden. There would, he knew, come
a time when he would be given over into other hands, and
would thus abandon any thought of himself as a distinct
being. He would become part of a species, and even in that
extremity would evoke little interest.

What was available to him now was more banal: a simulacrum of domesticity. Even this would be unconvincing,
yet he remained determined to make it work. The almost
abstract setting, the almost familiar woman, the discreet attentions of those appointed to tidy away the grosser aspects
of daily life, would, he hoped, be sufficient for a routine to
be established, one in which the physical life should not be
too obtrusively in evidence. They would meet for walks,
for meals, their changed appearance suitably disguised. In
time this newly constructed life might persuade them of its
reality. What he desired now was kindness, leniency, com-
prehension, the sort of reciprocity that two old acquaintances might recognize, and who, out of tact, would refrain
from unwelcome allusions to past intimacy, for they had in
fact never been intimate. Although his vision of Fanny was
that of a lost lover, that lost lover was himself. His former
hopes and expectations had, in the long run, amounted to
nothing. Fanny had been to him the embodiment of those
expectations, which had survived for a remarkable length

of time. He did not think himself excessively romantic, but it was true that he had long had a less than successful relationship with unalterable circumstance. The surge of memory and feeling was liable to overtake him at every turn: why else had he been willing to \set up this experiment? It would be prudent to view the real Fanny, the Fanny he was due to meet at Geneva on the following day, as a stranger, one to whom he would behave with respect, with courtesy, but no longer with ardour.

He no longer desired the sort of animated discussions he had earlier envisaged. What he desired was a smile to meet his own: that was still possible. He would allow her all her own fantasies, would humour her vanity as best he could, would permit her to see herself as sought after, but only on condition that in exchange she would sometimes let the poor worldly mask slip and favour him with unforced fondness, not for what he had once been, the humble suitor, but for what he was now, a fellow being easily frightened by the world as it was. For such a fond smile he would be willing to cross any distance. He was anxious now to get to a telephone, to talk to her, and if possible to detect in her voice some of the vulnerability that was now overtaking him, as he stood on the pavement, confused by the crowds, the traffic, the noise, and signalled for a taxi, his raised arm as heavy as lead. The great mass of the city, which he had always embraced, oppressed him. Once again he had a vision of Nyon, but of a place which thirty years earlier had appeared so caressing, so nurturing. It would have changed, as he himself had changed, but the vista across the lake would be unchanged, and the soft light, and the distant mountains. He would undoubtedly recover in such surroundings from the tiresome weaknesses which had plagued him in the last few months, would, if necessary, put himself in the care of a patriarchal Swiss doctor. And perhaps Fanny would act completely out of character and look after him. This, he saw, was not a prospect which would appeal to her. But he in his turn might act out of character and become testy, would insist on his regime being observed, would fashion her into the vigilant guardian he wished her to be. This prospect did not greatly please him either. But if they could both perfect their behaviour, or their performance, to the extent that each gave pleasure to the other he would count that as a great achievement.

He had taken note of her strain of melancholy, and her confession of past unhappiness. His worldly goods, with which he was prepared to endow her, would not efface her view of herself as a woman who had never known love. He could perhaps repair her pride, which, he knew, would once more come to the fore given a little encouragement. He would have to rely on what self-knowledge she might retain. It was possible, though unlikely, that she had gained a measure of wisdom in the intervening years, enough perhaps to enable her to treat him gently. That gentleness, as yet unproven, he now craved, as he had once craved love. In the jolting taxi he slipped a pill under his tongue and waited for his vision to clear. He had yet to pack, to tele phone Bernard Simmonds, to call on Sophie and Matthew and to wish them well. All this, however, took second place to his urgent need to reach Fanny, to know of her state of mind, to discover if she too were undecided.

In Chiltern Street he seemed engulfed in a rising tide of luggage, mostly Matthew's, his own modest suitcase a meek adjunct to the possessions of the new and rightful owner. It was clear that this was no longer his undoubted place. Nor did he want it to be. It had once represented emancipation from the dreariness of Edgware Road, from family commitments, from his marriage and divorce, yet that emancipation had not led to any kind of fulfilment. It was a refuge, nothing more, and as such had served him well. Now it seemed strange, already filled with another life. He welcomed his own impatience as he stumbled over Matthew's sports bag. Here was a sign of the testiness he hoped to evoke in other, more favourable circumstances. Here was a new persona in the making.

He dialled the Bonn number, let the telephone ring a number of times, able now to test his resolve. 'Fanny?' he said. 'How are you?'

There was a laugh at the other end of the line. 'I don't quite know, Julius. Quite nervous, to tell you the truth.'

'I am too. It's only to be expected. It's a long time since we last left home.'

'I hate to think how changed you will find me.'

'But, dear, we are changed; that is inevitable. In any event I have the strongest feeling that I shall know you straight away. What are you doing about your flat?'

'A friend will be staying here. Not indefinitely, of course, although she has once or twice mentioned that we pool our resources. But I have never liked the idea of living with another woman. I think I should rather be alone, though I have been very lonely.' Her voice trailed away, as if she had turned aside for a moment. When she came back to him he had the impression that she had had to make a conscious effort to retrieve her composure.

'I too have been lonely,' he said gently. 'I realize that

now that there is a prospect of company. This is a great up-
heaval for us both, Fanny, but we will still both be free
agents. There is no need to panic.'

'I do feel rather frightened,' she said. 'But, as you say, we
are both free. It's just that I thought it such a lovely gesture
on your part. And it will be good to have someone to talk
to after this long isolation.'

'You will soon forget about that. There will be people
around you.' Around us, he silently corrected himself.
'And plenty to do,' he added lamely. He wondered what
had become of her recently rediscovered authority. He
would have preferred her brisker, more authoritative, more
her old self. 'Is someone there to get you to the airport on
time? You were always a terrible timekeeper.'

She laughed. 'I'm afraid you remember me too well.
Yes, the friend I mentioned will see me off. And you?'

'Oh, don't worry about me.'

There was silence. Neither of them knew how to finish
this conversation, in which so much had been left unsaid.
Don't worry about me? he thought. But that is exactly
what I want you to do. I want, for once, to be greeted with
a loving smile, in response to which my own smile will
broaden without restraint. Instead he said, 'Well, I'll see
you tomorrow, then.' And Fanny, let us try to be happy.
This last remark he managed to suppress. 'Goodnight,
dear. Until tomorrow.'

For the pleasure of knowing that there would be a tomorrow he was willing to pay a great price. Briskly now he
set about his own arrangements, wrote a note to Bernard,
and one to Sophie. He did not particularly want to speak
to either of them, was anxious to keep any exchange of

news for Fanny alone. He passed, as he knew he would, a disturbed night, but told himself that this was inevitable. From time to time he felt the familiar discomfort of restricted breathing, but this was now so familiar that he accepted it as a mild disability, which must be disregarded. All efforts must be directed towards getting himself to Geneva. After that there would be time to take care, to take advice, to take precautions.

He looked round the flat for the last time, felt a little sadness, but not the sadness he had expected to feel. In the taxi he congratulated himself on making so discreet a departure. His breath was shorter now, but there was only one further effort to make, and then all would be taken care of. At the airport smiles of appreciation were directed at other passengers too distracted to return them. He succeeded in picking up his suitcase, negotiated all the hazards. He drank a cup of coffee at a small glass-topped table, newly indifferent to the effort he would soon have to make.

The pain began quite suddenly, unlike anything he had experienced before. When his flight was called he got up, fumbled for his pills. His shaking hand sent them flying, rolling across the dirty floor. Making an effort not to gasp he lurched forward, crushing the pills beneath his feet. Then, with the empty box still clutched in his hand, the ghost of a smile still on his face, he struggled mightily, exerting his last strength to join the other travellers on their journey.

## ABOUT THE AUTHOR

ANITA BROOKNER was born in London. She trained as an art historian and taught at the Courtauld Institute of Art until 1988. *Making Things Better* is her twenty-first novel.

## ABOUT THE TYPE

This book was set in Bembo, a typeface based on an old-style Roman face that was used for Cardinal Bembo's tract *De Aetna* in 1495. Bembo was cut by Francisco Griffo in the early sixteenth century. The Lanston Monotype Company of Philadelphia brought the well-proportioned letterforms of Bembo to the United States in the 1930s.